Due:

Tues
July 23

Praise for Sara Hoskinson Frommer's Mysteries

"*Murder in C Major* is a nifty first mystery, unpretentious yet none-theless impressive in its quiet way. ...a virtuoso debut by a new writer."

—*Washington Post Book World*

"Frommer's second mystery [*Buried in Quilts*] offers an entertaining family-centered murder investigation while examining the importance of quilts as a means of understanding women's history."

—*Publishers Weekly*

"*Murder & Sullivan*... invites you to lose yourself in a rollicking, old-fashioned, down-home Hoosier-style murder.... Frommer excels at creating a small-town ambience and connecting the storyline of the operetta to events aswirl on both sides of the stage curtain."

—*Chicago Sun-Times*

"The rich background [of *The Vanishing Violinist*], a quadrennial violin competition held in Indianapolis, combines with a strong puzzle and involving, mostly likable characters to create an enjoy-able reading experience."

—*Ellery Queen's Mystery Magazine*

"The prize here [in *Witness in Bishop Hill*] is the gently effective interpretation of the Alzheimer's scourge."

—*Kirkus Reviews*

"Frommer delivers [in *Death Climbs a Tree*] a solidly satisfying, character-driven, small-town cozy that addresses not only environ-mental issues but aging, workplace harassment, and the impact of death on family and friends left behind. A very enjoyable read."

—*I Love a Mystery*

Her Brother's Keeper

Her Brother's Keeper

— A Joan Spencer Mystery —

⸎

Sara Hoskinson Frommer

— 2013 —

PERSEVERANCE PRESS / JOHN DANIEL & COMPANY

PALO ALTO / MCKINLEYVILLE, CALIFORNIA

Copyright © 2013 by Sara Hoskinson Frommer
All rights reserved
Printed in the United States of America

A Perseverance Press Book
Published by John Daniel & Company
A division of Daniel & Daniel, Publishers, Inc.
Post Office Box 2790
McKinleyville, California 95519
www.danielpublishing.com/perseverance

Distributed by SCB Distributors (800) 729-6423

Book design by Eric Larson,
Studio E Books, Santa Barbara, www.studio-e-books.com

Cover illustration by Linda Weatherly S.

1 3 5 7 9 10 8 6 4 2

LIBRARY OF CONGRESS CATALOGING-IN-PUBLICATION DATA
Frommer, Sara Hoskinson.
Her brother's keeper : a Joan Spencer mystery / by Sara Hoskinson Frommer.
p. cm.
ISBN 978-1-56474-525-5 (pbk. : alk. paper)
1. Spencer, Joan (Fictitious character)—Fiction. I. Title.
PS3556.R5944H47 2013
813'.54—dc23
2012015566

To all good mothers and mothers-in-law,
especially Isabel Hoskinson and Magda Frommer

Special thanks to
David Canfield, David Edgerton, Carol Froelich,
Alice Fromm, Charles Frommer, Chris Holly,
Marni Hoskinson, Laura Kao, Joyce Kostelecky,
Susan Kroupa, Laura Lynn Leffers, and Celeste Schulman;

and to my agents, Shana Cohen and Stuart Krichevsky;

and my editor, Meredith Phillips,
who invited this book and did what the best editors do.

Her Brother's Keeper

Chapter 1

"NO!" HEADS jerked up all over the Oliver Senior Citizens' Center. "He can't!" The bridge game paused, and Annie Jordan dropped her ever-present knitting and hurried to Joan Spencer's assistance.

"What's the matter, Joanie? It's not Fred, is it?" Annie was an admirer of Joan's policeman husband.

Conscious of her audience, Joan pulled herself together and calmed her voice. "No, it's my brother."

Annie relaxed visibly. "I didn't even know you had a brother. What were you hollering about?"

"He wants to come to Rebecca's wedding."

"Did you invite him?" An unnecessary question. Joan was sitting at her desk keeping track of responses to the invitations she'd sent to her daughter's wedding. The "yes" pile was growing at an alarming rate, mostly from the groom's side.

"Well, yes, but I never thought he'd accept. Worse than that, he says he's coming early."

"Is that bad?"

"Annie, I haven't seen Dave since I don't know when. We didn't bother to tell him when Fred and I got married."

"There wasn't time," Annie said. "You took us all by surprise."

"That wasn't why. I didn't want him there. Dave's middle name is trouble."

"So why invite him this time?"

"Rebecca made me. With all the people Bruce's mother wants to pack into the church, Rebecca wasn't going to leave out anyone from our side. But having Dave show up isn't going to help

— *13* —

Rebecca's standing with her future mother-in-law. Elizabeth Graham is awful, Annie. And what will I do with my brother a week ahead of time? He thinks he's going to stay in our house. There's no way—" She fought her voice down to a reasonable level again. "There wouldn't be space for him with Rebecca here, even if I wanted him underfoot."

"Where are you putting Fred's parents? Didn't you say they're coming?"

"They'll stay in Ellen Putnam's bed-and-breakfast. His whole family will. But I couldn't put Dave there."

"Why not?"

"I couldn't do that to Ellen."

"Of course you can. Ellen's a big girl. She's open to the public."

"Well…" Joan felt herself weakening. Would Ellen ever speak to her again? But maybe Dave had mellowed. No matter what, he absolutely couldn't stay at her house.

She felt foolish for making such a fuss, but through the open doorway of her own tiny office, she could see that the old folks around her had gone back to their bridge and handwork. The exercise group upstairs probably hadn't even heard her squawk.

"You're right, Annie. I'll talk to Ellen. If she can stand Bruce's mother, she might as well put up with Dave."

—∞∞∞—

Ellen Putnam had put up with a lot, Joan thought that evening while walking home through the park. The Putnams had been in the throes of adding to their house when a tornado had destroyed the addition. Widowed shortly afterward, Ellen had enlarged the house and turned it into a bed-and-breakfast that was now supporting her and her children. She certainly had little competition in Oliver, Indiana, and she was always booked solid on Oliver College football weekends. But because Rebecca was to be married to Bruce Graham during the college's winter break, Joan had been able to reserve the whole house for the wedding guests. And Ellen, a superb cook, had agreed to feed them meals—even the rehearsal dinner, if Elizabeth Graham would stoop to holding it in Oliver. From the exchanges she'd had so far with the mother of the groom, Joan suspected Elizabeth would just as soon avoid having any part of the wedding in Oliver. Mrs. Graham was an elegant-hotel type, she was sure. But Rebecca wanted to be married in church, and from her mother's home. That pleased Joan, after the years in which Rebecca, asserting herself as an independent person, had kept her distance.

The bed-and-breakfast was just at the top of the hill beyond the park. The new addition and its extra bedrooms had more than doubled the size of their substantial home, using up most of the Putnams' lot. But beyond the picket fence that kept little Laura Putnam's dog in bounds, their view was of the park—all the advantages of a big yard, but no lawn to mow. Coming to it today, Joan debated warning Ellen about Dave. She could always just give him Ellen's address and phone number and let him do the rest himself. No. She owed Ellen fair warning.

Laura and the gangly mutt met her at the back door. "Mama, it's Joan!" Laura called into the house. Big new front teeth dominated her little face, and her fair hair threatened to escape its pigtails.

Ellen hurried to the door in paint-spattered jeans. "Come in, come in. I'm glad to see you."

"You're painting? Don't let me interrupt." Any excuse not to have to face this.

Ellen looked down at her pants. "No, that was last week. I think we're going to be ready for your wedding gang. Come, sit down."

Joan joined her on the big old sofa that dominated the living room. Now that the house was as much hotel as family home, the clutter of Laura's books and toys that she remembered had turned into a neat coziness, with just enough books to welcome a visitor and fresh flowers on a low table. The dog, its scraggly tail wagging, laid its head on her lap and drooled on her well-worn corduroy skirt. Joan reached out a hand to rub it between the ears.

"Take the dog out back, Laura," Ellen said.

"Yes, Mama," the child said. "Come on, puppy." She slapped

her leg, and the dog, its puppyhood long behind it, bounced in her wake.

Ellen looked after her. "I can't complain. That dog has made all the difference. She was headed for a real depression after she lost her father. But you probably didn't stop by to talk about Laura."

"Maybe a puppy would have helped Rebecca. She had a rough time, too, back when her father died. But you're right. I came to throw myself on your mercy."

Ellen waited.

Why was this so hard? "It's my brother," Joan said.

"Yes?"

"He's decided to come to the wedding. He wants to stay with us, but he just can't, not with Rebecca in the one spare room I have."

"We still have space."

"But you don't want Dave Zimmerman!"

"What is he, an ax murderer?" Ellen's dimples showed.

Joan suddenly felt silly. "Not that bad. At least, not that I've ever heard. And maybe he's matured. But when he was still living at home, he got into one scrape after another. Underage drinking, pot, reckless driving, gambling, even got picked up once for shop-lifting. I'm sure I didn't hear all of it—I was younger, probably too young to tell. But sometimes I heard my parents talking when they thought I wasn't listening. I haven't seen him for years. I don't know what kind of thing he'd pull now, but I wouldn't want to cause you any trouble."

"Don't give it a thought, Joan. He can't be any worse than some of the people who stay here. I didn't repaint the walls be-cause I changed my mind about the color, you know. You should have seen the stuff the last bunch threw at them."

"They didn't!"

Ellen shrugged. "I'm still in the hole for repairs."

"That's terrible!"

"The risk you take when you open a place like this. Good thing I can do most of the work." Ellen didn't sound sorry for herself.

"Oh, I forgot to tell you the worst of it!"

Ellen's eyebrows rose.

"He wants to come at least a week early. I'll pay you, of course." A wedding expense she hadn't anticipated.

"Good. It's the slow season. Nobody comes to Oliver right before Christmas. And I'll have a good week to show him who's boss."

Joan laughed. The set of Ellen's jaw made her believe that she might just pull it off. "Thanks, Ellen. I couldn't dump him on you without at least warning you. But I'm glad you're willing."

"You watch. By the time he leaves, he'll be washing dishes."

"It would do him good. He's probably just lazed around for years." But she wondered. She had no idea what Dave had been doing since their parents died. He'd moved out west and then to a town in Illinois, but his brief Christmas cards told her nothing about his life, and he never asked about hers.

Feeling a weight lifted, she swung along the rest of the way home with a lighter step. If only Bruce's mother were as easy to deal with. But at least there was no question of putting her up. She hadn't said a word about where she wanted to stay. She'd probably choose to drive from their home in Ohio the very morning of the wedding, or maybe spend a night in Indianapolis, if she didn't want to cut it too close. Not my problem, Joan thought.

What was her problem was tonight's orchestra rehearsal. Her very part-time job as manager of the Oliver Civic Symphony often threatened to take over her life, or so it felt sometimes. Last-minute calls from players begging off from rehearsal were a routine feature of her Wednesday afternoons. "The dog ate my homework" didn't apply here, but people came up with their own creative reasons for being unable to play. Some days Joan suspected they just couldn't face another evening of playing under their irascible conductor. Some days she wasn't sure she could, either. Even so, she climbed the steps to the front porch of her little house in a more cheerful frame of mind than usual.

Not even the blinking light on her phone message machine fazed her. She listened to the messages while changing from her work clothes to jeans and a sweatshirt. More comfortable for playing her viola, not to mention hauling those heavy boxes full of music folders. Her other part-time orchestra job, as music librarian, took more muscle than she had expected when she'd first agreed to it. Finally, she pulled a brush through her straight brown hair and fastened it back on top of her head in a loose twist, as usual when she was in a hurry.

Back when she'd first arrived in Oliver, money had been such a big worry that she would have agreed to almost anything short of selling her children. Now, with a regular job as director of the senior center, and married to Fred Lundquist, detective lieutenant in the Oliver Police Department, she felt less pressed. But she hadn't dropped any of her jobs.

No real bombshells on the answering machine tonight, thank goodness.

She thawed some burger buns in the microwave and zapped the filling for sloppy joes left over from a couple of nights before. While it heated and the teakettle worked itself up to whistle, she pulled out greens for a salad and cut up a tomato, as much for color as flavor, stuck forks into the salad bowl to toss later, and set the bowl on Grandma Zimmerman's old oak kitchen table. She had just sliced some fruit for another bowl when the phone rang and Andrew, her son, came through the back door. A scholarship student at the college, he still lived at home to save money.

"Get that, would you?" she asked Andrew. "My hands are wet."

He did, but immediately held it out to her. "It's Alex."

Joan wiped her hands on her jeans and took the phone. "Hi, Alex."

"You finally get the Mozart?" Whatever else you might want to say about their conductor, Alex Campbell, you couldn't say she didn't get right to the point.

"Yes, and the bowings are all marked." Might as well beat her to the punch.

"He'll probably want to change them," Alex said gloomily. Nicholas Zeller, the orchestra's concertmaster, had strong opinions about how the strings should bow their music.

"He's already seen them, Alex. I copied his bowings onto the other parts, so they're ready to hand out." It hadn't been as big a job as usual, since the music to Mozart's 40th Symphony had last been used by an orchestra that hadn't erased its bowings, and Nicholas had made very few changes on the parts for the first folder of each string section. "I'll see you soon, or was there something else?"

"Thanks, Joan." Alex hung up. Amazing. Thanks from Alex were rare and almost never unqualified.

Deciding to be grateful for small favors, Joan checked the sturdy plastic boxes of music to be sure she'd put the newly bowed parts into them, but of course she had. Good. The last thing she needed was to make a promise like that to Alex and then blow it. One collapsible box was built into the wheeled carrier she'd bought to ease the burden of hauling the folders to and from rehearsal, but it couldn't hold all the parts she needed to carry when they began rehearsing for a new concert, as they would tonight. She stacked a second, rigid box on top of the built-in one, tied them together with bungee cord, and hoped against hope the top one wouldn't fall off when she was pulling the whole contraption over a curb. At least the weather was clear. The folders, tall enough to hide any messy music from the audience in performance, stuck up out of the boxes too high for a lid to fit. She made do with an old rain poncho, but it had a habit of falling off at the worst possible times.

By the time she made it back to the kitchen, Andrew had set the table.

"Want me to put the rest of the food on, too, Mom?"

"Sure."

"Is Fred coming home for supper?"

"I'm here."

Joan hadn't heard the front door, but Fred came in from the living room in his winter coat and hat. When he kissed her, his nose was cold. He pulled off his hat and smoothed his thinning blond hair. A handsome man, even if he was balding. Blue-eyed and blond, Fred was all Swede. Andrew, as tall as Fred, was thinner, as his dad had been, with dark curls like his father's and Rebecca's.

"It's not fancy, but it's hot." Joan added the buns and sloppy joe filling to the table, and they sat down. Unusual on a Wednesday, eating together. They talked about nothing in particular. Then, for the first time since leaving Ellen's, she remembered her brother and was again filled with dread. "I have some news."

They both looked up.

"My brother's coming."

"To Rebecca's wedding?" Andrew asked.

"Yes, and he wants to come early. I about lost it at work today after I read that, but then I talked to Ellen. She says she'll risk letting him stay there."

"Whaddya mean, risk?" Andrew said.

Joan exchanged glances with Fred. "It's a long story, and I've got to get out of here. Tell you later."

"I'll get the music," Fred said.

"Thanks." She picked up her viola, and Fred, ignoring its handle, picked up the cart with its boxes as if they held feathers instead of heavy folders. "You going to be home?" she asked when they reached the car.

"Probably. Town's pretty quiet, with exams coming up at the college." He kissed her, gave her old Honda wagon a pat on its pockmarked fender, and waved her off.

Chapter 2

THE ORCHESTRA rehearsal went better than usual. Alex seemed to lack the energy to chew anyone out. Despite some clinkers in the Mozart that ordinarily would have enraged her, she just kept beating time, ignoring missed entrances as well as wrong notes and sloppy bowing that made what should have been clear and sharp ragged, instead.

"Not bad for a first reading," she said finally.

It wasn't the way it had been when she was in love with their narrator to Britten's *Young Person's Guide to the Orchestra*, when she'd praised them in ways Joan had never heard from her and even let the kid who played tuba join the piccolo in the "Stars and Stripes Forever" solo. It was more as if she just didn't care. She really is depressed, Joan thought, but the last thing she wanted was to become Alex's confidante, much less her counselor.

In fact, Alex was one of the first to leave after the rehearsal. Joan waited for the last slowpokes to sign out their music and then hauled the boxes of too many unclaimed folders out to her car, relieved not to have had to put out any orchestral fires. Nobody weeping about the concertmaster's heavy hand, nobody wanting to change seats, nothing.

Fred met her at home when she was unloading the car. "I'll take those," he said. "Phone for you." Joan gladly yielded the cart with its boxes to him and slung her viola over her shoulder.

"Thanks, Fred." She shucked her jacket and boots, tucked her feet under her on the old sofa, and picked up the phone, wondering whether the next shoe was about to drop. So far, the evening had been too calm.

"Hi, Mom."

Hearing her daughter's voice made her smile. "Rebecca! How are you doing? How is Bruce?"

"We're okay. But his mother is driving us both wild."

You, too, Joan thought. "What about?"

"Everything. She puts down everything we decide. Tells us we're doing it all wrong."

"You're talking about the wedding?"

"For starters, but I can see that she's not going to stop there. She's going to be like this our whole lives. No wonder Bruce keeps his distance."

"Uh-huh." A wonderful smell reached Joan's nostrils. Looking up, she saw Fred holding out a cup of coffee. She took it with her free hand and sipped cautiously. Just right. Fred's Swedish heritage came through in his coffee.

Rebecca launched into Elizabeth Graham's latest interference. "She wants me to buy my dress and the bridesmaid's dress from her dressmaker. Can't trust me to have any taste of my own. Do you have any idea how much that would cost? As if there were time to do it now, anyway."

"What did you tell her?"

"I'm getting better at dodging. I told her I'd think about it."

"Uh-huh."

"But she'll know as soon as she talks to the woman that I haven't done it."

"What are you planning?" Rebecca, as usual, had kept her plans close to her chest.

"I'm past planning. I've made my dress already, and one for you, Mom, if you'll wear it."

"Of course I'll wear it!" She could hardly believe what Rebecca was telling her. This late, she hadn't given Joan a clue what to shop for. Now she knew why. "Just promise me it's not beige lace."

"Mom! Would I do that to you?"

"I didn't think so." Joan sipped again. She had to trust Rebecca not to put her in a mini-dress, either. Did anyone even wear mini-dresses these days? Not that what anyone else wore would matter to Rebecca.

"My only bridesmaid will be Bruce's sister, and I've made her dress, too. I measured her the last time I saw her, without telling her mother. I know your size, but if I'm off, it will be easy to adjust when I'm there."

"What about Elizabeth?" Joan couldn't imagine dictating such things to Bruce's mother.

"She'll wear whatever she wants. Far be it from me to tell her how to dress. If she asks me, I'll tell her you're wearing blue, but if she doesn't, I'll just let her clash."

"You're learning." Rebecca was doing fine.

"So, are a lot of people coming?"

"Looks like it. We're going to have to hang them from the rafters. And oh, Rebecca, I heard from Dave today."

"Dave who?"

"Zimmerman. My brother. He's coming."

"Uncle Dave?" Rebecca's voice rose. "I know I said to invite him, but I didn't think he'd come. I don't even know what he looks like, except in your old pictures. That's exciting."

"I hope not."

"You what?"

"Dave used to be more exciting than I'd want at your wedding. That's why I wasn't going to invite him."

"I'm glad you did, especially if nobody from Dad's family can be there. Maybe this will bring the two of you together after all these years." Rebecca, the optimist.

"Maybe. I'm not counting on it."

"What did he do, torment you?"

Joan thought about it. "No, actually, that's the one thing he didn't do. He always had a soft spot for his little sister. Made our parents' lives plenty miserable, though."

"Well, then. It's going to be fine. You'll see."

My chance to tell her that her mother-in-law will turn into a sweetheart, too, Joan thought, but she couldn't make herself do it. "You picked a good man. I hope you and Bruce are very happy together. Do you know yet when you're coming?"

"A few days early, maybe as much as a week, if I can square it with my boss. We're driving out together, but after he drops me at home, Bruce will stay with his folks in Ohio before the wedding. Tradition and all that. When is the rest of the family going to arrive?"

"Most of them will be here the day before, for the rehearsal. But Dave wants to come a whole week early. Maybe more. I don't know, Rebecca."

"Good. Maybe I'll have a chance to get to know him. I hope you and he have time to feel like family again before the rest of them descend on you."

"I suppose." For better or for worse.

—∞∞∞—

But the first family member to arrive was neither Dave nor Rebecca. Instead, Elizabeth Graham roared into the senior center one afternoon three weeks before the wedding, as if taking it for granted that Joan would drop everything to cater to her slightest whim.

"What do you mean, she's not here?" Joan heard through the open doorway of the exercise class at the top of the stairs, where she was standing in for the curvy young woman the men in the group would much rather have had leading them. "She's supposed to work here!" Although she hadn't met Bruce's mother yet, there was no mistaking the officious voice she'd heard in far too many telephone conversations.

"That's right. And I'm not about to drag her down from upstairs for someone who won't so much as give her name," Annie Jordan shot back.

"Well, you'd better, if you know what's good for you."

Time to break that up, tempted as Joan was to find out which of these two stubborn women would resort to physical force. She apologized to the group, dismissed the class, and headed down the steps.

"Problem, Annie?"

Annie looked half-grateful to be rescued and half-sorry to give in. "Nothing I can't handle, Joanie. This—this woman seems to think you have nothing better to do around here than answer the door."

"In fact, I mostly do greet guests who come in," Joan said with a smile she hoped didn't look as phony as it felt. "But I'm lucky to have Annie volunteer when I'm unavailable. I'm Joan Spencer, director of the center. How can I help you?" As if she didn't know.

Wearing a silk shirt, trim tweed suit, and a frown, the slender woman didn't turn a perfectly groomed blonde hair. "I'm Elizabeth Graham."

"Elizabeth!" Joan smiled again. "How lovely to meet you at last. Do sit down, won't you?" Gesturing to the chair opposite her desk, she slid into the one behind it that Annie had just vacated. At least the desk hid her exercise sweats and sneakers. "Thanks for subbing for me, Annie. This is Bruce's mother. You remember Bruce."

Annie merely nodded and left the little office, her back as straight as one of her own knitting needles. Elizabeth sat, almost as unbending.

"What brings you to Oliver?" Joan asked. "Did your husband come with you?"

"No, he's seeing patients." Bruce's father was a physician, Joan knew. "But I wanted to make final arrangements for the rehearsal dinner. Seems to be about the only thing our family has any say in." Her sniff was inaudible, but visible in a tightness of her nostrils and lips.

"It is difficult, when we're all so spread out," Joan said as sympathetically as she could manage. "And Bruce and Rebecca have such definite ideas." Thank goodness.

"They certainly do," Elizabeth said. "But they don't know what they're doing. You and I have to set them straight."

"Oh? What did you have in mind?" She listened, not for the first time, while Elizabeth launched into how a proper wedding should be celebrated, with a full reception banquet, champagne, a band, and dancing.

"There's no venue in this dinky town to do it justice," the woman said. "I tried to tell them about the Indiana Roof Ballroom up in Indianapolis, but do you think they'd even hear of it?"

"Is that place still open?" Joan had no idea, though she remembered its huge wooden dance floor and starry ceiling from some long-ago occasion involving some of Rebecca's father's wealthiest parishioners.

"I don't know, but they wouldn't even let me check."

"Well." Joan's admiration for Bruce rose another couple of notches. Whatever Rebecca faced in dealing with this woman, her husband would stand up to his mother.

"They want to have the ceremony and the reception all in that church. Can you imagine—a wedding reception in the church basement? Nothing but wedding cake and little sandwiches, they said. You can't treat people like that!"

Joan smiled, remembering that she and Fred not only had treated their guests like that, but that those very guests had decorated the room and baked the wedding cake as a surprise gift. "We're planning to feed the family and friends who have to travel from a distance, and you may want to invite them to the rehearsal dinner, but you're right that the reception for all the guests will be very simple. It's what Rebecca and Bruce prefer."

"What do they know about it? You can't let them decide these things! How many weddings have they attended? They need a wedding planner!"

Joan stuck to her guns. "Rebecca's father was a minister, you know. She's seen more weddings in her short life than most people twice her age. She wants to marry Bruce in a quiet, traditional church wedding. No wedding planner's 'theme' and no dinner." And no crippling expenses.

Elizabeth glared at her. "I should have known you'd be just as bad."

How could she! "It isn't negotiable. Now, if you'd like to meet the woman who's agreed to do meals for us, you can discuss your plans for the rehearsal dinner with her." Poor Ellen. Sending Elizabeth to her was going to be worse than sending Dave.

Elizabeth sat stiffly. Had no one ever crossed her before? It was hard to believe. The woman played violin in the Canton, Ohio orchestra, Bruce had told them. Joan suddenly pictured her butting heads with Alex and had to repress the urge to laugh.

"I'll be glad to go over there with you, if you like."

"I'm sure I can find my way."

Good. It would give her a moment to call Ellen. "I'm sure you can," Joan said. "I usually walk through the park, but you'll probably want to drive around." She drew a quick map.

Elizabeth stuffed it in her purse without looking at it. "Thank you." She stood and left the office, barely glancing around as she threaded her way among the groups between her and the door.

As soon as the door closed, Joan reached for the phone. "Ellen? I'm glad I caught you. I wanted to warn you that Bruce's mother is headed your way. Yes, right now. She's fit to be tied because we aren't going to throw a reception that would break us. I hate to think what she's going to ask of you for the rehearsal dinner or whether she'll expect you to put her up for the night tonight. You'll have to decide how much you can stand."

"Don't worry about me," Ellen said. "I may charge her extra for the aggravation. I don't owe her the way I owe you."

"You don't owe me a thing!"

"Only Laura's life. If you hadn't protected her when that tornado roared through the park…"

"Oh." Embarrassed, Joan didn't know what to say. "I'm glad I was there," she finally managed.

"And I'll never forget it."

To think I was worried about sending Dave to her, Joan thought.

Chapter 3

"FOUND HIM, Lieutenant." Sergeant Johnny Ketcham stood in the doorway of Fred Lundquist's office holding a computer print-out. "He's been in prison."

So Joan's instincts were right about her brother. "What did he do?"

Ketcham's eyebrows rose above his wire-rims. "Could be worse, I suppose. There's nothing violent on his sheet, but it was his third conviction. This last one was for fraud."

"He serve time before?" Fred reached for the printout.

"Yeah. And this time he'd violated parole."

"No wonder Joan didn't hear from him," Fred said. "She said he used to phone her occasionally, but for the past few years I don't think she's had more than a Christmas card."

"So she didn't know?"

"No. Only address she had for him was a post office box."

"Probably had his mail forwarded."

"Or gave his box key to a friend he could trust. Same effect, but no records in the post office."

Ketcham nodded. "You gonna tell her?"

Fred thought about it. He and Joan had never kept secrets from each other. Oh, sure, he couldn't tell her about cases he was working on, but this was her family. None of his business at all, really, except that he didn't want this jerk to hurt her. "I'll have to."

"She won't appreciate it."

"No."

"You want me to…" Ketcham waved a hand in a general sort of way.

"Thanks, Johnny. Afraid I'd better do it myself." He folded the printout and tucked it into his inside jacket pocket. Maybe after supper, when they were relaxing together on the sofa. Soften her up with a cup of coffee first. Who was he kidding? She'd be mad no matter what he did. This wedding business had her stressed out as it was, and she'd been bent out of shape when all she knew was that Dave was coming. Had she suspected something of this sort? Maybe she'd be relieved it wasn't any worse.

When he pulled up in front of the house, she met him at the door, her face still rosy from her cold walk home.

"You're never going to believe who showed up today."

Was he too late? Was her brother in the house? "Who?" He bent to kiss her.

Her own lips curved in laughter. "Mother of the groom, that's who."

Just what he didn't need. He'd heard enough about Elizabeth Graham to dread this complication to an already complicated day. "Is she here?"

"Don't look so alarmed. No, she's not in the house. She may still be over at Ellen's, checking her out."

"Is she coming here?"

"She didn't say, and I didn't ask—or invite her, so I doubt it."

He grinned. "Not your favorite person."

"No. Even worse in the flesh than on the phone. Now I understand why Bruce never let his family come to his violin competitions. Or his professional concerts, now that he's making some progress in the musical world. I don't think it's his family—I think it's his mother."

He tipped up her chin. "I don't see any bruises."

She laughed out loud. "It wasn't that bad, though I thought for a minute she and Annie Jordan might come to blows. She showed up at the center and tried to throw her weight around, but Annie wasn't having any. I was all the way upstairs, but I could hear the two of them going at it in my office."

He put his arm around her slender waist. "Let's go in out of the cold, where I can listen."

Her face changed, and she let him lead her into the house. "Oh, Fred, I'm sorry. You're early—I haven't even made supper yet."

"Want to go out?"

"Not tonight. I'm going to throw leftover chicken and rice in the microwave."

"You do that. Then I have something to tell you, too."

She was always quick to catch his tone of voice. "What's wrong?"

"It can wait." With a show of casualness, he pulled off his warm hat and coat.

"Fred Lundquist, you tell me right now."

"Okay, soon as I change. You start supper. I'll be right back." Abandoning her to the kitchen, he went into their bedroom.

How to break it to her that her brother was an ex-con? He could hear her throwing dishes onto the table. Better go in there before she got so mad at him for making her wait that she broke something she cared about.

The back door slammed. Good. Andrew could run interference for him.

"Supper's almost ready," Joan called from the kitchen. Fred ran his fingers over his head, squared his shoulders, and went to face her.

"Hi, Fred," Andrew said.

"Andrew." Fred nodded at him, but kept his attention on Joan.

Andrew looked from one to the other of them. "Want me to make myself scarce?"

Joan shook her head. "It's all right, Andrew. Fred's about to tell us something, that's all. Unless it's personal." She looked at Fred.

"Nothing he can't hear."

"All right, then. Come sit down, both of you." In no hurry now, she began passing food around the table. She wouldn't ask again, he knew.

He helped himself to chicken. "We found your brother."

"Was he lost?" Andrew asked, reaching for the nearest bowl.

"Not exactly." He looked at Joan. "But you can't tell much from a post office box number, and that's all your mom had for him."

"So what's with Uncle Dave?" Andrew ladled chicken and rice onto his plate as if there were no tomorrow. How did he stay so thin?

Joan just sat there, waiting.

"He's been in prison," Fred said.

"Prison!" Andrew said.

Joan didn't look surprised. "What for?"

"Fraud."

"Is that all?"

"It's plenty, and this was his third conviction."

"But he didn't hurt anyone?"

"Physically, you mean?"

She nodded.

"No."

She didn't answer, but her eyes teared up.

"Are you all right?"

She patted her eyes with her napkin. "Oh, Fred, I was so worried."

"Why?" Andrew asked.

She smiled at him. "Dave was a wild kid, Andrew. I've hardly seen him since he went away to college, but I didn't think he changed much there, either. My parents used to talk about him when they thought I was asleep. I couldn't hear everything, but I know they worried about him. When I married your dad, Dave kept his distance from us. He showed up once in a while at family gatherings before you were even born, and sent you kids gifts a couple of times when you were little, but he never gave us any idea what he was up to. For years now, he's just sent us Christmas cards that looked like something he ran off on a printer. No note, nothing. No response to anything I wrote him. Now we know why."

"He could have written from prison," Andrew said.

"I imagine he was ashamed to let us know," Joan said. "To let me know. He hardly knew you and Rebecca. He probably thought your dad disapproved of him."

"Did he?"

"Not really. He wasn't the disapproving sort."

"Bad enough you married a minister. But then you married a cop." Andrew looked up at Fred.

"Yeah." Joan looked at him, too. "I told Dave, when I wrote to him last year, so he knows, but somehow he's decided it's okay to come to this wedding. You're not going to give him a hard time, are you?" But her face had relaxed. She was teasing him.

"I'll try not to let you down," Fred said.

Chapter 4

JOAN ALWAYS did her best to arrive in plenty of time before the rehearsal to supervise the setup of chairs and music stands on the stage of the Alcorn County Consolidated School, and this Wednesday, a week and a half before the wedding, she succeeded. Good thing, she thought, because the parking lot was already filling with high school basketball game traffic. Latecomers were going to have a hard time finding a spot.

Alex Campbell, who ordinarily gave latecomers plenty of grief, must have had trouble finding a parking place, because she still hadn't arrived when it was past time to tune. Nicholas Zeller climbed onto the podium and pointed his violin bow at the first oboe for the 440 A, as he did every week. The winds tuned first, then the lower strings, and finally the violins, with a fresh oboe A each time.

"You think he'll take over the rehearsal?" murmured John Hocking, the easygoing engineer with whom Joan shared the last stand in the viola section.

He might do a better job than Alex, she thought, but for the moment, at least, Nicholas took his seat in the first chair of the first violins. Next to him, Birdie Eads was studying the new music, her round face solemn. Could it be that she'd never played Mozart's 40th? Not likely. Birdie was serious most of the time. She seemed to spend most of her life looking the way Joan had been feeling all afternoon.

A few more players trickled in, but still no Alex. The orchestra was chatting, and the clock was crawling steadily on.

Joan stood in her place and raised her voice. "While we're

waiting for Alex, I'll remind you that the Mozart parts are rented, and they've threatened us with a stiff penalty if we leave markings on the music. So please erase all the pencil marks after the concert, even the ones you didn't make. We can't afford the penalty." And she didn't want to do all that erasing herself. She wondered whether the last orchestra had been charged. Having their bowings left in had ended up saving her a lot of work because she'd had to change so few, but of course the rental company might have charged the penalty without doing anything to the music before sending it out again. "And be sure to sign out your folder and return it after the concert. They really hit us hard for lost music. Any other announcements?"

An orchestra board member in the horn section stood. "We've never yet charged dues to play in this orchestra. But we have to pay Alex and Joan, not to mention the phone bill and renting music and the school, printing programs, and setup for concerts. At the moment the budget is in the red. I don't know about you, but I'd miss it something fierce if it folded for lack of funds. Please donate what you can. We need it!" He sat down to a smattering of applause and a certain amount of muttering. Joan couldn't help thinking of the people whose arms she'd had to twist to fill out the sections.

As if on cue, Alex blew in from stage right, bringing a blast of cold air with her. But she looked as downhearted as she'd been looking all fall. She shed her coat and hefted herself onto the podium, where she sat up in the tall chair that let them all see her baton better than when she stood, short as she was. "We'll start with the Mozart."

"I still haven't practiced the fast bits," John confessed to Joan. "She's gonna yell at us, you watch."

"Me either, with the wedding stuff landing on me. But I don't think Alex's mind is on such things." Alex was still mourning the sad end of what might have been her only romance ever. Joan couldn't help her and was glad she hadn't asked for help in that department.

The symphony began at what felt like breakneck speed with

the famous tune to which her children had sung, "It's a bird, it's a plane, no, it's Mozart."

Alex didn't seem to notice the violas' errors tonight, even when Joan struggled with fingering the string crossings of the second set of *divisi* "deedle-deedles," as her father had called them. I don't belong in this orchestra, she told herself, not for the first time. But they keep letting me play. And paying me for the work I do, to boot. She scribbled a penciled star by the measures before letter *C*, to work on the accidentals that went by too fast for her slow fingers to catch.

The lyrical second movement required less of her fingers and more of her soul, and the Menuetto was straightforward, and not too fast for comfort. But the final movement charged ahead again, and Joan scrambled to keep up. More stars.

Alex took time to work through a few problem spots, and then they went back and played the symphony straight through. The last movement was less ragged than before, but Joan thought it still had a long way to go. I'm going to buckle down as soon as the wedding is over, she promised herself. She leaned over to copy her scribbly stars onto the copy in the folder she'd take home to practice.

Then she heard clapping. Someone was standing out in the center aisle of the dark auditorium, clapping hard.

Alex whirled around and peered into the dark, shielding her eyes with her hand. "Who's out there?" she barked. "This is a closed rehearsal!"

"I'm sorry," said a deep, resonant voice. "I was looking for Joan Spencer, but the Mozart was so beautiful I couldn't help applauding."

Joan knew that voice. She handed her viola to John and squeezed her way between the stands in front of her to look down over the apron of the stage.

"Dave?"

"Joanie!" Now he was close enough for the stage lighting to show him standing there with a battered suitcase at his feet. Even after all that had happened to him (and because of him), he was

Back in her own seat, Joan reclaimed her viola from John, who looked bemused. "Happen often in your family?"

"People showing up out of nowhere, you mean?"

"Well, yes, or your brother winning over an old grouch like Alex."

"If it's a woman, I wouldn't doubt it. Dave always used to have that effect on girls."

"It seems to have done her good." John was looking at Alex.

Joan had to agree. Alex looked happier than she had in months, even though Dave had told her he was leaving soon. Maybe all she needed was for some man to treat her like an attractive woman, Joan thought. Could it be so simple?

When the rehearsal finished, she dealt with the usual details, digging extra folders out of the boxes for the string players to take home, signing them out, packing up the rest, picking a plastic water bottle and a Styrofoam cup up off the floor, and shooing the stragglers off the stage under the baleful eye of the custodian who was being paid extra for cleaning up after them but who nevertheless acted personally affronted by having to wait, even though they hadn't run late. She stacked the now-empty extra box on top of the one that still weighed more than it should, stuffed the poncho into the empty one, tied them together again, and rolled them out to where Dave was standing.

"Swap you my stuff for all that?" he offered.

"Thanks." She picked his old suitcase up and led the way to the car, where he loaded the music carrier into the backseat and tossed his case in beside it. "How did you get here?"

"Took a taxi from the bus station."

"Hop in, then."

Sitting in the dark car in the parking lot, she watched while he buckled up and wondered how to break it to him that she wouldn't take him home tonight.

It was Dave, staring straight ahead, who broke the silence. "You might as well know. I've been in prison."

"What happened?" She leaned toward him, hoping she looked like someone who wasn't going to throw him out of the family.

"I got overextended and yielded to temptation. Oh, hell, who'm I kidding? I broke parole and had to serve a longer sentence the next time. The last time. Don't worry, Joan, I won't disgrace you here. No way am I going back to that place again."

"Good. Are you broke?" She'd heard they discharged prisoners with practically nothing. Might as well know the worst up front.

"I'm okay. I've been working in a friend's print shop since I got out. Not someone I knew inside—a guy I knew before all this happened. Doesn't pay all that much, but if I don't do anything stupid, I can make it. I won't be asking you for money." He sat straight and proud, or as straight as the seat belt permitted.

She reached her hand over to him, and he took it. "That's not what I meant." But maybe it had been. "You won't have any expenses while you're here, anyway. With Rebecca home, our house will be full, but we're putting family up in a bed-and-breakfast owned by Ellen Putnam, our neighbor near the park, and she's expecting you."

"I can't let you do that."

"Of course you can. It's only because we live in such a little house. Fred's parents will stay at Ellen's, too, and his brother and his family, and we'll have all our big family meals there. Besides, Ellen's almost family. She'll have you walking the dog with her daughter if you don't watch out."

He smiled. "How old is her daughter?"

Joan tried to do the math. "Laura must be about seven by now. It's her dog, you understand, but I have the impression her mother gets stuck with it a lot."

"Just like you at that age."

"Who, me?" Sometimes Joan felt as if she'd been born adult.

"You never had a dog, but I remember a kitten, and a rabbit or guinea pig—something that lived in a cage, anyway. You'd beg and promise anything to talk Mom into letting you have pets, and then it was like pulling teeth to get you to take care of them."

"I did take care of them—didn't I?" Suddenly she wasn't so sure.

He grinned at her. "Uh-huh. When Mom hollered at you for not cleaning the litter box, you bribed me to do it."

"What did I have to bribe you with?" Back then, he'd stood almost as tall as her father and had ridden his bike around town freely, while she was still limited to their immediate neighborhood. The gap between their allowances must have been just as large.

"More worthless promises, I imagine. But I didn't care. You were my cute kid sister."

She was touched. It fit with her memories of Dave taking her by the hand to show her off to his friends, twice as old as she was. That he'd taken her anywhere at that age was amazing.

"I'll drive you past our house, so you'll see where it is. You'll sleep at Ellen's, but until the crowd arrives for the wedding, you'll eat at our house."

"Any way you want to do it is fine with me."

It wasn't far—nothing in Oliver was far, for that matter. She pointed out her house and then drove the most direct route from it to Ellen's, though on her walk home from work, she often meandered through the neighborhood for variety.

The lights were on at the bed-and-breakfast, including one that lit up the sign decorated with an evergreen swag.

"And here's Ellen's." Laura's dog, which looked as if it had some beagle in it, barked at them from the front porch, but as soon as they came close and talked to it, it wagged its tail along with the barking. Joan was nevertheless glad to see that it was on a leash, tied far enough from the front door to leave them a clear path.

Laura ran out of the house. "Hush, puppy!" she told it. The dog hushed and wagged its whole rear end. "I'm sorry, Joan. We're trying to teach him to behave. He's okay with us, but if he doesn't know you, he makes a fuss."

"Not a bad thing to have a watchdog," Dave said mildly.

"He won't bite you. He just barks."

"Laura, this is my brother, Dave Zimmerman."

Hanging on to the dog's collar, Laura pulled the storm door open. "Come on in. Mom said you were coming early."

"Early?"

"For the wedding, I mean. We're still fixing the house up, and I'm gonna have to behave like a lady that whole weekend."

"Laura! What are you telling them?" Ellen called from inside the house.

"Just the truth, Mama." She pushed the door shut and released the dog to frisk around them, tail wagging furiously.

Ellen came into the living room. Gone were the paint-covered jeans. Today's trim pair looked brand new, and Joan wondered who had knit the elegant Aran sweater she wore so casually over them. Either somebody loved her, or the bed-and-breakfast was doing well, indeed. Or she'd taken good care of the clothes left from her previous life as a judge's wife.

Joan introduced them.

"Mrs. Putnam," Dave said, turning on the smile.

"Call me Ellen, please."

"Ellen, then. I'm Dave."

"We were expecting you. You get to choose your room. You're first to arrive, and Laura's right that we've been getting ready for everyone. But tonight's a school night, and she needs to go to bed." She looked Laura in the eye. "I'll be there in a minute, honey, just as soon as I give Dave a tour of the rooms."

"Yes, Mama." Laura led the dog out, shutting the living room door behind her.

"Oh, I don't need anything fancy."

"Good thing." Ellen dimpled up at him. "What with Scott, Amy, Laura, and now Laura's dog, there's no point in trying for fancy. We're saving the biggest rooms for families, but most of the smaller ones overlook the park."

"I'd like that."

They followed her. Joan admired the new rooms she hadn't seen since the house had been finished after the tornado and the remodeling Ellen had done more recently. Downstairs, the public areas had been enlarged, and the big living room flowed into the huge new dining room. Together they would host the buffet dinner Joan planned after the reception, for family and people who came from a distance. They climbed up to the second-floor bedrooms available for able-bodied guests. Ellen waved a hand at one downstairs for people who couldn't handle the steps.

"They're beautiful!" Joan said, peering into one tastefully decorated room after another. Each had its own individual flavor, some modern, others furnished with what might even be antiques. Ellen had found them at auctions and secondhand shops and refinished them herself, Joan knew.

"Thank you," Ellen said.

"How do you make them look so—relaxed?"

Ellen laughed. "A whole college-football–season's worth of fans staying here, for starters."

Dave didn't waste much time choosing. He parked his bag in a bright single room with a patchwork quilt–covered brass bed and came downstairs after Ellen showed him which bathroom to use. "Very nice. I'm sure I'll be comfortable."

"Until the others come, you can walk over to our house for breakfast," Joan said.

"Or help yourself in the kitchen here," Ellen said. "We keep it stocked for people who get up early and for days I don't serve a cooked breakfast. I won't be doing that until later in the week."

She led them into the kitchen, where a woman who looked a little older than Rebecca was putting away supplies. "This is Chrissy. She and her mother have been working like troopers this week. Chrissy, Dave will be staying in the yellow room. Would you give him the key to his room, please, and show him where to find things in the kitchen? Then go home. You've done more than your share today."

Joan was glad to see that Ellen didn't depend on the honor system to keep her guests' belongings safe. She wasn't as worried about Dave's things as about those of the others staying at Ellen's.

Leaving Dave to Chrissy, Ellen excused herself to supervise Laura's bedtime routine.

Dave was flirting openly with Chrissy now, who was responding as if he were an eligible bachelor. As far as Joan knew, he was, even though he was old for Chrissy. All Joan didn't need now was to worry about hearts he'd leave behind in pieces. As she remembered, he'd generally had a string of girls hanging on his every word when he was in high school. Not my problem, she told herself. Chrissy was clearly old enough to look out for herself.

But what was Joan going to do with him? It wasn't as if she could take more than a week off work to entertain him. She'd planned to take the last Friday off, and maybe part of Thursday, if things were under control at the senior center.

"I imagine you have things to do between now and the wedding," he said, as if reading her mind.

"Well…"

"That's all right. So do I. Mom and Dad left me something I need to check on while I'm in town."

Of course. They wouldn't have neglected him while leaving the house to her. Back when the accident had killed them both so suddenly, she must have known what went to Dave, but for the life of her, she couldn't think of it now, and he didn't say another word about it. All right, if he wanted to be mysterious, she could live with that.

And Dave, like Joan, had lived here that sabbatical year of their dad's, when she was in sixth grade and he was a high school senior. He probably remembered more people in Oliver than she had when she'd first arrived here a few years earlier. If nothing else, he'd probably want to check out all his old conquests.

"But you have time for supper tomorrow?" She suddenly hoped he hadn't already made a date with Chrissy.

"Of course. Will Fred and Andrew be there, too?" He sounded very relaxed asking about Fred, cop or no cop.

"Sure, unless Fred gets stuck with something."

"Good. I look forward to meeting them. I haven't seen Andrew since he was little."

Maybe it would be all right, after all.

But soon it was anything but all right.

Chapter 5

TRUE TO his word, Dave kept out of Joan's hair between his own arrival and that of the rest of the out-of-town family a week later. Oh, he came to supper, and he got along with Fred and Andrew. But during the day, he didn't bother her.

On the first day after his sudden arrival, though, he showed up at the senior center near the end of the afternoon. Joan waved through the office doorway and went to meet him as he came through the activity room.

"So this is where you work." He looked around as Elizabeth hadn't bothered to do. Many eyes met his. The bridge players and handicrafters stared openly. "You run this place?"

Joan laughed. "They mostly run themselves. Everybody, this is my brother, Dave Zimmerman. He's come for my daughter's wedding, and I'm very glad to see him." She knew the word had spread that she was worried about his coming. Let them wonder now.

A few people waved to him, and then they all returned to what they'd been doing. They wouldn't stare anymore, at least not for him to see.

But Joan could feel their eyes on her back when she escorted Dave into her office. Annie, as she so often did, sat knitting and minding the telephone. The sweaters she knitted these days were considerably larger than the ones her grandchildren had worn only a few short years ago, when Joan took over the center, though the odd piece she was working on now didn't look like anything that could fit one of them.

"Annie Jordan, meet my brother, Dave Zimmerman. He's here for Rebecca's wedding. Dave, we couldn't manage this place without Annie. They pay me, but she does it for love."

"Thank you for taking care of my sister." He flashed her the smile with which he'd captivated high school girls when their family had lived in Oliver.

"We love her to pieces," Annie said, smiling her own sweet smile and laying down her knitting to give him her hand to shake. He held it just long enough to be personal.

"What are you making?" he asked.

Annie held up the red thing Joan had wondered about. "A sweater for my daughter's dachshund. That's why it's so long and skinny."

He laughed.

"I'll have to add a couple of straps to hold it on, here and here." She pointed to the spots.

"Uh-huh. I learn new things all the time." Pulling a slip of paper out of his pocket, he quickly sketched a low-slung dog wearing a sweater and carefully added straps where she showed him they should go. He tucked it back into his pocket.

"You let me know when you're ready for knitting lessons," Annie said.

"I might just take you up on that." Again that great smile.

He'd already charmed the socks off Annie. How did he do it? But Joan could see how. Who could fail to respond to what appeared to be genuine interest?

She reminded herself that he had defrauded someone—several someones—to land in prison. Easy to see how he'd won their trust. Surely he wouldn't pull anything on her stomping ground. But how could she be certain?

"I'll leave you two to catch up," Annie said. She slipped delicately out of the room.

Joan held up the schedule to her retreating back. "I want to give this to her."

"Don't worry about me." Dave eyed the card players. "Maybe I'll kibitz."

"Good." Half an hour later, she was ready to leave. By that time, he had the bridge players eating out of his hand.

"You never told us you had such a handsome brother," Berta said, looking up from the ace, king, and queen of spades, plus some little ones. "Why didn't you bring him by sooner?"

"He doesn't live near enough. But he's here for my daughter's wedding."

"Oh, that's right. Will we meet your whole family?"

Not unless they all show up this early, Joan thought. "Dave's the only family I have besides the ones you already know," she said. "I don't know who else will stop in here. My daughter, probably."

"She's the quilter, isn't she?"

"That's right." Rebecca had brought her controversial Adam and Eve sleeping bag to the Oliver Quilt Show awhile back. And she'd helped some of the women there finish the edges of the orchestra quilt.

"And her fella's the fiddler," said Muriel, Berta's lucky partner.

"Yes." That was putting it mildly. Bruce Graham, Rebecca's fiancé, had visited Oliver when he was competing in the high-powered International Violin Competition of Indianapolis. "I imagine you'll have a chance to see both of them. But right now I want to take my brother home to meet Fred and Andrew."

"You'll like them," someone said.

"I'm sure I will," he said, and they escaped.

Outside, he looked around. "Where's your car?"

"Home. I need the exercise."

"I can use a walk, too. After that bus ride yesterday, I'm about sat out." He didn't say where he'd come from, and Joan didn't ask. He swung along beside her while they walked through Oliver's little downtown. She wondered how much walking he'd been able to do in prison and imagined a crowded yard, with men standing around doing nothing. Old movies, she thought. I hope it's better than that.

She pointed when they came to the church. "There's the church where the wedding will be. I hope we can cram all the guests in there. Bruce's mother had a list you wouldn't believe. We haven't heard from a lot of them, even this late. Maybe there'll be some no-shows. I only hope they won't all want to come this far."

"Where do they live, anyway?"

"Bruce and Rebecca are in New York. His parents live in Ohio, but they have friends all over."

"You could set up a big video screen out on the steps, like the major tennis matches."

She laughed and led him into the park. He sniffed the cold air as if being outdoors felt good. How long had he been out of prison? She couldn't bring herself to ask, much less how long he'd been inside. For all his charm, her original doubts were returning. What was she letting them all in for, having Dave here? How far could she trust him? Would even Rebecca's wedding gifts be safe?

You're borrowing trouble, she told herself. He promised. And he told me himself he'd been in prison. But wouldn't he? He knows I'm married to a cop. He probably knows Fred could find out, so he told me the truth to look open and trustworthy. I can't let myself think about it.

"There's Ellen's B-and-B," she told him when they reached the other side. "We're kind of in her backyard here."

"Some backyard!" He looked back at the park they'd just crossed. "How big is it, anyway?"

"I don't know how many acres the park has," she said. "Fifty or sixty, maybe. There used to be a lot more trees, before the tornado, but they've planted saplings. They'll grow."

"It looks fine now."

"My problem is that I remember how it used to look. They did cut up the wood to use in the fireplaces in the park shelters like the one over there." She pointed. "Most of it's stored somewhere else, but they keep some here where it's handy."

"I noticed."

Dinner went well. Fred and Andrew treated Dave like family, not an ex-con, and Dave told stories about Joan as a child. She knew she'd be teased about them later, but right now she enjoyed hearing them.

As the days passed, she began to relax, or at least to trade mother-of-the-bride worries for any misgivings she'd been having about her brother. Elizabeth Graham called her several times a day with one complaint after another, and the people who mattered were beginning to arrive. Bruce and Rebecca came first, although Bruce managed only to drop Rebecca off before leaving to cope with his mother, back in Ohio. He didn't even have time to help open the wedding gifts Joan had been storing in Rebecca's room.

———∞∞∞———

Thursday evening after supper, a week after Dave arrived, Joan was trapped on the phone with Alex, who seemed to think she was supposed to be managing through Christmas, even though the orchestra was taking almost a month's break.

"No, Alex, they're not going to charge us extra for the music. We negotiated the extra time in advance. "

She found it hard to keep listening as Alex went though a laundry list of concerns about players she found less than fully cooperative with her musical priorities. Having long since learned that there was no point in suggesting that Alex take up her issues with the players concerned, Joan knew it was easier just to wait her out.

But she had concerns of her own. Rebecca was as full of nerves tonight as if she and Bruce hadn't been together for years now. Joan watched Dave take her to a quiet corner of the living room for a chat. They were sitting with their heads together when she ended her call and tuned in to what he was saying to her daughter.

"So throw the guy over," he told her. "Run off with me, instead."

Rebecca actually giggled. "Oh, Uncle Dave!"

"Can't you call me Dave? 'Uncle Dave' makes me feel a hundred years old."

"Sure, Dave."

"Much better. Now give me a kiss and don't worry about old what's-his-name, much less his mother."

She giggled again and reached up to kiss him on the cheek, but he grabbed her, hard, and claimed a long, probing kiss. When he finally released her, she wasn't giggling. Visibly shaken, she said, "I think I'd better go upstairs," and escaped to her room.

Dave stood and looked after her, but made no attempt to follow her.

Joan trembled with fury. "How could you? Even you!"

Dave shrugged it off. "It was all in fun."

"Maybe for you, but not for her. You keep away from my daughter!"

He backed away, open hands raised. "Sure, boss."

It took every ounce of Joan's self-control to turn her back on him. If he'd been anyone else… As it was, she followed Rebecca upstairs. "You all right?"

Rebecca was sitting in her room, which ordinarily functioned as a guest room. All around her were recently opened wedding gifts and the thank-you notes she'd begun writing for Joan to mail after the wedding. Now, though, she was pulling a hairbrush through her dark curls.

"Thanks, Mom. I'm fine. It's not as if no one ever came on to me before. I didn't expect it from my own uncle, that's all." *Brush, brush, brush,* the fierce strokes belied her calm words. Tears came suddenly to her eyes. "If you're not safe in your own family…"

"Oh, honey!" Joan ran to her and hugged her. "Dave wouldn't hurt you!" Or would he? Had he? That kiss hadn't been innocent, no matter what he claimed.

"It's all right, Mom, really." Now Rebecca was comforting her mother. Joan's face must have given her away. "Tell you what, let's look at what you're going to wear on Saturday." She hopped up as if nothing were wrong and ran to her closet.

Bless her heart, Joan thought. What if it doesn't fit? But maybe it will distract her. As for Dave, I'll have to talk to Fred about him. "Sure, honey," she said. "I'd love to."

Rebecca unzipped the garment bag she had brought with her and pulled out something long in Joan's favorite soft blue.

"I thought a light wool might be good for a winter wedding."

Joan shed her work clothes and slipped it over her head. Wool it might be, but so light it floated. The simple neckline was low, and the long sleeves hugged her upper arms and floated down to her wrists. In the same way, the long gown clung to her upper body and relaxed in soft folds below her hips. "Rebecca, it's beautiful! Where did you find the pattern?"

Rebecca smiled. "I didn't. It's my own design."

"I should have known. And it fits exactly."

"Mine is almost the same, only cream-colored—looks a lot better on me than stark white. And I made Sally's rose, because that's what she looks good in."

"Would you like to wear my pearls?"

"Oh, Mom, what a sweet offer. But you'd better wear them yourself. Bruce is giving me my own as his wedding gift."

"Lovely. Does his mother know?"

"About the pearls?" Rebecca grinned. "I doubt it. It's his money."

"No, about the dresses—yours and Sally's."

"I told her they were being created especially for us by a New York designer. That sounded fancy enough that she couldn't object. She didn't ask who the designer was, and I'm not about to tell her."

"Why did I ever worry about you?"

Rebecca hugged her. "Thanks for trusting me, Mom. It's the difference between you and Bruce's mother. She doesn't think we know enough to do any of this, as if this were even the part that mattered."

"I'm so glad you know that. Have you and Bruce met the minister?"

"Only by email and phone. We'll talk to him tomorrow afternoon before the rehearsal. We haven't had his usual premarital counseling, he says, but we had a good three-way phone conversation with him, and what he said and asked us made sense. He's been a big help about Bruce's mother."

"How's Bruce's dad?"

"Busy. Fine, I guess. Seems supportive enough. But he doesn't get in the middle when Elizabeth's throwing her weight around. How can such a thin person throw so much weight around, anyway?" Rebecca was smiling when she hung her gown back in the closet. Joan reluctantly took off the blue wool and stroked its softness as she held it out to her daughter.

"Don't you want to keep it in your own closet?" Rebecca said. "It's not as if it needed any alterations. And it's yours, you know."

A happy thought. And as Rebecca had surely known, she had just the right shoes for it. "I'd love to. Are you coming back down?"

"No, I think I can use some time alone. But you know, in an odd way, I feel better now. Not as uptight as I was when Uncle Dave tried whatever he was trying." Her dimple was showing.

I know exactly what he was trying, Joan thought, and so do you. "Okay. You know where to find me. And Rebecca, I love the dress. You've outdone yourself."

She went downstairs to hang it in her closet and to hang her brother out to dry, but as she passed through it, the living room was empty.

Andrew wandered in from the kitchen. "You looking for Uncle Dave? He said to tell you he was going back to Ellen's. Something about overstepping. Does that make sense?"

"Too much." She turned her back on him and went into her room, giving the blue wool one last stroke before closing the closet door.

"You mad, Mom?" he called from the living room.

"Sorry." It wasn't fair to take her anger at Dave out on Andrew. She went back into the living room and curled up on the big leather sofa. "Not at you."

"What's he done now?"

"What do you mean, now?" Was he going after her son, too? She'd have to get rid of him, that's all there was to it.

"Oh, you know."

"No, Andrew, I don't." Joan patted the sofa, and he sat down at the other end,

"Besides the phone and all. All those phone calls he's been making. He said you didn't mind."

"Did you hear his calls?"

"Not what he said. But I could hear that they were long distance from all the numbers he was hitting. And he used our phone, not a cell phone or anything."

Probably couldn't make a long-distance call from Ellen's. "This was in the middle of the day?"

"Yeah. I didn't have any classes, so I was home. Upstairs, some, and I had lunch. I kept hearing him hitting all those numbers. Sometimes the phone rang, and he answered. But mostly he was doing the calling."

"You said 'all those calls.' How long do you think he was on the phone?"

Andrew shifted his weight on the sofa. "I don't know. As I said, I was in and out. Maybe it wasn't as long as it seemed."

"Make a wild guess."

"Couple of hours? Probably not that long. And maybe they weren't all long distance."

Well, it wouldn't break them.

"He didn't ask, did he?" Andrew said.

"No." What would she have said if he had? She couldn't imagine herself telling Dave not to use the phone. But he'd made it sound to Andrew as if they'd at least talked about it. One more reason not to trust him. Again, she wondered whether the wedding gifts were safe up in Rebecca's room. Joan had already arranged to take Friday off from work, but she couldn't stand guard here all the time.

"Andrew, you don't have any plans tomorrow, do you?"

"Nope. No classes now till January—I'm all yours."

"Good. I'll have to spend some time with the Lundquists and the Grahams. But one of the family needs to be here, and I don't mean Dave. Whatever my brother is cooking up, I don't want Rebecca's gifts to disappear. I'd already hired someone to be here during the rehearsal dinner and the wedding. But I wasn't thinking of protecting the house from one of the guests, only from outsiders."

"Now you are?"

"Now I am."

"You telling Fred?"

She sighed. "I guess I'd better."

She put off saying anything until they were in bed, but Fred wasn't impressed by the phone calls.

"If that's the worst he does while he's here…"

She thought for a moment about telling him what had happened with Rebecca, but somehow she couldn't. Had she blown it out of proportion? Part of her wanted to give him another chance. Until now he'd behaved like a gentleman. She'd think about it tomorrow.

"It isn't the phone calls that bother me. It's that he lied to Andrew about them. Told him I'd said it was fine."

"I know." Fred curved himself around her. "Let it go, Joan."

"I don't want to have to be on my guard. Not now, of all times. Can you imagine what Elizabeth would say if he pulled something on her?"

He nibbled her ear. "You want to suggest it, or should I?"

She laughed and relaxed into his embrace. But as she was sinking into sleep, she imagined Dave grabbing Sally Graham, or Kierstin Lundquist. She'd better watch him like a hawk around the other young women at the wedding.

———

On Friday afternoon Ellen called and reported that Dave was helping her at the bed-and-breakfast. "I told you he would!" she said. "This morning I had him peeling vegetables for tonight, and this afternoon he and Laura went out in the park with the dog. He's great with her—says she reminds him of you at that age."

"That's what he told me, too," Joan said. Should she warn Ellen about his behavior with Rebecca? As inappropriate as it had been, it hadn't suggested that he'd do anything wrong to a child. And there were plenty of eyes in the public park.

"But that's not why I called," Ellen said while Joan was still dithering. "The Lundquists have pulled in from Illinois. They're getting settled in their rooms right now."

"Great. I'll be right over." Fred's family were the only other family Joan was expecting. She had invited Rebecca's aunt, uncle, and cousins on her father's side, but they'd claimed to be unable to come. Maybe it was true, she thought on her walk through the park to Ellen's place. Along with their good wishes, the aunt and uncle had sent a crystal vase that would be a challenge to transport to New York without breaking, though Rebecca had probably saved the bubble wrap it came in.

By now Rebecca and Bruce must be having their talk with the minister. Joan had no idea where Bruce's parents were staying, if they would even stay in Oliver. Not at Ellen's, she knew. So only the bride's side of the family would be at the bed-and-breakfast, and most of them would be Fred's family. Very cozy.

She couldn't help wondering how far her mother-in-law had declined since they'd first met. Helga's mind had been failing then, even though she was in her own house, in the tiny community of Bishop Hill, Illinois. By comparison, even Oliver would feel huge, and any new place would be hard for her to adjust to. Staying at Ellen's with the rest of her family ought to help, but the wedding itself could put a big strain on her.

It was one more reason to be grateful that Bruce and Rebecca had kept it simple.

At Ellen's, it was Laura, wearing an honest-to-goodness dress and tights, who opened the door. No dog indoors today. Good.

"Come in, Joan. Mom's already got the company working."

Ellen hurried into the living room, a no-nonsense apron covering most of her jeans and shirt. "Laura! You're not supposed to tell all our secrets."

"You already told me Dave was hard at work in the kitchen," Joan said.

"I mean Mrs. Lundquist," Laura said, her eyes huge.

Helga. Joan couldn't think of a better thing to do than let her help with food. "I'm sure she wanted to."

"She did," Ellen said. "And the rest of the family seemed relieved. Your brother's helping her put salads on the salad plates. He's sweet with her. Of course, it probably doesn't hurt that Chrissy's working in there, too. He doesn't seem to care how old they are, as long as they're female."

Deciding the kitchen crew could do without her, Joan went to meet the rest of the family. Oscar, Fred's father, his shock of hair even whiter than before, if that was even possible, greeted her with a warm hug and a totally appropriate kiss on the cheek. "How's my boy been treating you?"

"Just fine, Oscar. I'm so glad you were able to come. Ellen tells me Helga's already in there working."

"Can't keep her down. But she'll fold pretty soon. I hope she can last long enough to eat whatever it is she's fixing."

Joan did, too. They wouldn't start dinner until after the rehearsal, and that was likely to throw Helga. "Would she take a nap, do you think?"

"Nap? Helga? Not on your life. She'd be afraid she'd miss something. Me, now, I'll drop off first chance I get."

"You two don't have to attend the rehearsal, you know. I wouldn't go myself if I didn't have to sit where I was told."

He nodded. "I was kinda hoping there'd be a way to get out of it. She seems right at home here."

Until Elizabeth Graham roars in and treats her like hired help, Joan thought. But with luck Elizabeth won't deign to notice the help.

"It should be fine. You take your nap and trust Helga to Ellen. Where are Fred's brother and his family?"

"Walt and Ruthie are up changing clothes. But I'm surprised their Kierstin isn't down here asking about your boy. She sure is excited about seeing him again."

The beautiful Kierstin, younger than Andrew and as blonde as he was dark, had turned out to be a big plus during their visit to Fred's old home. "He'll be glad to see her, too."

At least tonight he wouldn't have to worry about guarding their house from whatever Dave couldn't resist. Dave would be right here with the rest of them. And it would be no punishment for Andrew to spend time with Kierstin.

Chapter 6

JOAN LEFT the Lundquists in Ellen's good hands and went home to change for the rehearsal and dinner. She found Bruce's sister up in Rebecca's room with her, trying on the rose-colored bridesmaid's dress.

"Mom, this is Sally Graham."

"Sally, you look lovely," Joan said. It was true. Rebecca's design did as much for this slender teenager as for the mother of the bride. And this dress was exactly the right color to enhance Sally's young features. Like Bruce, she had red hair. Who would have thought rose would look so good on her? But Rebecca had seen beyond the obvious.

"I can't believe she did this," Sally said. She, too, was stroking the soft wool. "And it fits me exactly. She didn't even have a pattern, you know? She just made it up."

"But we're not telling your mother that!" Rebecca reminded her.

"I wouldn't dream of it. Lots of times, what Mom doesn't know makes my life a lot easier."

Joan could believe it. Was that how Rebecca had felt during the years when she'd kept her distance from her own mother?

"You're so lucky to have your mother," Sally told Rebecca. "Bruce told me how much she helped him when he was playing in the Indianapolis competition."

Joan beamed. "I like him, too," she said. She'd done what she could, but it was good to know he'd said such a thing about her.

"Time to get ready for the rehearsal," Rebecca said, and began helping Sally out of her dress. "I'll bring it to the church tomorrow. Tonight the minister will show you the room they have for the bride and bridesmaid to change clothes."

Joan left them to it and went to do what she could to neaten her own appearance. As mother of the bride, she wouldn't have a big role, but she couldn't help the way she felt about Elizabeth Graham. It didn't help that the only time the woman had seen her, she'd come straight from that exercise class in sweats that had more than lived up to their name. *Anyone else, and I wouldn't care,* she thought. *Except maybe Fred, even though Fred would tell me I looked beautiful in them, bless his heart.*

"Don't you have to be somewhere?" Sergeant Ketcham asked Fred.

What would he do without Ketcham? He picked up his phone and called home. "Joan? You mind going over to the church alone? I'll be there as fast as I can. Yes, I promise. We're tracking down— never mind what we're tracking. Nothing important, but it's tied me up all day, and I let the time slip away from me." He shook his head at the pile of folders on his desk. "There's no way."

"Don't worry about it," Ketcham said. "We'll deal with this. And if Altschuler raises a ruckus, I'll tell him you—"

"I'll tell him myself. Thanks, Johnny." He pulled on his jacket and went down the hall to Captain Warren Altschuler's office. Altschuler, chief of detectives, was generally a reasonable man, and he and Fred got along well. But Fred knew better than to cross him.

He knocked on the frame of Altschuler's office door and watched him look up.

"Fred." Altschuler's gravelly voice matched his pug-ugly face. "Take a load off. Progress?"

Fred shook his head and remained on his feet. "It's slow going. Just when we think we've nailed these guys down, we lose 'em again."

"You came to tell me that?" Altschuler's face was turning red.

"No, sir, I came so my sergeant wouldn't be tempted to lie for me."

Altschuler's eyebrows rose.

"Barring another murder, I have to take off for several hours. You know my wife's daughter is being married tomorrow."

"You take as much time as you need tomorrow. But tonight?"

"I have to show up for the rehearsal and the dinner afterward. If I weren't giving the bride away…" Fred knew the red he felt rising up his face would betray how awkward he felt about being honorary father of the bride. Not that he wasn't fond of Rebecca. Somehow, though, he felt out of place. But her real father was dead. How could he turn her down?

"Then go, man. Get the hell out of here!"

Fred grinned. "Thanks, Warren. Ketcham's in the picture."

"Don't worry about it. This case'll be waiting for you when you come back. I don't want to see your face around here till Monday."

"Thanks," Fred said again and left.

They hadn't waited for him, he was glad to see when he arrived at the little church. Reverend Eric Young was talking the wedding party through the service.

"Fred, you're just in time," he said as Fred hurried down the aisle. "You've already walked the bride down the aisle, and when I ask, 'Who gives this woman to be married to this man?' Rebecca says you'll answer."

"Yes," Fred said. He smiled at Rebecca. "She wants me to say, 'Her mother and I do.'"

Rebecca tucked her arm through his and nodded emphatically.

"Then you go back and sit with her mother."

Fred did, and he thought his part was finished. "Who walked her down?" he whispered to Joan. Andrew was standing up by Bruce, and the redheaded girl by Rebecca must be Bruce's sister.

"Nobody. So far they're just talking."

"You mean they're going to go through the whole thing again?" He and Joan hadn't bothered with a full-fledged rehearsal when Eric Young had married them in this very church, with hardly more people than were scattered around it now. He waved to his brother, Walt, sitting near the back door with his wife, Ruthie.

"You'll live."

Across the aisle, the woman emphatically clearing her throat had to be the infamous mother of the groom. Fred smiled and nodded in her direction as if the words he was sure she intended weren't in his vocabulary.

"You're awful!" Joan whispered.

"I try," he returned out of the side of his mouth.

Then the unforgivable happened—his cell phone rang. He hit the Mute button, looked at the number on the screen, and slid out of the pew to retreat up the aisle to the back door. "What?"

"I'm sorry, Lieutenant," the 911 dispatcher said in his ear. "I knew not to bother you. But when they said it was your family, I—"

He cut her off. He hadn't seen his parents in the church, but hadn't worried until now. "What happened? Where are they?"

"At Ellen Putnam's. Something about a knife was all I could get. Ambulance on the way, but I thought you'd want to know."

"Oh, God," he groaned. It had to be his mother. "I'll be right there."

Joan had turned around. He scribbled a note to her and handed it to Ruthie. "Come on," he said to Walt, who looked surprised, but followed him.

"Carol didn't make this trip?" Fred asked him once they were outside.

"No, they were glad to get some time to themselves. You know how it is, with Mom and all." Fred did know. Their sister and her husband shared the care of their parents with Walt and Ruthie, but the demands of Walt's restaurant meant that Carol bore the brunt of it. Walt looked alarmed. "Is Mom all right? Is Dad? Where are you taking me?"

"Back to Ellen's. And I don't know. Whoever called 911 said it was my family, so I figured Mom. Here's my car." He'd parked his Chevy smack in front of the church, illegally, knowing no Oliver cop would bother it.

Because the college was taking its break, the streets were empty. They covered the short blocks in minutes that felt like hours.

Two squad cars were flashing lights outside the B&B. The ambulance hadn't arrived when they pulled up, but the siren was close.

Beside him, Walt sat mute and tense.

"Come on," Fred said, knowing Walt had to dread what they'd find as much as he did. Walt followed him in.

"In the kitchen, Lieutenant." Officer Wampler pointed the way.

"Hang in there, Walt," Fred said. "She probably cut herself." The dispatcher had mentioned a knife, and he had to prepare Walt for that, at least.

But he himself wasn't prepared for the sight that met them. Her apron and hands covered in blood, Helga stood alone beside a table covered with what looked like individual salads arranged on plates, waving a bloody kitchen knife at all comers. Armed, the police were keeping their distance. Then Fred saw the man's body crumpled at her feet, face down. The table kept him from seeing the head, but the source of the blood was obvious from what he could see.

"Good God, Mom!"

"Fred. I'm glad you finally got here. Tell these people to leave me alone." She waved the knife at the police again. "They don't understand. I had to do it."

"Do what, Mom?" Churning, he forced himself to ask it quietly.

"Take the knife out," she said as if it were obvious. "It was going to kill him."

Taking it out probably finished the job, Fred thought. "We'd better see how bad it is," he said. "Let's let the doctors check him, okay?"

"Okay," she said. Fred went to her side.

"Tell them to come in," he told Officer Chuck Terry, who nodded and gestured behind him. Two EMTs hurried in and knelt by the body.

"Let's give them room to work, Mom," Fred said. "I'll take the knife." He reached his hand out to Officer Jill Root. "Evidence bag, Jill."

"Yessir."

He held the open bag out to his mother, who put the knife into it without protest. Fred passed it to Root as if it didn't matter.

"Mom, are you hurt?"

"No, but that poor man…" she said, leaning on the table and craning to look.

Fred stood in her way and faced her. "They'll take care of him now. Let's get you cleaned up." He held her hands out to the sink and ran water over them, just in case. No, no cuts. She, at least, was uninjured.

"Walt, can you take Mom to her room and help her clean up? We'll get this apron off right now." He pulled the blood-soaked thing over her head and held it out to Root, who slid it into another bag.

"Sure," Walt said, with amazing calm. "Come on, Mom." He led her out of the room, unprotesting. Fred wondered how often Walt had to help his mom in less dramatic circumstances. Their roles seemed to come naturally to them both.

Did she have any idea what she'd done? And exactly what had she actually done? Could she have reported that accurately?

"Lieutenant, I know she's your mother and all, but somebody's got to talk to her," Jill Root said. Not you, she clearly meant.

"Of course. Ketcham can do it, unless Altschuler wants someone else. But you're not going to get anything useful out of Mom. You could see how she is."

Root nodded. "Is she always that way?"

"Pretty much. Up and down, not always the same. Stress makes her worse. I haven't seen her since last year, so I'm not up to date. We'll see what she's like when Walt gets her changed, but I'll be surprised if she can be much help. You call Ketcham yet?"

"He's on the way."

"Good."

The EMTs had turned the body over and were still working on it, but showed no signs of packing it up to transport.

"You know who he is?" Fred asked, keeping out of their way. All he could see were the man's feet, toes now pointing up.

"Ellen said his name is Zimmerman," Root told him.

"Zimmerman! Dave Zimmerman?"

"That sounds right."

Fred groaned. Now he had to see for himself. No longer worried about the EMTs, he went over for a close look.

"You know him?" Root asked.

"He's Joan's brother. Here for the wedding. He's staying here, too."

"So why were they in the kitchen?"

"No idea. You'll have to ask Ellen. Where is she, anyway?" The only people he'd seen on the way into the kitchen were cops.

"She called us and took her staff and kids to her private quarters. This is really going to cramp her style. She's supposed to be putting on a big dinner here tonight."

"I know."

Root looked horrified. "It's not—"

"Afraid it is. In fact, they're over at the church now, for the rehearsal. That's where the dispatcher reached me." What Ellen would do—what any of them would do—about the rehearsal dinner concerned him less than what he needed to do next. Should he go back to the church, break the news about her brother to Joan? Or would whoever would be in charge of the investigation want to speak to her first, see her reaction? No question about it, someone else would have to handle it.

He was relieved when he finally saw Ketcham enter the kitchen.

"What's up?"

"My wife's brother just got himself stabbed." Fred gestured to the EMTs, still working over the motionless body on the floor.

"Alive?"

"Don't know. But when we came in, my mother was standing here, covered in blood and holding the knife."

Jill Root held up the two evidence bags.

"So there's no way I can deal with this one," Fred said. "Did Altschuler put you in charge?" He hoped so. Ketcham was steady and competent. He knew his way around Oliver and how to handle people.

"Yeah, but he didn't say why. I'm not sure how much he knew. The dispatcher did say something about your family and a knife. That was enough to tell him he couldn't leave it to you. So what did you learn so far? And where's your mother?"

"She's not hurt. My brother, Walt, took her up to her room. She told me she had to take the knife out to save his life. But we all know how much that's worth."

Ketcham knew about his mom. "Who else was in the kitchen?"

"When Walt and I got here, only cops—Root, Terry, and Wampler."

Root said, "She wouldn't let us come close. We were afraid she'd stab him again. Or us." She looked apologetically at Fred.

"It's all right, Jill. She looked pretty fierce."

"Where were the staff?" Ketcham asked her.

"When we arrived, Ellen had put them in her private quarters. She directed us to the kitchen and then joined them. You'll have to ask her who was here when it happened."

"I'll do that." Ketcham looked fierce himself.

Fred didn't envy him.

One of the EMTs stood up. "He's gone. We'll transport him and keep up the CPR, just in case, but between you and me, he's not coming back."

Ketcham checked his watch. "Was he breathing when you arrived?"

"Nope. No heartbeat, either."

"And that was…?"

"I forgot to time it." The man blushed. "Maybe ten minutes ago."

"More like fifteen," Fred said.

"The dispatcher logged the call half an hour ago," Ketcham said.

Fred had missed being at the station when it came in by mere moments.

"You can go back to the church."

"And say what to Joan?" A decision he was glad to palm off on Ketcham.

Ketcham looked at the blood on the floor, still not clotted. "She was probably at the church well before the call came in. No way was she involved. Still, we ought to go by the book, notify her ourselves. Maybe you'd better stick around. Or do they need you there?"

"I'd better go back. I'm giving the bride away. I'll keep it to myself."

Ketcham nodded. "All right, then."

"And what about the rehearsal dinner?"

Ketcham looked blank.

Fred pointed to the salads on the big kitchen table. Odds were good his mom had been helping make them. It explained the apron.

"It's here?"

"Would have been. Now it's a crime scene."

"We'll do our best." The EMTs had already contaminated the scene, of course. Ketcham didn't need to spell it out.

"Thanks." So he didn't have to tell Joan, and he could be there to comfort her when she found out. He could imagine Elizabeth Graham's reaction to the news, though. All Rebecca would need was for her mother-in-law to blame her family for a stabbing. Or a murder, more like it. Time to face the music. They had to be wondering what had happened to him.

"Tell Walt I went back to the church. Someone will have to let us know about the dinner."

"We'll sort that out with Ellen as fast as we can. Let her call you. She know your cell?"

"If she doesn't, give it to her."

Chapter 7

AT THE church, the rehearsal was thrown into disarray by Fred's disappearance. Ruthie brought Fred's note up to Joan, so they knew where he'd gone. At first, it was no problem. With the minister and Sally and Andrew, Rebecca and Bruce talked through the exchanging of vows and rings and what to do with the bouquet. But when it came time to walk through the whole thing, Rebecca insisted on waiting for Fred. Behind them, Elizabeth Graham was jangling her bracelets impatiently, but Bruce stood firm.

"Don't worry, Mom," he said. "They're not going to kick us out of here."

"Certainly not," Eric Young said. "I haven't met your mother yet, Bruce. You think you could manage an introduction?"

Bruce obliged gracefully, introducing both his parents, sister, and brother to the minister, and then the other members of his family who had shown up for the rehearsal. Elizabeth had probably invited still more to the dinner.

Joan wondered whether the dinner would be delayed by whatever emergency had dragged Fred over there. At least it was something to do with his mother rather than the kind of police emergency she'd hoped to be spared this weekend.

Now Eric was doing a beautiful job of making the wedding party feel comfortable, asking them about their interests. Joan held her breath, but Rebecca clearly had no intention of mentioning her interest in dress designing in this company.

The bracelets were beginning to jangle again.

At last Joan saw Fred running down the aisle toward them, breathless. "Did I make it in time?"

Helga must be all right, Joan thought. Probably just scared to be in a new place.

"Sure, Fred," Eric said. "We've just been chatting. Okay, let's get this show on the road. Places, everybody."

"Come on, Fred," Rebecca said, linking her arm in his and smiling up at him as if he'd never left. Bless her heart, Joan thought. Having him run out on her like that and then Elizabeth's reaction to the disruption—it all has to be hard on her. Fred didn't smile back, but he patted her arm with his other hand.

Bruce, Andrew, and the minister came in from the door near the front of the church to stand facing the center aisle, where Sally waited to precede Rebecca and Fred. Finally, the organist began the traditional march.

"I know it's corny," Rebecca had said, "but I want to hear it like everybody else."

"If you want it, it's not corny," Joan had told her.

But when Rebecca and Fred were a few slow steps down the aisle, the organist suddenly switched into a very different kind of march, one Joan and her children knew just as well. Instead of "Here Comes the Bride," Peter's theme from *Peter and the Wolf* came bouncing down from the organ loft.

Joan saw her daughter change from a solemnity that threatened to give way to tears to startled recognition and then open giggles. Rebecca's eyes met hers, but Joan raised her palms and shook her head in innocence. Glancing back at the groom, though, she saw a sparkle in Bruce's eyes that gave him away. Good for him!

Rebecca murmured something to Fred. Holding hands like children, they skipped the rest of the way down the aisle, though Fred's face looked incongruously grim. Ahead of them, Sally Graham, still trying to match the traditional hesitation step to Peter's theme, barely beat them to the front of the church.

Elizabeth Graham was glaring, but her husband's eyes mirrored Bruce's sparkle. That was encouraging. Joan didn't know him yet, but she'd wondered more than once how he'd stayed married to the woman.

Then Eric asked, "Who gives this woman to be married to this man?"

Fred answered, handed Rebecca to Bruce, and came to join Joan in the first pew. Rebecca passed the frilly bouquet she'd made of wedding gift bows to Sally and turned to Bruce. Andrew patted his jeans pocket when it was time to produce a ring for his sister, coming up with a pull-tab from a soft drink can, and Sally found a rubber washer in hers for Rebecca to give to Bruce. Eric gave them a few last instructions, and it was all over but the Mendelssohn.

While Bruce and Rebecca led the march back down the aisle and general conversation broke out, Joan turned to Fred. "I'm so glad you got back. I would have hated for you..." But the look on his face stopped her. "Your mother. Did something happen?"

"She's okay. I left Walt with her."

"But?"

He shook his head. "I can't tell you the rest. It's a police matter. But I'm afraid the dinner will be delayed."

"By a police matter? Oh, Fred, that's terrible." But she knew better than to ask him for more details.

His cell phone rang then, and he saw Elizabeth's head swivel around, even though it couldn't matter now. "We're still in the church," he said. "Rehearsal's just over. Okay, we'll wait for you."

He stood up. "I have an announcement for all of you."

"Make it short," Elizabeth snapped. "You delayed the rehearsal, and we're due for dinner in just a few minutes now."

"That's the announcement," Fred told her. "The rehearsal dinner is going to be delayed by a police problem. We're asked to stay right here for now. I hope that's not going to cause any difficulty for the church," he said to the minister.

"No," Eric said. "It's warm in here. You wait as long as you need to."

"Is that it? A police problem? We're supposed to take your word for it?" Elizabeth was working up a lather now. Joan wished again that Rebecca could have been spared Bruce's mother.

"No, ma'am," Fred said. "Sergeant Ketcham is on his way over now."

"Hmph." She turned her back on him.

Joan wondered whether she even knew that Fred outranked the sergeant. She hoped not. Let Ketcham take the heat. She squeezed his hand when he sat down again, and he returned the pressure.

The young people were visiting among themselves, but she and Fred sat together in silence. She hoped whatever had happened wouldn't make him have to go back to work on the weekend. Clearly, he'd made a point of coming back for Rebecca's sake, but from the way he looked, it had to be something serious. She wouldn't even try to guess what.

"There he is!" someone cried, and she turned to see Sergeant Ketcham coming down the aisle, followed by a tall black officer she'd met. Chuck Terry, that was his name. Rather than stop to speak to the whole group, Ketcham headed right for Joan and Fred.

But he didn't speak to Fred. Instead, he said seriously, "Joan, I need to talk to you."

"Please, sit down," she said. What on earth?

He sat beside her in the front pew and peered at her through his round wire-rims. "I'm afraid I have bad news."

"About the dinner?"

"About your brother."

"Dave? What did he do?" She looked from him to Fred, who obviously knew.

"It's what someone did to him." Ketcham looked her in the eye. "Your brother has been killed."

"Killed? Dave? I don't understand." It made no sense. Dave did things to people, not the other way around.

"When did you last see him?"

"I...I don't know. Yes, I do. He was at our house for a while after supper last night." What an awful way to remember him. "But Ellen Putnam said he was alive and well this afternoon. He was...he was helping her in the kitchen. What happened?" How could Dave be dead, just like that?

"That's what we're sorting out." Ketcham looked more

relaxed now. Had he expected her to fall apart? "It seems someone killed him in the kitchen."

"I thought there was some problem over there with Fred's mother, not Dave."

Ketcham turned on Fred. "You told her that?"

"I left her a note when I went over. The dispatcher mentioned my family."

"Mrs. Lundquist was in the kitchen with your brother."

"But Fred said she was okay," Joan said. "When he came back."

Again, Ketcham looked at Fred as if he'd told tales out of school.

"That's all I told her, Johnny."

He nodded. "She's not injured."

"So…what?" She didn't even know what to ask. He wasn't telling her anything.

"When did you arrive at the church?" Ketcham asked her.

"Me? You think I'd kill my brother?" She could hear her voice rise, but she didn't seem to be able to stop it.

"Just tell him," Fred said. "It's a routine question. He has to ask you."

"I don't even know. About ten minutes before you came, the first time." She looked around her. The rest of the wedding party was staring openly. "Can anyone tell me when I arrived here?" she called to them at large.

"You were late," Elizabeth Graham said. "We were supposed to be here by five. Everyone else was here—well, almost everyone." She glared at Fred.

"Simmer down, Elizabeth. She walked through the door at five on the dot," Dr. Graham said.

"You're sure?" Ketcham asked him.

"Yes. Some clock outside was tolling the hour."

Joan no longer noticed the courthouse clock when it chimed, but she was glad this visitor had.

"And she was the last to arrive?" Ketcham asked.

"Except for her husband."

Ketcham nodded. "That's very helpful." He turned to Officer Terry. "Take down the names and where they can be reached. Then they're all free to go. I need to get back to Ellen's." Leaving Terry to it, he walked out of the church.

Terry pulled out a notebook like the one Fred always kept in a convenient pocket and began making his way around the room.

"Does that mean we can have the dinner now?" Elizabeth asked.

"Elizabeth," her husband said. "He's just told Joan her brother was murdered."

"Murdered! How dare anyone murder anyone at a time like this!"

Fred stared at her.

Now he'll know I was right about her, Joan thought. Then she wanted to kick herself for even thinking about Elizabeth. But Elizabeth had a point. Who knew how long it would take to sort out what had happened to Dave? Joan didn't understand her own emotions. She felt guilty about celebrating a wedding, as if it weren't fair to Dave, but Rebecca and Bruce had waited a long time. Their wedding was long overdue. And who wasn't being fair, anyway? Dave, for coming to do some kind of secretive business in Oliver under the guise of attending the wedding? Had he gotten himself killed? What had all those phone calls been about? She'd have to remind Fred about them.

"They'll get word to you as soon as it's possible to hold your dinner," Fred told Elizabeth. "The police have promised to do whatever they can. They know about the wedding."

"What do you mean, *they*? Aren't you in charge?"

"No, with my family involved, I can't investigate this time."

"I don't see why—"

"Elizabeth, hush," Dr. Graham said, and to Joan's astonishment, Elizabeth hushed.

"I'm sure Ellen will know as soon as anyone when she can feed your guests," Fred said. "You'll want to be sure she knows how to reach you."

Dr. Graham nodded. "We'll talk to her. Come on, Elizabeth."

It was an order. He took her by the arm and led her out of the church.

"Come on, Joan," Fred said, but more gently. "I'll take you home."

"You go, Mom," Rebecca said, holding Bruce's hand tightly. "We'll be fine."

"Do you want me to come with you?" Eric asked.

"That's good of you," Joan said. "But I don't think so. Later, maybe."

"Call me when you need me," he said. "I'll be home. I wasn't going to the dinner anyway."

Joan nodded, remembering. Ken Spencer, her minister husband, had ducked most such invitations, too, back when Rebecca and Andrew had been small. As little as she'd attended church in Oliver, she didn't know anything about Eric's family, she realized. Never mind. Paying no attention to her grown children now, she walked with Fred out to his car.

On the way home she realized he was saying something.

"At first I thought it was Mom because of all the blood."

"What? Fred, I'm sorry. I spaced out."

"I'm not surprised. I was telling you I thought Mom was hurt when I first saw her. But she was fine."

"I'm glad." It would have been harder to lose Helga Lundquist than Dave Zimmerman, she thought. Was that disloyalty? But Helga had given her life to her family. Dave…she didn't know what Dave had given his life to. She hated to think. "So why did you think it was your mother?"

"You didn't hear a thing I said, did you?" He patted her knee. "Her apron had blood on it. Then I saw the knife."

"Knife?"

"She was holding a big kitchen knife."

For the first time, Joan was horrified. "Fred, you don't think she…" She couldn't say it.

"I don't know what to think. But that's why I can't be in charge, even if Dave weren't your brother."

Chapter 8

IT WAS beginning to sink in. Someone had stabbed Dave in Ellen's kitchen. Then why wasn't his only sister feeling anything?

"You're sure he's really dead?" Joan asked Fred in the car on the way home.

"The EMTs thought so when they took him to the hospital, and Ketcham says he was pronounced DOA there."

She sat still. "Am I supposed to go there and identify him?"

He pulled up to the house. "Not unless you feel the need to see him yourself. There's no doubt about who he is. I saw him. And I'm even a relative. So it's up to you."

"No, I don't need to see him." She felt a little lost, though, as if having a job to do would make some kind of difference.

Had Fred's mother really killed Dave? She couldn't imagine it of Helga, at least as she had been when they visited her and Oscar in Bishop Hill a year ago. But why had she been holding the knife?

"Did she say anything?" Joan asked as they climbed the steps to their front porch.

"Only that she had to take it out, or it would have killed him." He held the front door for her.

"But wouldn't that..." Doctors would have been very cautious about removing a knife stuck in a wound, she knew, for fear the bleeding would increase.

"Probably."

"You don't think she knew?" Joan pulled her coat off when the indoor warmth hit her. She didn't bother hanging it up, but tossed it on the sofa.

"Not these days." No, Helga didn't know much of anything these days.

"You home already?"

Joan jumped when Gary, the boy she'd hired to watch the house, came down the stairs, but she pulled it together enough to talk to him.

"We've had a family emergency," she said. "We don't know what time the dinner will be."

"Want me to come back? It's no trouble."

"Thanks. We'll call as soon as we know." She wondered what else she'd forgotten.

Fred closed the door behind him.

This whole business was upside down. She'd been worrying Dave would do something to harm someone else, and instead someone had killed him.

Ellen had said Dave was being very good with Helga, working together with her to make the salads. There was no way that cooperation could have turned into a murderous rage. But something had happened. Who could have barged in on them? Laura had been minding the front door, but what about a kitchen door? Joan tried without success to picture it. And who else had been in the kitchen? She didn't know that, either.

"You going to be all right?" Fred looked concerned.

She was standing in the middle of the living room, still feeling lost. Like Helga, maybe. She could see why Helga welcomed something to do with her hands.

She plopped down on the sofa, and he joined her. "Oh, Fred, I don't even know. I don't know how I feel about Dave, but this is all wrong."

"Yes," he said. "It always is."

"And with your mother...and Rebecca's wedding..." She couldn't think how to end her thought. Maybe that was because she had no idea how any of it would end, or how it had started.

He stood up and started pacing.

"What about you?" she asked. "This has to be hard for you, too. Do you want to go back there, check on your mom?"

He shook his head, but he kept pacing. "Walt's with her, and Ketcham won't give her a hard time. She's probably forgotten the whole thing by now."

Maybe she has, Joan thought. But Fred hasn't, and he can't distance himself from it by doing his job. Doing nothing has to be hard on him, too.

⬦⬦⬦

"Time to change, if you're going to."

"Huh?" She sat up straight, rubbing her eyes. How had she managed to fall asleep?

Fred was putting his phone into his pocket, but she hadn't even heard him talking on it. "Ketcham just called. He said the crime scene was so messed up by the time the EMTs left that they've got about as much out of it as they can. He told Ellen to go ahead with the dinner."

"Oh." Could she even face the dinner? And the rest of it? But for Rebecca... How could she not?

"You go ahead and get ready." He nudged her gently. "I promised to call Elizabeth."

"You know where they're staying?"

"Ketcham told me. Elizabeth's been on his back."

Joan smiled then. "She would be. Bad as this is, I can't help being glad it's Ketcham and not you."

"Come on, get ready. I'll call Gary back, tell him we're leaving in what, fifteen minutes?"

"I can do it in ten. I hadn't planned to change again." But she hadn't planned to sleep in these clothes, either.

"Take fifteen. Knock 'em dead."

She kissed him and ducked into their room. She checked the little makeup she wore, smoothed her hair back into the twist she'd chosen for the evening, and tucked a simple, pleated silk blouse smoothly into the skirt of her best winter suit. She'd worn the skirt to the rehearsal, but with a sweater. Neat, but not gaudy, as her mother used to say. She swiped the toes of her shoes with the brush from Fred's shoe polishing kit. Nothing much she could do about the look on her face.

No, that wasn't true. This was Rebecca's party. She'd worried for weeks that Dave might do something to mess it up. Dying wasn't what she'd expected of him, but it wasn't fair to Rebecca to let his death ruin her wedding. Think about her, instead, she told herself. The notion of Rebecca fooling Elizabeth Graham about her New York designer gown brought the smile she needed. Slipping her suit jacket on, she stuck some extra cloth hankies in her pocket and joined Fred and Gary, who was already back.

"You sure you're up to it?" Fred asked.

She nodded. "I'm not going to let Rebecca down."

"All right, then." He held her coat for her, shut the door behind them, and kissed her solidly. "If you change your mind, I'm on your side. You know that."

Tears stung her eyes. "You're a good man, Fred Lundquist." Taking his arm, she felt ready to face the world, even Elizabeth Graham. "Let's walk over. It'll feel good."

Conversation in Ellen's living room died suddenly when they came in. Rebecca ran to greet them.

"We didn't know whether you'd come!" she cried.

"I'm so sorry," Joan said, and hugged her. "I didn't want anything to spoil your wedding."

"Don't worry about us. Are you all right?"

"I'm going to be fine. How is Ellen holding up?" She could hardly imagine putting on a dinner of this size after having the last-minute preparations interrupted by real disaster, much less finishing those preparations in a room even Fred said was bloody.

"She's amazing."

The conversational buzz picked up, but not before Joan heard Elizabeth at it again across the room. "I don't know why we didn't simply call it off. The dinner's bound to be ruined."

When her husband said something to her, she subsided, but the look on her face left little to the imagination. Joan was relieved to see Ellen come into the room and speak to them.

"Dinnertime," Dr. Graham announced. He held his arm out to his wife, and they led the way into the dining room.

At least this room hadn't been disturbed. Joan's stomach lurched at the thought of what had happened only a few feet away. How could she possibly eat? She willed herself to concentrate instead on the banquet table, which she had never seen opened out to its full length or set with formal linens and shining glassware and silver. Neat place cards told them all where to sit. At one end, Bruce and Rebecca took their places side by side, flanked by their parents. Joan and Fred also sat side by side, but across the table from the Grahams for easy conversation, if such a thing were possible with Elizabeth. On Fred's other side, his parents were surrounded by their sons and Walt's wife. Good. That should help Helga's inevitable confusion. For the moment, at least, she looked cheerful and was chatting with Oscar as if they were at home. She'd obviously forgotten all about what had happened in the kitchen. Beyond the Grahams were what must be relatives and close friends of theirs. The young people, including Andrew, Sally Graham, Tom Graham, and Kierstin Lundquist, sat at the far end of the table.

Joan was grateful to be directly opposite Dr. Graham—she'd have to start thinking of him as Don, which she knew was his name, but so far this was her first chance to exchange two words with him. And how could she make small talk now, much less here? His eyes looked kind, she thought.

"You must be very proud of your son," Fred said to Bruce's mother.

Of course. "I felt so lucky to hear him play in the violin competition," Joan said to his father.

"You heard him?" Elizabeth pounced. "We're not allowed to, you know."

How could she have forgotten? Rebecca had told her he didn't let his family hear him compete. A sore spot, obviously, though now that she'd met his mother, Joan could see why he didn't want her anywhere around. "That was probably my last chance," she said. "After tomorrow, I'll be family, too."

Don Graham smiled at that, but Elizabeth frowned.

They were spared further attempts at conversation by the arrival of the main course. Chrissy and an older woman who looked familiar, probably her mother, from what Ellen had said, began serving the plates at their end of the table.

"Beef bourguignon!" Bruce exclaimed. "My favorite."

"Mine, too," Rebecca said. "What a great choice."

And one that could survive the wait, Joan thought. Sure enough, the beef was fork-tender and still moist, the mushrooms fresh, and the sauce delicious. The vegetables on the side must have been cooked at the last minute. Instead of the individual salads Ellen had said Helga and Dave were fixing, there were fresh fruit plates for the table to share. Last came baskets of hot rolls, three or four different kinds.

"Wonderful, Elizabeth," Joan said, and meant it. "Thank you for this lovely dinner." Even Elizabeth looked satisfied.

Peace reigned for a time.

"So," someone down the table on the Grahams' side asked Fred, "what do the police think happened here?"

"They're not telling me," he said. "I'm at a party."

"But won't you—"

"Not with his mother here!" someone shushed the questioner.

Helga seemed oblivious to the exchange. Good, Joan thought. It might make the job of the police harder, but she doesn't need to be involved.

"Isn't this delicious, Mom?" she heard Walt say.

"It doesn't taste very Swedish," Helga answered, and all the Lundquists laughed.

"We all know you're the world's best cook," Oscar told her. "But this will do fine. I don't think most of this crowd would enjoy Swedish lutefisk."

"Especially me!" Kierstin said from the far end of the table, and they laughed again.

"Isn't that the horrible stuff you people do to fish?" Elizabeth said, but Don shut her up with a couple of quiet words Joan couldn't hear. How could he stand being married to her?

They got through the rest of the dinner pleasantly enough, but Joan was glad to escape as soon as it was over.

"You don't think anyone minded that we left?" she asked Fred on the walk home.

"Not a bit. Sets 'em free to talk about what's really on their minds."

"At least no one came up and said sorry for my loss."

"No."

"We'll get through the wedding, and then I can collapse."

"And a funeral?" he reminded her.

"Do we have to? I don't know who'd even show up." That hit her hard. "Oh, Fred, he may not have a friend left in the world. Maybe the guy he worked for, wherever that was. But I don't know how we'd let him know. And I didn't really know Dave at all." She grabbed for the handkerchiefs in her pocket, but they were hidden by her coat.

"Here," he said and offered her the big one he pulled from his coat pocket. Why were the few women's hankies she could find to buy these days so small, anyway?

She wiped her eyes and blew her nose hard before sticking the sodden thing in her own coat pocket. "Thanks."

"Anytime."

The funeral would be the least of it, she thought as they walked. The police would be talking to her before then, she knew. And she had no idea what she could tell them. "I wanted to kill him myself" would hardly do.

When she could see their house, she didn't recognize the car in front of it, but Fred clearly did.

"Ketcham's here," he said.

Chapter 9

JOHNNY KETCHAM swung his car door open when they approached. "Fred, Joan," he said.

"Come on in," Fred told him.

"I rang the bell, but the kid who answered the door told me you weren't back yet."

"Yeah, we walked."

Ketcham nodded and got out of the car.

"I'll pay him," Joan said. She ran up the steps and went in.

Fred stayed behind. "You getting anywhere?"

"I couldn't tell you if we were," Ketcham said. "But we spent some time with your mother. She was more out of it than I expected."

"She'd revived some by suppertime, but all she talked about was food."

"Figures. She have a diagnosis?"

"It's gotta be Alzheimer's. I don't know that Walt and Carol have had her worked up yet. Joan keeps pushing me to get them to do it. Can't see it'll make much difference to put them all through the tests. They can't be sure until she dies, anyway."

"Could be something treatable. You know that."

"Yeah." Fred didn't want to tell his brother how to manage their mother. Not from southern Indiana, so far away from them. "So anyhow, where do we stand?"

"We aren't having this conversation," Ketcham said.

"Right."

"Okay, then. The knife your mother was holding did the job,

all right. A regular knife out of Ellen's drawer—seems she makes a point of keeping them good and sharp. All kinds of prints on it. Your mother's on top, of course. We're taking prints from everyone who works there, but she rested her bloody hands on the table top, so we got almost a full set and don't have to bother her. Only question is whether we'll find prints unaccounted for by the kitchen workers."

"Unless one of them did it," Fred said.

"Yeah."

"Access from the outside? Is that back door locked?"

"Nope. Seems it never is when people are working in there. Handy for taking the garbage out. It's the one they use when they arrive, and the one delivery people use, so as not to bother the guests."

"Somebody sure bothered the hell out of Dave Zimmerman."

The boy came down the steps and left. Joan stuck her head out the door. "Are you going to stand out there in the cold forever?"

"Be right there," Fred called. "Anything else I oughta know?" he asked Ketcham.

"You're not supposed to know any of it. But we're just getting started. We gave you time for the dinner. I've got people over there now asking Ellen and her staff preliminary questions while they prepare for the reception and meals tomorrow, and I'll go back shortly. I wanted to talk to Joan myself, thought it might be easier on her if I came here first."

"Thanks." Fred had known Ketcham would understand.

"You think she's up to it?"

"So far." Fred waved Ketcham ahead of him, and they went into the house.

Joan was back on the sofa, but this time she'd stashed her coat somewhere. Her color looked better, too. She smiled at them. "I won't ask what brings you here."

"I'm sorry to have to come," Ketcham said.

"Thanks. Have you had anything to eat? The leftovers are over at Ellen's, of course, but I could—"

"I'm fine." He looked more awkward than Fred could remember seeing him. Fred pulled up a chair for him and sat down with Joan.

Ketcham sat, but he didn't take out his notebook. Instead, he took out a handkerchief, wiped his wire-rims, and slipped them back over his ears. "What can you tell me about your brother?" He leaned forward and began to look more like himself, his face relaxing, the glasses somehow contributing to his usual calm.

"So little it's sad," she said, but without tearing up. "I mean, I remember how much trouble he got in when we were growing up, and I wasn't really surprised when Fred told me he'd been in prison, but I've been out of touch with him for years. When he arrived, he told me right away about being just out of prison, but he promised he was going straight now—said he didn't ever want to go back there. He was his sweetest self with me and with the old people at the center, and I found I was glad to have him here, after all."

"Uh-huh," Ketcham said.

"Ellen said he was good over there, too. He was good with Laura Putnam when he met her; I saw that myself."

"We'll talk to Ellen."

She nodded and paused. "I almost don't want to mention it, but…"

"Yes?"

"Two things happened yesterday."

Ketcham waited without looking impatient. He's good, Fred thought.

"First, only I didn't find out about it till later, when Andrew told me, Dave made a bunch of long-distance calls from our phone. That would be no huge deal, but he lied to Andrew, said I'd told him I didn't mind."

"When you did?"

"When he hadn't asked me."

"Andrew say what the calls were about?"

"No, he didn't hear. Just long enough numbers he could tell they weren't local. Dave did tell me he was going to be doing something about what our parents left him in their wills."

"You know what that is?"

"I don't remember, if I ever knew, but I have the wills somewhere. I can look."

"I'll help her find them," Fred promised.

"Okay with you if we check your phone records?"

"Yes," she and Fred said in unison. They could get a court order, Fred knew, but permission would speed up the process.

"We'll look into them." Now Ketcham did pull out a little notebook like the one Fred used and made a brief note. "This was yesterday, you say?"

"At least. You probably ought to check the whole week."

He made another note. "Okay. And the other thing? You said there were two."

For the first time, she looked away. Fred resisted the temptation to take her hand. Ketcham just waited.

"Last night he was teasing Rebecca. At first that's all it was, teasing. He made her laugh, and she needed it." Now she met Ketcham's eyes. "She'd gone all nervous about Bruce and the wedding."

"Uh-huh."

"Then he kissed her. That doesn't sound like anything, but what started out as gentle teasing turned into the kind of kiss you wouldn't want your daughter's uncle to give her."

Ketcham nodded.

"She ran upstairs to get away from him. I couldn't believe it. Right there in our living room, right in front of me, what did he think he was doing, anyway? I gave him what-for."

Ketcham waited.

"Then I followed Rebecca. When I came down, he'd left. Today Ellen said he was helping in the kitchen. When I got over there, someone told me he and Fred's mother were making salads together. I didn't go in the kitchen, didn't want to confuse Helga. I never saw him again." Now the tears came, and she fumbled for a handkerchief and blew hard. "Before he got here, I worried that he was coming. After yesterday I was worried all over again. How could I trust him if he'd lie? And make Rebecca feel like that?

What else would he pull? You saw Gary here—the kid we hired to watch the gifts. I told Andrew to watch them while Dave was here and I was at work, too. Felt silly about it till last night. Then I was glad I had."

"I didn't know that," Fred said.

She looked up at him. "I don't tell you everything. Besides, you didn't take it very seriously."

"No, I didn't. I'm sorry, Joan."

She took his hand. "It's okay."

Ketcham looked around. "Andrew here?"

"No," Fred said. "I think the kids are hanging out together tonight. He's with my niece, probably. And maybe Bruce's sister and brother, unless their parents dragged them off to wherever they're staying."

"Yeah, we got that." Ketcham patted the pocket where he'd stashed the notebook. He looked at Joan. "Anything else? Anything I should have asked you but didn't think of?"

"I don't know. It's all a jumble to me."

"You know how to find me. Anytime, day or night. He may have been an ex-con, but we're taking this as seriously as if he were one of us."

"Thank you," she said, and her smile lit up the room.

No wonder I fell in love with her, Fred thought. Now he did pat her hand. "I'll see Johnny out."

Ketcham stood and held out his hand.

Joan took it. "Thank you," she said again.

"You call on me for anything they'll let me do," Fred said at the door.

"You bet," Ketcham said.

And he was gone. What an odd feeling it was, to be on the other side like this. Fred went back to Joan.

"You know Helga didn't do it," she said.

"I know." Almost. Who knew what his mother was capable of these days? And how would they ever sort it out, when she'd been holding the weapon and was covered with blood herself?

He sat down by her, checked his watch from force of habit.

"It's not even ten yet," she said. "Feels like midnight. But I couldn't possibly go to sleep. Way I feel now, I'll never sleep again."

Another night, he might have made a suggestion, but tonight he hardly dared touch her.

"Take me for a walk?"

"Sure, if you want. You'll have to wrap up. It's supposed to hit zero tonight."

"And Fred? Hold me tight?" She reached up to him, the tears flowed freely, and they didn't need the walk after all.

Chapter 10

JOAN SMELLED the coffee first.

"Rise and shine. Big day today."

Groggily, she rose to consciousness and opened her eyes. There stood Fred, holding a mug of his good coffee just beyond her nose. She propped herself on one elbow and then slid up against the head of the bed.

"Thank you." She reached for it.

"Careful, it's hot."

"Mmm." Sipping, she was glad he'd warned her. "What time is it?"

"Almost nine. Rebecca's still upstairs."

"I never did hear her last night."

"She rolled in around one. Andrew didn't beat her by much. He and I have been sitting in the kitchen, talking. I think he's going up pretty soon to drag her out of bed."

"She'll love that."

"He said she asked him to."

"I'd better get my shower in now, then, before she takes over." She sniffed again. "Is something baking?"

He nodded. "Sweet rolls. Thought I ought to do something to celebrate the day. Andrew's been asking for lessons, so he helped."

By the time she'd showered, thrown on a pair of jeans and a sweatshirt, and braided her wet hair, the rolls were out of the oven. She was enjoying her first one when Rebecca, still sleepy-eyed, came down in pajamas and robe.

"Andrew told me he was baking sweet rolls. Is that true?"

"You don't have to eat any," he said. "Leave more for the rest of us."

Fred poured Rebecca's coffee and held out the basket of rolls. "It's true."

She bit into a roll. "Andrew, I take back every mean thing I ever said or did to you."

The roll in Joan's mouth lost its sweetness. The last thing she'd ever said to her own brother had been hateful. She saw Fred looking at her with a gentleness she could hardly bear.

"I'll be back," she said, and she managed to escape to her room before the tears erupted again.

"Is Mom okay?" she heard both her children ask.

"Let her be," Fred said. But a few moments later, she was grateful to feel his arms supporting her.

"It's all right," he told her. "They'll understand if you weep in front of them."

"But I don't want to cry on Rebecca's wedding day!"

"All mothers cry at their daughter's wedding. It's expected. Tradition."

She managed a wobbly smile. "I suppose." He had a point. The wedding guests who didn't know about her brother would think she was dripping tears about losing her daughter.

When she rejoined them in the kitchen, Rebecca gave her a big hug.

Andrew held out his rolls. "Try another one, Mom."

"They're great. It wasn't your baking, before." She took one and this time was able to enjoy it.

Rebecca was humming something that sounded almost familiar, but Joan couldn't place it.

"What's that?" she asked.

Rebecca actually blushed. "Just something Bruce plays for me to tell me he loves me."

"What are the words?"

"I don't know that there are any. It sounds a lot better when he plays it."

"I'm glad to hear it."

"You making cracks about my singing?" But Rebecca clearly didn't mind.

"He plays for you, but not for his mother. That says something."

"More about her than about me. Can't you just imagine what it must have been like to grow up in that house? Tom's glad to be in college, and Sally can hardly wait to leave."

"You were like that, too."

"I was, wasn't I? But that was me, not you. You never gave us a hard time. You were great, Mom, don't you know that?"

Joan's eyes stung again, this time for a good reason. "Rebecca, that's the nicest thing I think you've ever said to me."

"High time," Andrew said, and Rebecca socked him on the shoulder. They might have been ten—at most, no older than fifteen.

"What's the schedule today?" Fred asked.

"The wedding's at five," Rebecca said. "The women will go over at four, four-thirty to dress. The men dress at home, so all you have to do is show up before five. Well before five, please, or I'll have a heart attack."

"I'm meeting Bruce at the church about half past four," Andrew said. "Check the ring and all that."

"Ellen's feeding a light lunch to whoever wants to eat with the Lundquists. Will the Grahams go?" Joan asked Rebecca.

"I doubt it."

"Kierstin will be there, though," Andrew said. "And I promised her I would."

"That's why you dragged in so late last night," Rebecca said. "You two serious?"

"Nah, she's just a kid."

"That's not how it looked last night. She likes you a lot, Andrew. Don't set her up and dump her."

Joan and Fred exchanged a wordless conversation across the table from each other.

"How long do people have to be married before they can pull that off?" Andrew asked.

For the first time since hearing about Dave, Joan laughed.

"It comes with the vows," Fred said deadpan. "Sometimes even before. But only in a good marriage." His eyes crinkled at her.

"You watch your sister and Bruce the next time his mother makes one of her cracks," Joan said.

Andrew nodded. "I'll do that."

"Want to come up and help me with the wedding gifts?" Rebecca asked him. "I have to write the notes, but there are some I haven't even unwrapped."

"Sure." Snagging another couple of warm rolls, he followed her upstairs.

Joan heard the mail slot in the front door flip open and the day's mail hit the floor. Now that the responses to the wedding invitations were no longer flooding in, the mail was back to its usual puny quantity. Puny if you didn't count bills and junk mail.

"I'll wash the dishes," Fred said. She knew he hated to open mail.

"Thanks." She bent down to pick up the messy pile inside the front door and quickly sorted out the few pieces that needed opening instead of recycling, mostly bills. "Would you believe it, here's one more response to our invitation?" Opening it, she was relieved to see "regrets" checked on the response card. She took it over to her little desk at the far end of the living room and tucked it into the others of its kind after checking off the name of one of the few people who hadn't yet replied.

Then she pulled out her checkbook to pay the bills. The gas and electric weren't as high yet as they would be in January, when the cold and dark hit hardest. But the phone bill was unusually high. Flipping down the itemized calls, she suddenly realized why.

"That was quick," she said.

"What was?" Fred said, drying his hands on the dish towel.

"It's only Saturday, but this bill includes calls from Thursday." He looked over her shoulder.

"Fred, those are Dave's calls, the ones Andrew told me about."

"The ones we gave Ketcham permission for," Fred said.

"Uh-huh. If he doesn't have them yet, we could let him copy the bill."

"It might save time." Fred picked up the phone. "Ketcham in? Lundquist here. Tell him we have our phone bill. If he still needs to see those calls, he can copy it." He listened for a moment. "Okay, then."

"What did they say?"

"They'll tell him. I wouldn't worry about it."

"But…"

"No buts. Leave that job to the pros."

He had a point, but she muttered under her breath while she wrote the check for the bill. She tucked it into its envelope, stamped it, and set it on the little table by the front door to put out for pickup on Monday. After writing the check number on the bill itself, she stuck it into her jeans pocket with the others to file upstairs.

The filing cabinet was in Rebecca's normally empty room. Joan knocked at the open door. "Mind if I come in?"

Rebecca looked up from her notes and stretched. "Any excuse for a break."

"What happened to Andrew?"

"He opened the last of them. Left kind of a mess." She pointed to the floor. "I had to stop him before he separated the cards from the gifts. I would have been thanking people who sent us our good stainless for a cookie jar shaped like a violin." She pointed to it.

"Do you mind doing it?"

"Not really. I didn't expect so many people to care. Of course, a lot of them are friends and relatives of the Grahams. People I don't even know."

"Are they coming?"

"Some of them. But I don't expect to remember them after today. If I write now, they won't expect me to know them yet. I say I look forward to meeting them at the wedding."

"I'll mail them first thing Monday."

"Thanks, Mom."

Joan started filing the bills, but her hand stopped before she could slide the phone bill into its folder. "Rebecca, may I borrow your cell phone?"

"Sure, why?"

"This phone bill lists the calls Dave made the other day. I was worrying how to find out who his friends were, so I could invite them to whatever service we decide to have for him. I'd like to try those numbers, see what they answer, but I don't want anyone with caller ID to see my phone number, just in case."

"In case the calls are connected to what happened to him?"

"Exactly. You have a Manhattan number, don't you?"

"Yes."

"Good."

"What are you looking for?"

"Well, he said he was working for a friend who owned a print shop."

"So you're looking for the print shop."

"Yes."

"And if you find it?"

"I haven't thought that through yet. I suppose I could tell them my daughter's getting married and ask for their price on invitations. At least that's something I know enough to talk about."

"Is it in Manhattan?"

"No…oh, I see your point. I'll think of something."

"And if you get someone else, not the print shop?"

"Wrong number. But I'll write down what they answer."

"What does Fred say about this?"

"Fred doesn't know, and you're not going to tell him."

"You be careful, Mom."

"I will." She knew what Fred would say if she told him. Don't, that's what. He'd have a point. But with Rebecca's phone burning a hole in her pocket, Joan was sorely tempted to make a few calls.

It's not as if I were going to talk to anyone about Dave, she thought, and went downstairs to sit on the sofa.

"You going in to work?" she asked when Fred came out of the kitchen, drying his hands on his jeans.

"Captain said to take the weekend off. Why, don't you want me here?" He bent over the back of the sofa and nuzzled the back of her neck.

She reached up and stroked his unshaven cheek. "Of course

I do. But I'll be fine, Fred. I'm not going to fall apart again. You don't have to watch over me."

"I'm not. Just enjoying a little rest before I have to make like a father again."

She looked up at him. "You were very sweet with her yesterday. Skipping down the aisle, for goodness sake."

He blushed as only a blond Swede can. "It was her idea."

"I know. That's what I mean."

He wasn't budging, and cell phone or no cell phone, the house wasn't big enough to make those calls with him around. She could, of course, go up to Rebecca's room, but on her wedding day? It didn't seem fair. The calls could wait, even if she had to use a phone that would betray her location. She looked at Fred again. He probably knew exactly what was going through her head. Without saying a word, he would stop her from going through with it. But who said she had to stay home?

"Maybe I'll take a little walk. Rebecca doesn't need help right now, and with Ellen doing lunch, I can't just twiddle my thumbs."

"Sure," Fred said. "Mind if I come along?" She caught the twinkle in his eye.

She sighed. "You know, don't you?"

"I have a fair idea. Might as well give her back her phone, and let's go walk it off."

"Were you listening?"

"Didn't need to. I know you so well."

"Uh-huh." It was second nature for a cop to listen, and she didn't remember closing Rebecca's door. "I give up. Here, you take it to her." She held it out.

He laughed. "Rebecca? We're going out for a little walk. Your mom's leaving your phone down here." He set it on the table by the sofa and held Joan's coat for her.

"Okay." Rebecca didn't need to shout for her voice to float downstairs.

As Joan knew hers must have done, too.

Chapter 11

IN SPITE of herself, Joan enjoyed the brisk walk through the park with Fred, but by the time they'd rounded it a second time, she was chilled through.

"Let's stop in at Ellen's for something hot," she said.

"This early?"

"She won't mind, and wouldn't you like to spend a little time with your family?"

He raised one eyebrow.

"Don't worry, I won't dump you there and run home to play with Rebecca's phone."

"It crossed my mind," he admitted. "But yes, I'd like to check on my mother, especially."

Personally, Joan couldn't imagine Helga remembering anything now if she'd managed to block it out by the rehearsal dinner. Still, you never knew. Memory was a funny business, especially once it became as unreliable as Helga's. And it would be good to talk to the other members of the family without Bruce's mother there to make life difficult.

For that matter, she hadn't had a chance to exchange more than a word with Ellen Putnam and had no idea what Ellen could tell her about what had happened in that kitchen. She squared her shoulders.

"Let's do it, then."

Laura welcomed them at the door, her flyaway pigtails now neat french braids. "It's not lunchtime yet," she said.

"I know," Joan said. "But Fred wanted to visit with his family, and I wanted to talk with your mama."

"Come on in." She held the door wide. "Don't worry, we're keeping my dog in his doghouse while so many people are here."

"Good idea." She was glad to see that Laura seemed unaffected by what had to have been considerable hullabaloo in her house on Friday. And she had known Dave. How was she dealing with his death? Did she realize that he'd been murdered?

"Mama's in the kitchen," Laura said. "Chrissy and Patty, too. All our guests are upstairs." She turned to Fred. "Would you like me to show you?"

"Sure," he said. "I wouldn't want to get lost up there."

She wrinkled her brow at him. "Are you teasing me?"

"A little bit. But I don't know who's staying in what room."

"I do." She led off confidently, and Fred followed.

Joan smiled. Times like this made her think she ought to give him at least one child of his own. Could she face starting over now? Could he?

She pushed such questions to the back of her mind and went into the kitchen, dreading what she'd see there. To her amazement, the room showed no sign of having been a crime scene. Dave had been stabbed here, but she couldn't even smell the blood. How had they cleaned it up so fast? Ellen and her crew must have done it themselves as soon as they got permission; there hadn't been time to call in a professional cleaning crew before the rehearsal dinner. Maybe the horror she'd been imagining when she was trying so hard to focus on that dinner really hadn't existed by then.

"How're you holding up?" she asked Ellen, who was cutting oranges onto a platter as if it were a perfectly ordinary day.

"Joan!" Ellen smiled a welcome. "We're doing fine, thanks." She waved her knife at the other two women in the room, who were slicing meat and cheese onto other platters. No question of letting Helga wield a knife along with them. "You've met Chrissy Chitwood, and this is Patty, her mom."

"Hi, Chrissy, Patty." Joan looked hard at the older woman. "Do I know you, maybe from a long time ago?"

Patty nodded. "I wondered whether you could possibly remember. You were so young."

"In sixth grade. And you were in high school—what, a senior?" Dave had been a senior the year their family lived in Oliver.

"That's right."

"And you and Dave…" Had they gone steady? Or was she imagining it?

"We dated."

"That's what I thought. And now this. I'm so sorry."

Patty waved it off. "It has to be worse for you. He was your brother."

Joan nodded, suddenly unable to reply. Finding her voice again, she said, "I've been telling myself I can't think about him until we get through this wedding. I owe that to Rebecca."

"How is she this morning?" Ellen asked.

"Fine. Fred and Andrew lured her out of bed with fresh sweet rolls."

"They made them?" Patty looked as surprised as she sounded.

"Fred's a baker from way back," Joan said. "Learned it from his dad. Oscar owned a bakery until he retired, but they both still bake."

"You knew that, Mom," Chrissy said. "Fred used to bake for Catherine Turner."

"That's right." Patty looked sideways at Joan.

"It's okay," Joan said. "I know about Catherine. They had some kind of falling out before we were married. But we've ordered Rebecca's wedding cake from her."

"She'll take that directly to the church for the reception," Ellen said. "Just as well. It would be in the way here."

"I suppose," Joan said. She wasn't going to worry that Catherine might take out old grudges on her daughter.

"She'll deliver," Ellen said, as if reading her mind. "It would be bad for her business if she ever were late with a wedding cake. And hers are delicious, not just beautiful. We'll have some here later, for the buffet."

Joan's mind had already moved away from food and squabbles with Fred's old girlfriend. "I suppose the police have talked to you about what happened yesterday." She ducked saying more.

"Yes."

"Could you tell them anything?" Fred wouldn't like her butting in here, either, but Fred didn't have to know.

"Not really. Chrissy and I were both setting the table for dinner, and Patty was delayed at home. So only Helga and your brother were in the kitchen after we left the room."

Joan was horrified. "You mean she might really have done it?"

"Or someone could have come in the back door. With Dave here, I wasn't worried about leaving it unlocked. Not in the daytime."

If you only knew, Joan thought. But Dave hadn't stolen or helped some confederate steal from Ellen or hurt Fred's mother. In the end it was Dave who was hurt. Never mind hurt—he was killed. Murdered. Why was it so hard even to think *murder* about her brother?

"Don't worry," Ellen said, looking at the door. "It's locked now. I'm only so very sorry it wasn't locked yesterday."

"So you don't think it was Helga?"

"Oh, no! She thought she was saving his life."

"That's what Fred said. She seemed to have forgotten all about it by suppertime."

"There's good and bad in everything," Chrissy said.

Even murder? Joan thought. But she means Alzheimer's. She nodded.

"Will you eat lunch with us?" Ellen asked.

"I imagine so. I need to clean up a little first."

"It's going to be very informal."

Joan glanced at her watch. Late as it was, was it worth going home? She was still cold. "Any chance you could spare a cup of something hot right now?" It was, after all, why she'd asked Fred to stop there.

"You poor dear!" Patty said. "You're shivering." Setting down her knife, she quickly poured a mug of hot coffee. "Cream? Sugar?"

"Black is fine." Joan wrapped her hands around the mug and

inhaled the warmth before taking her first sip. "Mmmm, thank you."

Patty was hovering. "You're sure you'll be all right?"

"I'm fine now, thanks." She smiled at her. "This is just what I needed."

Patty nodded and returned to her cheese slicing.

"I should probably go up and say hello to Fred's family," Joan said.

"Might as well," Ellen said. "You may not get much chance later on today."

"How was Helga this morning? Did she come down to breakfast?"

"She sure did. Ready to give me lessons in making Swedish pancakes."

"Did you take her up on it?"

"No, I let her make do with my plain old flapjacks."

"Nothing plain about 'em," Chrissy said.

"Maybe sometime when this all dies down, we'll treat ourselves to an overnight and sample your breakfast." It held a certain appeal, though Joan doubted that Fred's sweet rolls had much to fear from the competition.

Fortified by the hot coffee, she left the mug in the kitchen and made her way up the stairs. "Fred?" She didn't know what room he was in.

He stuck his head around a door and stepped out of the room. "Right here."

"Everyone okay?"

"Sure. Dad's taking a pre-lunch nap, and Walt and Ruthie are keeping Mom out of the kitchen. She thinks she ought to be doing something, but we're not letting her back downstairs till lunchtime."

"Good."

"Kierstin's more than a little interested in walking over to our house."

She grinned. "I can't imagine why. You call Andrew?"

"He's expecting her. She's putting on her things."

"Me, too." Joan zipped her jacket and pulled her hat down around her ears before pulling her mittens on.

"Back soon," Kierstin called back to her parents as she rounded the door, which Fred quickly closed behind her. Her fine blonde hair swung fashionably straight around her shoulders this year, and she carried a warm-looking parka over one arm. "Hi, Joan. Farmor really wants to go down and help fix lunch. It's all they can do to distract her."

Farmor—Swedish for "father's mother," Joan had learned. And Kierstin called Oscar Farfar.

"Maybe we ought to bring her with us," Joan said.

"We could try it after lunch," Fred said. "Right now she's got a one-track mind."

"You having a good time?" Joan asked Kierstin on the walk home.

"Not really. I felt cooped up. Thanks for springing me."

"You're not usually in the bosom of your family anymore. How's college?" Kierstin was in her first year at the University of Illinois.

"Oh, it's okay." Looking appropriately cool, Kierstin tossed that off. "Actually, it's great. I'm so glad to get away from Bishop Hill and meet some people." She pulled on her parka and mittens when they left the house, but let her hair hang free.

"Anybody interesting?"

"A few, but nobody serious."

"I'm glad to hear that. Way too soon for serious."

Kierstin tossed her hair. "This time last year, I was feeling pretty serious about Andrew."

"Were you now?"

"He was really sweet to me. Last night, too."

"I'm glad to hear it. I'm sure he'll be glad to see you again."

The hair toss again. "You think so?"

"Ask him yourself." No way was Joan getting in the middle of that one.

Kierstin giggled. "I don't think so."

"Well, it's good you're coming over now. He'll have to spend most of his time from now on with Bruce's sister, because he's the best man and she's the maid of honor." If anyone paid attention to such things these days, Joan thought as soon as she'd said it.

"Oh, I know that! But I met some cute guys last night."

"I noticed that." The young people had seemed to be having a good time at the far end of the table. And who knew what they'd done afterward.

"Where all did you go after we left last night?" Fred asked.

"Oh, here and there. Over to the campus, for one thing. But it was pretty dead, with the students gone and all. Andrew wanted to show us around anyway. It's pretty, but it's awful little compared to U of I."

"I seem to remember you were pushing to come here last year," Fred said.

"Was I? I'm glad I ended up at Illinois."

Joan and Fred had another of those wordless exchanges over her head.

Andrew met them on the porch. "Kierstin, hi. Glad you came. I couldn't very well bring you over here last night. Abandon Sally to her mom."

Kierstin rolled her eyes, and he grinned.

"Just as well you didn't," Fred said. "Sergeant Ketcham came over to ask us questions."

And then he left, Joan thought. It was good you weren't here then to cramp our style.

Andrew took Kierstin up to show her his room or his etchings or whatever they called it these days.

"I'll go check on Rebecca," Joan said. Ignoring the phone still on the table by the sofa, she climbed the stairs to her daughter's room.

Fred, left alone downstairs, called Ketcham. "Any progress?"

"Hi, honey," Ketcham said. "I can talk for a couple of minutes, but we're swamped with this murder."

"Altschuler's right there, is he?" Fred asked. It was going to be one of those conversations.

"That's what you get for marrying a cop."

"You get anywhere on those phone numbers? Joan's chomping at the bit to try 'em herself."

"It wouldn't hurt. But you're not likely to find anyone home of a Saturday."

"So I might as well turn her loose?"

"Sure, that would be fine," Ketcham said. "I'm too busy, but you might try an old friend or two. That's what you really wanted, isn't it?"

"Yes, the print shop where Dave worked."

"He's open for business. The rest of them, all we got were message machines and voice mail."

"Altschuler finally out of range, huh?"

"For the moment. He's keeping close tabs on this one, though. Sure wish you could work it."

"You and me both. Sorry Mom couldn't keep her hands off it. Anything else you can tell me?"

"Afraid not. Gotta go now, sweetie." Ketcham hung up. No way to tell whether he could have said anything more if Altschuler hadn't returned just then.

Fred picked up the cell phone and took it upstairs. "Knock, knock," he said outside Rebecca's door.

"Come on in," she told him. She was sitting at her desk, pen in hand, and Joan, cross-legged on the bed, seemed to be doing something to the wedding gifts.

"I brought your phone back. And Joan, I cleared it with Ketcham. It's okay to make those calls. He said most of them won't be in on Saturday, but the print shop is open."

"I don't suppose he told you which number that was?"

"No, Altschuler was standing right there, and it's clear he's not supposed to be talking to me."

"But he did?" Rebecca said.

"Indirectly. Made me sound like his wife."

She snorted.

"Cops know how to be sneaky when they have to."

"Thanks," Joan said.

"My pleasure. But you don't have a lot of time. Not if we're going back to Ellen's."

She looked at her watch. "He's right, Rebecca. I suppose I could skip lunch."

"Don't!" Rebecca looked flustered. "I mean, sure, if you want to. But the wedding's just a few hours from now. And then we leave. Can't you wait till we're gone?"

"Of course I can. I can use my own phone."

"Use mine," Fred offered.

Her face melted. "You'd do that for me?"

"C'mere, woman." He held out his arms, and she walked into them.

Chapter 12

THERE WASN'T much time left to make those calls, if they were going back to Ellen's. Joan pulled the numbers out of her pocket and settled down with Fred's phone to try them.

"Realty," a pleasant woman's voice answered. "Our office is open Monday through Friday, eight to five. Please try again at that time."

"Midwest," the second one said. "At the tone, please leave a message."

"J and S Investments," said the third, also unavailable on a Saturday.

"Cooper Hardwood," said the fourth, a man. "Highest prices for standing timber. Professional land clearing. *Beep.*"

She took notes, but at least there was no need to speak to anyone. Maybe Dave had inherited land from their parents—that rang a bell—and he'd been checking into what to do with it. But why long distance?

"Yeah?" said the fifth.

"Oh," Joan said, startled. "What number did I reach, please?"

"Who'd you want?" the man's voice growled at her.

"I must have the wrong number." She ended the call, her heart pounding. That one didn't sound like a business. Not a legitimate one, anyway. Maybe she really had reached the wrong number. And maybe not. She wouldn't try twice. He'd sounded too tough to want him annoyed at her. Someone had, after all, murdered Dave.

Shaken, she tried one more number.

"Pete's Print Shop," a cheery man answered, not sounding like a recording at all. Finally.

"Dave Zimmerman works there?" she asked.

"Dave's off till next week."

"This is his sister, Joan Spencer."

The man sounded puzzled. "He said he was going to your daughter's wedding. And I thought he called from there."

"He did. And—I'm sorry, is this Pete?"

"Yeah."

"Pete, Dave said you were his friend."

"Thought I was." She could hear his suspicion.

"There's no easy way to tell you this." She fought to steady her voice. "Dave is dead."

"Dead! He was fine when he left here."

"He was murdered."

"Oh my God, lady. The guy survives years in—he told you where he's been?"

"Yes."

"So what could have happened to him in your little burg that didn't happen there?"

"Somebody stabbed him. That's all we know."

"And the cops don't care because he's an ex-con."

"They care. My husband's a cop, and he and Dave got along fine." No point in telling him Fred was excluded from the police investigation, much less why.

"I hope so. For all his troubles, he was my good friend."

"Pete, I hadn't seen Dave for so long, I don't know his friends. I don't even know who would care enough to come to his funeral."

"I'll be there." Just like that. "Close the shop if I have to."

She was touched. "Are there enough other people where you live to make it worth putting in the paper there?"

"Probably not. I can tell the ones who know him—knew him. How about the place he grew up in?" Of course.

"Thank you, Pete. Why didn't I think of that?"

"Thing like this—it's hard to think."

"Yes."

"You know when it will be?"

"No. The wedding is today. And they haven't released Dave's—body yet."

"No hurry, honey. You hang in there. Give me your phone number, would you? If I come up with anything more, I'll call you."

She told him her number and thanked him. Time to stop. Fred was right about the other calls Dave had made. Pete was the man she'd wanted to talk to. It was good to know her brother still had one real friend in the world.

"Mom?" Rebecca called downstairs. "You ready to go?"

"Almost." She went into the bedroom and swiped at her face and hair. She wouldn't mess with changing clothes for lunch. At least the Grahams weren't expected.

Fred came up behind her and began massaging her shoulder muscles, as she loved. "Feel any better?"

"I mostly got machines."

"Uh-huh."

He already knew she would, of course. "I did reach Pete, though."

"Who's Pete?"

"The printer who hired Dave. He didn't know about Dave, so Ketcham didn't talk to him yet."

Fred's strong fingers tensed up and stopped. "You ask him about enemies?"

"Didn't cross my mind. I asked him about Dave's friends."

His fingers relaxed and pressed into her shoulders again. "What did he say?"

"He said he'd tell the ones there—I still don't know where 'there' is—and I ought to tell the paper in the town where he grew up. That's Ann Arbor, of course. But on Monday I'll talk to the people here. There's no way Margaret Duffy won't know who taught him when we lived here. And I can ask Patty today."

"Who?"

"She works for Ellen, but she and Dave dated that year."

"I imagine Ketcham's already talked to her."

"Oh."

"I'll mention it to him."

"I thought he wasn't talking to you."

"He's not. You didn't hear me say that."

"He wouldn't have asked her about Dave's friends. That's what I'm trying to find out, remember?" She turned around to look up at his face. "You don't trust me, do you?"

"Not as far as—" Swinging her off her feet, he kissed her.

"Mom! Time to go!" Rebecca sounded much closer this time.

Joan was laughing now. "Be right there. You tell Andrew and Kierstin?"

"They already left."

Fred set her down, and they left the bedroom like an old married couple.

At Rebecca's request, they drove the short distance. "I don't want to be rushed right before the wedding," she said.

"It's your day," Fred told her and held the Chevy door for her.

Casual was indeed the word at Ellen's. The Lundquists were already congregating around the table in the dining room, which had been pushed against the end wall. Chairs clustered near the edges of the room. Last night's white linen and shining china had been replaced by the table's gleaming wood and casual pottery plates and mugs. Chrissy and Patty were carrying in trays of sandwich makings and baskets of bread.

"Come and get it," Ellen announced. "Let me know if you want anything you don't see on the table."

"When did they do all this?" Helga asked, her clear voice carrying all the way into the living room. "Nobody asked me to help."

"We had lots of extra help today," Ellen told her. "Your family wanted to see you."

"Hi, Mom," Fred said, going over to her.

"Fred! Where did you come from?"

"I had to pick up the bride."

"Are you getting married?"

And they were off. Joan watched Rebecca hug Helga and accept a kiss from Oscar. Greeting them briefly, she filled her own plate and found a corner to sit by herself. She was glad to see Rebecca welcome other people as they arrived. Whatever social graces she herself possessed had deserted her today. At least nobody seemed to expect anything of her. Andrew and Kierstin came in with her parents, all four engaged in lively conversation. Joan was relieved when they, too, let her vegetate in her corner. It wasn't the way she'd expected to feel on her daughter's wedding day.

But it wasn't only a wedding day. It was the day after a death in the family. The day when traditionally people would come to offer comfort and support. And food.

"Did you have enough to eat?" She looked up to see Ellen standing in front of her. Then down at her empty plate.

"I must have. I know it was full when I sat down here. But I don't remember eating any of it." Was her memory going, too?

Ellen nodded. "That kind of thing happened to me all the time after…"

After her husband was killed, she had to mean. That had to have been much worse than a brother you hardly knew anymore. Joan reached out a sympathetic hand. "Does it still?"

Ellen shook her head. "Hardly ever. You'll get through this. You don't know how, but you do."

"Thanks, Ellen."

"Want me to take your plate? Maybe bring you another cup of coffee?"

"Thanks." If she sat there with something in her hand people would be less likely to fuss over her. "Would you tell Patty I have a question for her?"

"Sure."

Patty brought the coffee. "Black, right?"

"Right. Maybe you can help me."

"Oh?"

"I need to plan some kind of service for Dave, and I don't know who his friends were. Do you remember?"

Patty frowned. "They're mostly long gone."

"Uh-huh."

"I'll try." She looked around. "We're kind of busy."

"Sorry. I thought this might be my only chance to ask you. I'm in the phone book, if you think of anyone."

But when Patty went back to the kitchen, Joan wondered whether she'd ever call.

The rest of the day flew by. Rebecca's nerves were a thing of the past. By the time they left for the church, Joan could feel her daughter taking her in hand, when it should have been the other way around. They dressed together with Sally Graham in the beautiful dresses Rebecca had made. Joan kissed her daughter, and Bruce's brother, Tom, ushered her past all the people she didn't know to the front pew during the last Bach the organist played before the wedding march. She remembered to stand when she heard the strains of *Lohengrin*, and except for not skipping, the rest went as rehearsed, with Fred joining her after handing Rebecca to the groom.

Before the vows, though, they had a surprise. Andrew left his post as best man to bring Bruce's violin and bow to him from a hiding place behind the pulpit. Bruce checked the tuning of the strings lightly with the tip of the bow and then turned to Rebecca. "For you," he said, and he started playing.

Elizabeth Graham's gasp was audible across the aisle, probably all the way to the back of the sanctuary, Joan thought, and it was a good thing Rebecca couldn't see her face. She recognized the melody Rebecca had tried to hum that morning. It was Massenet's "Meditation" from *Thaïs*, beautiful for solo violin, and Bruce caressed it into a love song. When he finished, he handed the instrument back to Andrew, took Rebecca's hand, and looked into her eyes.

Joan squeezed Fred's hand.

In no time, they'd exchanged their vows, the organist was playing Mendelssohn, and they all marched back out into the narthex. Joan and Fred followed Andrew and Sally.

Joan kissed her daughter and new redheaded son-in-law. "Welcome to the family, Bruce."

"Wasn't it beautiful, Mom?" Rebecca said. "I didn't know he was going to do that at all."

"Who's watching your violin?" Elizabeth asked Bruce, peering back into the sanctuary.

"A good friend."

Joan could see the minister near the pulpit. Uh-huh.

"He'd better be," Elizabeth said. Not a word for Rebecca. It was Don Graham who kissed her and whispered something that made her smile.

"We'd better get out of the way," Fred said. "The wedding guests are trapped in there till we do."

Joan doubted that would cut any ice with Elizabeth, but she was glad to lead the way down the stairs from the narthex to the basement. She hadn't noticed the flowers in the church, even though she had ordered them from the florist, but now evergreens and white roses softened the edges of the fellowship hall. And Catherine Turner had come through, after all. A tall white cake, elegant in its simplicity, dominated the refreshment table, though Catherine, if she was even there, was invisible. Rebecca and Bruce had arranged this part of the day. Joan sat in her blue gown at a table dressed in white and let the guests mill around her. She hardly had to do more than smile and nod. She certainly made no attempt to socialize with the Grahams. From time to time someone came over and said, "Lovely wedding" or some such, and Fred stuck close by.

"You all right?" he asked.

"Uh-huh."

"Holler if you need me."

"Your parents all right?" she remembered to ask.

"They're with Walt and Ruthie. It's okay. You can let go."

"Thanks."

So she did. As simple a reception as Bruce and Rebecca had chosen, it didn't last long. They cut the cake but didn't smush it on each other's faces. Ellen's helpers cut the rest of it and served it to the guests. To Joan's astonishment, Andrew managed to toast the happy couple like a real best man, and Rebecca threw her bouquet to all the young women, but that was it.

They changed into traveling clothes, the guests blew soap bubbles at them instead of rice, they kissed their families, and they were off.

And we're left to pick up the pieces, Joan thought.

Chapter 13

NOT THE LEAST of those pieces was dealing with the people who'd been invited to supper, including the Grahams and the many out-of-town guests from their side of the aisle.

Joan hadn't changed out of her blue woolen dress, and she was pleased to see Sally show up in her rose, too, though she'd parked her bouquet somewhere. Andrew, minding his manners, paid good attention to her, even though it left Kierstin high and dry with her parents and grandparents. He probably didn't mind; Sally was only a little younger than Kierstin and certainly attractive, especially dressed so becomingly.

Then Joan heard him suggest that they look for the other young people they'd enjoyed visiting with at the rehearsal dinner. Sally responded immediately, with the result that Andrew soon had Kierstin on his other arm. He looked up at his mother and winked.

She didn't think she could return the wink in the present company, but gave him a motherly smile.

"Slick, isn't he?" Fred said at her elbow.

"Just doing his job," she said, but he certainly didn't make it look like a chore.

"It's a rough life," Fred said.

To Joan's relief, Elizabeth stuck with her own guests. Don, though, came over and thanked her. Again, Joan wondered how he put up with his wife. She hadn't seen any obvious intimacy between them, but those three children came from somewhere, and they all looked like their father. His graying hair still had a sandy tinge to it, for one thing. He must have been a redhead like Bruce.

"It's hard on her, losing her firstborn," he said in answer to her unspoken question.

"Yes, I'm sure it is," Joan said. "But we're glad to welcome Bruce into our family, and it's a joy to see Rebecca so happy."

He smiled and nodded. "She's a dear. We'll try not to give her too rough a time."

Bless his heart, Joan thought, he was promising to be the cushion between Rebecca and her mother-in-law. "Thank you," she said.

The supper was far less formal than the rehearsal dinner, but no one would have to go home hungry. The top layers of the wedding cake had been brought over, both to grace the table and to accompany ice cream for dessert, if anyone had space for it.

With no appetite for what looked like excellent food, Joan picked at her plate. Chrissy, carrying a coffeepot around, came over to her.

"You all right? Need any more coffee?"

"Thanks, Chrissy." She accepted a refill. "You've all done a great job. I'm so grateful to you. I'll have to make a speech to Ellen."

"We wanted to do our best anyway, but especially the way things turned out. And I'm feeling sad."

"Oh?" She looked somber enough, but it warred with the cheery-hostess manner with which she was pouring coffee.

"I got fond of your brother over last week. So I just wanted to tell you how sorry I am. For you, but for myself, too."

"Thank you, Chrissy. I appreciate your telling me." There was no way to hug a woman carrying a coffeepot, and Joan didn't even have a hand free to pat her arm, but she did her best with a smile.

"I've got to keep moving, or they'll get on my case."

"Don't forget to tell everyone how pleased I am."

"Thank you. I will." And she moved on, hostess face back firmly in place.

Joan parked her plate on the table and went over to spend some time with the Lundquists. Fred was already back in the bosom of his family, but she'd given them short shrift.

"Joan, come say hello to my parents," he said. "Mom, you remember my wife, Joan. It's her daughter who was married today, and her son who is over there with Kierstin."

"I didn't know you had any children," Helga said to him.

"Now I do," he said, and she accepted that without explanation.

"I'm glad to see you again, Helga," Joan said. "Oscar." She smiled at both of them, but was relieved when Oscar didn't claim a kiss. Helga wouldn't have appreciated it, she knew.

"It was a beautiful wedding," he said. "Especially when he played the violin for her."

"Was I there?" Helga asked.

"You bet, Mom," Fred said. "We couldn't have a wedding in the family without you."

She looked satisfied. "Kierstin will be next. Maybe that nice young man who's with her tonight. They'd make a beautiful couple."

"Yes, they would," Joan said, looking over at Andrew.

"How are you holding up?" Ruthie asked. "I've been thinking of you ever since yesterday afternoon."

"I don't even know. Today I've been trying to get through the wedding. That's enough. Will I see you all in the morning?"

Ruthie looked at Walt.

"I want to get started early," he said. "It's a long drive, and some of us don't tolerate it well, especially late in the day." He looked at his mother. "She did very well coming."

They had arrived in early afternoon, Joan remembered. "Good planning. We'd better say good-bye now, then. I'm usually a night owl, but I'll probably wipe out soon as my head hits the pillow tonight."

"You and me both," Oscar said. "My prayers will be with you, dear." He took both her hands in his.

"Thank you, Oscar." It was the first time she'd ever heard him say any such thing. "Thank you all for coming."

"We wouldn't have missed it," Ruthie said. "Besides, Kierstin was dying to visit Andrew. She's having a wonderful time."

Joan was tempted to offer Kierstin a longer stay, but considering what she had to do next, she restrained herself. Besides, gentleman that he was being, Andrew might not want her to decide his social life for him.

"I hoped she would," she said instead. "I'm glad it's worked out. Maybe another time, our life won't be so torn up."

"Better get you home." Fred put his arm around her.

Joan surveyed the room. The guests were thinning out, and she didn't know anyone else she owed a social effort. "I won't argue. Good night, folks. Have a safe trip."

"Are we going somewhere?" she heard Helga ask as they left the room.

"I'm wiped out," Joan told Fred on the ride home, just the two of them. Andrew could find his own way when he was ready. From the look of him, he'd hang around the girls until they left with their families, or Kierstin went upstairs with hers.

Snow was beginning to fall now, the first of the season. It was past time to think about Christmas, which had been low on her list, close as it was, with Rebecca's wedding to prepare for. But first a funeral.

"I'll have to call the minister. Find out what I'm supposed to do next."

"Tomorrow," Fred said. "Plenty of time."

"Tomorrow's Sunday."

"He won't care."

"I suppose not." Joan yawned hugely, remembering how many times her minister husband had been called out by sick parishioners or grieving families on Sundays after he'd given his all in the morning. "But you're right. There's no hurry. He knows all about it. Might as well let him rest a little." No way would she call him on a Saturday night. He could even still be writing his sermon, if he left it till the last minute. Ken had always said it was when he took that risk that one of the children would spike a fever and keep them up all night Saturday.

She began thinking of people right there in Oliver who would remember Dave. Her old classmate, Nancy Van Allen, even if she'd been too young to know him, probably would be able to suggest others his age. So would Margaret Duffy, their retired teacher who was on the board of the Oliver Senior Citizens' Center.

And Gil Snarr, now director of the funeral home his father, Bud, had run when they were growing up together. Between them, the Snarrs knew everyone. They'd also know what she needed to tell the newspaper—or would they do that themselves? Joan couldn't remember how that worked. They'd need information from her, in any case. His current employer would know his Social Security number, if that mattered. Maybe it didn't, unless he were collecting retirement income from them. But he wasn't old enough for that. Would Social Security pay a death benefit? What would she have to do about it?

Fred pulled up in front of the house. "What are you thinking?"

"All those details I need to know about Dave."

"They'll wait. You've had enough for one day."

⸺◦⊰⊱◦⸺

In the end, she didn't plan to call anyone on Sunday, either, or even to show her face at church. She woke up Sunday morning thinking of the bare bones she did know about her brother. His birth date, for one, and the day he died. Their parents' names, Samuel and Hannah Zimmerman. Where he was born, Ann Arbor, Michigan, and where he died, Oliver, Indiana.

He'd never married, he'd told her that. She supposed she and maybe her children could be counted as his survivors. The paper's fudge words were "Survivors include," which covered it in case anyone was omitted. Sometimes a correction was published to add someone miffed at being left out. These days she'd seen people's pictures and whole life stories in the local obituary columns—a source of income for the paper, she was sure, but she couldn't add much to Dave's life story that was appropriate to publish. She had no idea whether he was a member of any organization that should be mentioned. Sometimes people listed where charitable donations should be directed, but she didn't know what he'd want about that, either. That left only a funeral to announce, or the lack of one, if she couldn't face it. Still, Pete from the print shop seemed to want to be there. Maybe he had other old friends who would, too. And maybe some of hers would find that the easiest way to show their support for her.

So many things to consider. In her grief after Ken's death, she'd been surrounded by supporters, and there hadn't been any question about whether to have a service for him. In fact, she'd hardly had to do more than stand back and let his parishioners take over. There must have been decisions, but she knew she'd been spared many of them.

This time it would be up to her and the minister to decide. But she wasn't drowning in grief. For that matter, her children, instead of clinging to her in their own confusion and sorrow, were old enough to give her support.

So what do I feel? she asked herself. Shock? She supposed so. Anger, mostly. As much at Dave as at the person who had done this...this thing to him. Was that fair? Maybe not, but it was honest.

The room wasn't light yet when the phone woke her. She grabbed it, for a wonder, before Fred budged.

"Joan? Nancy Van Allen. I just read about your brother. That's awful! I'm so sorry. If there's anything I can do—"

"How could you read... I was just thinking what to send to the paper."

"Oh, you mean for the obit? No, I mean the front-page story."

"Front page!"

"Right below the fold. I was a little surprised there wasn't a picture. Even if the police won't let them in, those photographers usually manage to get some pictures. Oh, wait, I'm wrong. There's one of Ellen's sign. Hope it doesn't hurt her business. Is that where it happened?"

"Nancy, I can't talk about it." Her teeth clenched around the words.

"No, I suppose they won't let you. Well, you have my sympathy. I saw him when he walked into orchestra rehearsal, remember? But I remember him back when you lived here. He was handsome when I saw him the other night, and he was handsome in high school, too. I was way too young then, of course, but I had kind of a crush on him, even so. Let me know when the funeral will be, okay? And how did the wedding go? The paper didn't say how you managed."

"Good-bye, Nancy." Joan hung up on her without a qualm, even though she knew she wanted to pick Nancy's brain before long.

What time was it, anyway? She pulled on jeans and a sweatshirt to make a quick run down the front walk for the paper. Gary was pretty good about getting it on the sidewalk, anyway.

One look out the door made her swap her sneakers for a pair of boots. Overnight more snow had fallen, and from the look of the paperboy's fresh tracks, it would top her ankles.

She pulled the orange plastic bag out of the snow and was unfolding the front section before she'd closed the door. No point in bothering Fred. Dumping her boots on the rug to drip, she wrapped her cold feet in a blanket and curled up on the sofa.

The story could have been worse, she told herself, but only by including Helga's name. Maybe the cops would protect Fred's mother from the press. But Dave's criminal record was right there for the whole world to read. Joan was named as his sister, and Rebecca and Bruce, whose wedding was given as the reason for Dave to end his long separation from his family. Elizabeth Graham was going to hate that, if she ever knew about it.

Who had spoken to the press? Joan hadn't had a single phone call from a reporter. And if any had shown up at the wedding, they'd kept their mouths shut then, too. Had that been Fred's doing? Or was the press in Oliver that civilized? Come to think about it, why hadn't the story appeared on Saturday? He'd died on Friday.

The phone rang again. She grabbed it, glad Fred, at least was managing to sleep through it.

"Joanie? You okay?" Annie Jordan. Would all her old people call?

"Hi, Annie. As okay as I can be, considering."

"I was so sorry to read about your brother. I really liked him."

"Thanks, Annie." Me, too, sometimes.

"Hope I didn't wake you."

"No, I was up."

"I won't keep you. But I had to give you my love."

Better than Nancy's prying, only thinly disguised as sympathy.

When she hung up the phone, Fred was standing in the bedroom doorway. "What's going on?"

She held out the paper and pointed to the story.

Scarcely looking at it, he nodded. "I should have warned you."

"You knew?"

"I could guess. Ketcham said they were all over him. He held them off as long as he could. Didn't identify him on Friday, anyway."

"Is that why they let me alone?"

He smiled. "For a mild-mannered cop, he can be tough."

"Is it going to be like this all day?"

"Not if you take the phone off the hook. Anyone you can't live without talking to?"

"Not today."

Smiling, he lifted it off. "It won't beep at you for long."

Chapter 14

FRED KNEW he couldn't protect her from all the fallout, but he could shield her from the worst of it.

She looked him in the eye. "Is it safe to leave the house?"

"You want to go somewhere?" He looked out the window. "In this snow?"

"I want to know what will happen if I do."

"Probably nothing. They don't know your face, and I don't see anyone parked on the doorstep."

"Can you find out what Ketcham's learned so far?"

"Who, me?"

"He talks to you—I know he does."

He considered denying it, but knew it was useless. Ordinarily, she didn't push him about police investigations, but this was different, he had to admit.

As if in answer to her question, the cell phone in his pocket rang. When he answered, Ketcham apologized for calling so early on a Sunday.

"We were awake."

"She up to talking this morning?"

"She'd probably welcome it." He mouthed Ketcham's name at her, and she nodded. "Come on over."

In ten minutes, Ketcham was slogging up their still unshoveled walk. Fred had thrown on jeans and brewed a pot of coffee. "Heat up some of those sweet rolls for him," he told Joan.

"I'm way ahead of you." Behind him, she'd already set cups and plates out on the old oak table, and now she pulled the butter out of the refrigerator.

Ketcham shed his outdoor gear in the living room, sniffed, and followed Fred back to the kitchen.

"You read my mind," he said as Fred pulled the tray of left-over rolls out of the oven.

Licking his fingers, he told Joan some of what they knew and a few new things. Dave had been healthy. The wounds were not self-inflicted. The knife came from Ellen's kitchen. Helga Lundquist's prints had smudged those below them, but they'd been able to identify prints of all the various kitchen workers. "With all the smudges, we can't be sure there weren't still more. But people do know about gloves."

"Was Helga holding the murder weapon?" Joan asked.

"Yes. No sign of wounds from anything else. But that doesn't mean she did anything more than she said she did. There's no question about the time of death. He was seen alive only a few minutes before he was found the way you saw him." His eyes met Fred's.

"After she pulled it out," Joan said.

He nodded. "I can believe she'd do that."

"But not attack him," Joan said.

"The other workers don't think she would," Ketcham said. "That's all we're going to know, unless we find someone else."

And evidence to go with him, Fred thought gloomily.

Ketcham reached for another sweet roll. "So the crime scene's no help. We need to look outside it. Like those phone calls he made."

"I thought you had those numbers," Joan said.

"We do, and we tried them. Mostly, we got recorded messages. One didn't answer at all, and one was the print shop where he worked."

Joan nodded.

Without saying anything about what Fred had already report-ed to him, Ketcham continued. "We were able to identify several of those businesses, and it looks as though your brother might have been trying to sell some land. Maybe timber, too. Did he own land in Indiana?"

"I think so," Joan said. "That's what I meant to do today, go up and hunt for my parents' wills. I think they left him land somewhere when they left me this house."

"Do that, would you?" Ketcham said. "It would help us."

"All right," she said. "And I made those calls, too. I got those messages, and I reached Dave's friend Pete at the print shop. I was hoping to find his friends, for a funeral. Pete sounded really shocked and sorry."

"So you'll call him back," Ketcham said.

"Yes, and he suggested telling the paper in Ann Arbor. Dave was born there and lived there a lot longer than he was here. I can do that and maybe talk to someone at the high school there tomorrow, and I can talk to retired teachers at the senior center about when he was here. I do know one old girlfriend of his—she works at Ellen's."

"Yes, we spoke to her. Did you reach anyone else by phone?"

Her eyes looked troubled, and she took Fred's hand. He patted hers and didn't let go.

"One man. He—he scared me."

"Scared you?" Ketcham asked, not leading her.

"He sounded nasty. Almost threatening."

"What did he say?"

"It wasn't what he said so much as how he said it. I asked what number I'd reached, and he asked who'd I want. That's when I hung up." Her eyes were big now. "It sounds silly when I tell it, but he frightened me."

"Can you show me which number that was?"

"I'll go get the phone bill." She left the room.

"Whaddya think?" Fred asked.

Ketcham shrugged. "Maybe she caught him on a bad day. But she might be right about this creep. She hung up so fast, let's hope he thought it was a wrong number. Now, if it's the number I think it is…"

Joan ran back into the kitchen, waving the phone bill. "I thought I left it in our room, and there it was." She held it out to Ketcham, pointing to one number.

He pulled out his notebook. "That's the one where we got no answer. Man probably has caller ID. Wasn't about to answer the cops."

"You mean, you think he did it?"

"Doesn't mean anything. Maybe he wasn't there when we called. And ask Fred how many people won't talk to us."

"It's true, honey," he told her. "Some people are scared, and some people just hate cops."

"Don't worry," Ketcham said. "We'll track him down."

"Sorry to be such a wimp."

"You're no wimp!" Fred told her.

But Ketcham took another tack. "I want you to think back to other times you were scared in Oliver." And before she could answer, he added, "Think way back."

"You mean, to when we lived here before?"

"Yes, when you and Dave were kids in school."

She smiled. "You're not interested in the things that scared me in sixth grade."

"Try me. Anybody ever threaten you in any way?"

Good for Ketcham. Fred hadn't thought of such an approach.

"Or Dave, you mean?"

"Or Dave, if you know."

"That's the problem. He was so much older. But there was this guy, this big kid, older and tougher, maybe a dropout…"

Fred didn't let so much as a finger move. He could feel hers tremble.

"I used to ride my bike to school. I had a new three-speed and thought I was something. Dave had his license by then, but my parents didn't believe in giving cars to kids, and Dave hadn't saved the kind of money he'd need even to buy an old, beat-up one. He rode his ten-speed to high school, and he couldn't give me a ride on that. So I was alone, part of the way, anyhow."

Ketcham nodded, the sunlight through the kitchen window glinting off his glasses.

"The first time, this big kid knocked me off my bike, and no one came to help. I was scratched up, but it hurt worse that my new bike was scratched up, too. I was afraid to climb back on, but I had to get to school on time, so I did. The kid kept threatening me from behind all the way to school, but he didn't hit me again, not that day. After school, Dave fussed about my bike and my torn-up knee. I told him what had happened. So the next morning, he followed me to school, and when the same guy came after me again, Dave rescued me. He wasn't as big, but he was furious, and got him to back off."

"Was that the end of it?" Ketcham asked.

Fred had been wondering the same thing. It sounded like a good memory of Dave, not something she'd remember as a threat. Still, she had been trembling.

"No," she said. "The next day, he came back with a bunch just like him. They were all yelling insults at us and threatening what they'd do to us."

"Insults?" Ketcham asked.

"I didn't understand them at the time. They were calling us kikes. I guess they thought a name like Zimmerman meant we were Jewish. One of them even waved a little swastika flag on a stick."

"You get any names?"

"Not me. Dave eventually found out a couple. The first guy was Bud something."

A big help in southern Indiana, Fred thought.

"Only Bud I know is Bud Snarr," she said. "He owned the funeral home back then, before Gil grew up and took over. But it's not that Bud. Closer to Gil's age, anyway, but older."

"These guys come back again?" Ketcham asked.

"Sometimes. Mostly just Bud, when I was alone. Dave couldn't be there all the time. It made him late to high school, and he got into enough trouble at school. But one day Dave got some of his friends together, and they lay in wait. For a change, they were on the attack when Bud and those guys showed up, expecting to make me miserable. Instead, they got chased by a bunch of boys closer to their own size. Scared 'em good. They turned tail and ran." She smiled, remembering. "Bud and his gang let me alone after that. Even so, for weeks I didn't feel safe going to school."

"You went anyway?" Fred said.

"I had to." She said it naturally, and he thought, not for the first time, how many people would have curled up and given up after things she'd lived through. Giving up didn't seem to occur to his wife—hadn't, even back then.

"You ever report any of this to the school, or to your parents?" Ketcham asked.

"No, and I don't know why not. Only to Dave. A skinned knee didn't worry Mom, and she didn't know the rest of it."

"I don't suppose you could recognize any of them again, after all these years."

"Not most of them. Boys change a lot more when they turn into adults than girls do. But Bud—I might know him."

"Why?"

"He was tall and blond, though who knows what will have happened to his hair by now. But really tall, maybe six-five—he looked gigantic to me back then. And there was something wrong with his hand." She paused. "He was missing a piece off the end of his right index finger."

Ketcham was writing in his notebook. "I'll see what I can find out."

"You don't seriously think a thing like that would make a man come after Dave all this time later and murder him."

"I don't think anything. But your brother humiliated him at an age when kids like that don't take kindly to humiliation."

"Then Dave showed up in town again, after all this time. But I've been here for years."

"You were his victim. Dave was his enemy."

"Oh."

"And he could have found out Dave's name—probably knew it all along. Yours had changed."

"But today the paper told the world he was my brother."

"As I said, Dave was the enemy, not you."

She didn't look much comforted.

"Anything else come to mind?" Ketcham asked.

"Not here. My dad had a student up in Michigan go after him once with a railroad spike, or something he thought looked like one, anyhow. Kid he flunked. Dad showed up at home with a bandage on his head, blood all down his shirt, and a big smile on his face. They'd treated him at the university hospital. Scared Dave and me. Mom was cool about it, though, once she saw he was okay."

"You know anything more about that student?"

"No, but there might be records at the university. You could ask the anthropology department, where Dad taught."

Ketcham nodded and made another note. "Let those memories keep coming. No telling what will turn out to matter, so don't hesitate to call me if you think of something else, or something more about Bud and his friends."

"I will."

Fred walked Ketcham out. "Good job," he told him out on the porch.

"Thanks. That finger…someone will remember him. I almost do myself."

"It'll come, then."

"He'll probably turn out to be long dead, but we can hope."

"And that business about the student who went after their father in Michigan," Fred said. "And all the years Dave lived there. Joan was thinking of people to tell he'd died. I was wondering who up there already knew all about it."

"Yeah." Ketcham jammed his hat on his head and his hands into his gloves.

"Keep me posted."

Ketcham met his eyes. "When I can."

"And Ketcham, thanks for holding them off her yesterday."

"Sure. How'd the wedding go?"

"Not bad, all things considered. I gather you gave my family permission to take Mom home."

"No point in keeping her here. And we don't know whether she saw it happen, or just found him on the floor and pulled the knife out. Even with her memory as bad as it is, she could seem like a threat. She's safer out of here."

"Thanks."

They both knew she could be hauled back, but Fred knew Ketcham was doing everything he could to keep that from happening. It wouldn't make a bit of sense, and it might indeed put her in danger.

"You think they'll get her diagnosed now?" Ketcham asked, drawing with the toe of his boot in the snow on the porch.

"If I have anything to say about it," Fred said, wondering how much he would have to say.

"Might make her happier, if they can treat it, even for a while. My aunt's on Aricept and another one now, Namenda. Didn't stop it, but it helped some at first. They say it's better if you don't wait too long."

"Yeah." Would they listen to that?

After Ketcham left, Fred felt useless. He might as well get out the snow shovel.

"Do you mind if I desert you to clear the walk?" he asked Joan.

"Oh, please. Do next door, too, would you?"

"Sure." The old guy on the corner was long past it, and they routinely included his sidewalk with theirs.

It was a relief to move his muscles, clearing the walk and the steps up to the porch, but he found the snow wetter and heavier than he'd expected, and he rested on the shovel a few minutes before starting in next door.

"Okay, my turn." It was Andrew, finally awake, trotting down the front steps.

"I wondered when we'd see you."

"I wasn't in any hurry to get up, but Mom said you were out here, and I couldn't let you get the best of me."

"You're welcome to it." Fred passed him the shovel. "What time did you take those girls home?"

"Sally left early with her folks, but I hung out pretty late with Kierstin. She can sleep on the way home."

Fred had been pushing the heavy, wet stuff ahead of the shovel, but Andrew was tossing it over his shoulder.

"You still like her?"

"She's all right. A kid."

Fred smothered a smile. "Thanks, Andrew. For the shoveling, but also for showing her a good time."

Chapter 15

JOAN FELT relief at having told Ketcham about her childhood tormenter. Odds were good the man was long gone, but the memory of how Dave had come to her defense back then cheered her, rather than increasing her feeling of loss at his death. You weren't all bad, she told him. I'm glad you came, even if you didn't get to see Rebecca married.

He may have protected Helga from being attacked in the kitchen, she suddenly thought, but surely that would have occurred to Ketcham. It wasn't something she needed to tell him, especially since she didn't really know what had happened in that kitchen. Telling how he protected me from Bud, though—that was something he couldn't figure out on his own.

Bud…no matter how she tried, she couldn't make the rest of his name come, if she'd even known it. She was glad she'd remembered the critical detail about that finger.

Comforting as Ketcham had tried to be, she couldn't help wondering whether Bud, or whoever had killed Dave, if it was someone out of their past, would come after her next. At least Rebecca would be a long way off, hidden in the big city, whether she changed her name to Bruce's or not. But Andrew was right here in Oliver. Ketcham would think of it, too, and Fred was here to protect them. But could he? Could anyone?

She heard Fred now, stamping the snow off his boots on the front porch. He came in and shed them by the door.

"Andrew's doing the neighbor's walk."

"Good for him. I was hoping you'd remember."

"I did, but that stuff's heavy. I was glad to see him."

He hung up his jacket and hugged her, rubbing his cold hands and nose against her warm cheeks.

"It's early still," she said. "Are you up to a walk after all that work?"

"Why not?"

"I'll hang up the phone again. Let 'em leave messages."

They bundled up and set off. With so few walks shoveled and no traffic to dodge, they walked in the street, where the snow plows had left a smooth single lane.

"Want to go over to Ellen's, be sure your folks got away?"

"Not unless you do."

"Good." She had no desire to revisit the scene of her brother's murder. Tucking her arm in the crook of his elbow, she followed his lead. She wasn't surprised when he eventually headed for the park. The path through it wouldn't be cleared, but it wouldn't matter where they walked. Anywhere ought to be beautiful.

Sure enough, snow crystals glistened on every twig, and it took no skill at all to follow the little footprints of rabbits and squirrels throughout the park. But she was surprised to see deer tracks, too.

"Look!" She pointed. Then she felt his hand on her chin, turning her head. "Ohhh," she breathed. Three deer, their heads bent to the ground, seemed to think themselves invisible behind a single leafless tree. She supposed that before the tornado the trees in the park had been dense enough to provide cover.

Standing still, they watched the deer until something startled them, and they bounded off, grace itself.

"I didn't know we had deer right here in the middle of Oliver," Joan said.

"They wander in from time to time to forage in the park."

"I suppose they're safe here from hunters."

"I wouldn't count on it. They're a nuisance, and some people in town think we ought to go after them."

The cops ought to know, but even that grim thought failed to lessen her pleasure at knowing there were deer grazing on her way to and from work every day. She'd never again walk through the park without half expecting to see them.

Nothing that happened the rest of the day came close. They walked awhile longer, but after they went home to warm up, the rest of the day was routine. The telephone was blessedly silent.

Joan caught up on laundry and other chores. She cleared out the clutter she'd told Rebecca not to worry about leaving in her room, most of it recyclable packing from gifts that had been mailed to them. In one corner stood a stack of gifts she'd promised to send Rebecca and Bruce in a few weeks, after they'd had time to decide which of their old furniture and other belongings would go into the apartment they were going to live in. Joan had been interested to hear that they had chosen to give up both their old apartments and set up joint housekeeping in a place new to them both. A good sign for the marriage, she thought, but it had to make more work than if one of them had simply moved in with the other on a permanent basis. She wasn't surprised they hadn't found time before the wedding to decide and deal with what they weren't keeping.

What did people in the big city do? Hardly a garage sale, she thought.

She'd carefully kept her mitts off their decision making, but she could only imagine Elizabeth Graham's intrusiveness. Hang in there, Rebecca, she thought. The wedding was only the beginning.

Still, Rebecca had managed well. So far, so good. And watching Don Graham's quiet authority had reassured Joan. He could control Elizabeth. Joan suspected Bruce would follow his father's lead when necessary to protect his wife.

Late in the day, she finally remembered her promise to Ketcham and went back up to Rebecca's room to dig into the box in which she kept old records and important papers. The wills would be there, she knew, as she sat on the floor in front of the box. But nestled against the wills she turned up an old family photo. There stood her parents, glowing with health. And there she was in front of them, still too young to go to school, much less worry about bullies. Her brother stood beside her, already so tall he had to lean down to hold her little hand.

The tears came. Tears for her parents, tears for Dave, tears for herself. Holding the picture in her hand, she wept without trying to stop.

I'm the last of the family, she thought when the tears finally slowed. There's no one else left. I'm all alone.

"Mind if I join you?" Fred said and sank to the floor behind her. He held out a clean handkerchief, and she took it and blew her nose.

"Thanks, Fred."

"Andrew wanted to come up, but I pulled rank on him."

She laughed.

"How're you holding up?"

"Better, now you're here."

"Ketcham's a good man."

"I know."

"He'll get him."

"I hope so. I can't live scared like this." She held out the wills and the photograph. "Here are the wills. And here we all are."

Ignoring the wills, he took the picture. "That's you and Dave?"

"Hard to believe, isn't it?" Now she could smile.

"And your folks. You know, I don't think I've ever seen them."

"Really? Somewhere in a closet up here I have some old albums. I should bring them down. Andrew won't remember them, either."

"Sounds like fun." He looked down at the wills. "You want to give those to Ketcham? You can do it yourself, you know. I'm not in on this case."

"I know." He was right, she thought. With him not in charge, she should act like a grown-up. "Okay, I'll call him." She slid the wills into her pants pocket and went down to make the call from her favorite spot in the living room.

"I'll be right over, if that's all right," Ketcham said.

In her corner of the big sofa, Joan assured him that it was. Then, for the first time in years, she read her father's will again, knowing that her mother's was the same in everything that applied after they both had died. Sure enough, in addition to leaving her the house and its furniture, they had left Dave a sizable piece of land some miles from Oliver. She had a vague memory that her father had hoped to find something there of interest. Would he have told Alvin Hannauer about it? It was Alvin whose research had brought him to Indiana in the first place, and they'd worked together during her dad's sabbatical. She could ask him when she saw him at the senior center. But from the phone calls Dave had made, he must have been planning to sell it, maybe to timber it first. He'd probably used up his share of their parents' savings, though there hadn't been much in the bank. At least they'd owned the house and the land free and clear.

When Ketcham arrived, she invited him in.

"Can't stay this time, I'm afraid," he said, but he came inside to let her shut out the cold.

Joan pointed out the relevant passages in the will.

"All right if I borrow this?" he asked.

"Sure. It's long since probated—I already have the house. Dave's land is the only part that matters now. It's probably all he owns—owned—that amounted to anything."

"Did he have a will?"

"I have no idea." It had never occurred to her. She wondered who his lawyer was, and where.

"You might inherit."

"I don't want to!" It burst out of her. Her fear returned. "You think someone might have killed him for that property? If he left it to me, I'd be next, and then my children! They inherit from me."

"Don't get ahead of yourself."

It wasn't much comfort. She let him out and then started worrying all over again. What if that awful man Dave had called went after him for his land? And now he'd come after her? Instead of a blessing, would their parents' gift to Dave be a curse to them all?

Maybe she needed to talk to the minister after all. Sunday evening shouldn't be too terrible a time to call him. Before she could back out, she picked up the phone again.

"Of course I'll come," Eric said.

"Would you rather have me go to your house? I wouldn't mind."

"You would when you got here. The kids are wild today."

"And they don't need to be shushed," she said, remembering times when she'd had to keep Rebecca and Andrew out of the way when some parishioner had shown up to consult their father about a personal problem.

"Well…" He wouldn't say it.

"That's fine. You come here, whenever you're ready."

Chapter 16

ERIC YOUNG rang their bell at half past eight.

"Hope I'm not too late for you folks," he said when Fred let him in.

"Of course not. I'm glad Joan called you. It's been a little hard to know how to support her. Take your coat?"

"Thanks." Shrugging it off and giving it to him, Eric looked around the little house. "I'm sorry it's taken something like this to make me pay a pastoral call."

Joan came downstairs from Rebecca's room. "I thought I heard the doorbell. Thank you for coming, Eric."

"Joan, how are you holding up?"

She took the hands he held out to her. "Amazingly well, most of the time. Then I fall apart. I never know when it's going to hit me. Please, sit down." When she curled up in her usual spot on the sofa, he sat in the comfortable chair she was pointing to.

Fred joined her on the sofa, glad to see that she wasn't playing hostess for a man who might be able to help her as he didn't know how to do. He hesitated to reach for her hand. Better follow her lead.

"You made it through the wedding," the minister said.

"I did, didn't I? But that was for Rebecca. Now she doesn't need me anymore."

"And you're all right about that? Some mothers find that a loss in itself."

Fred looked at her. Her face was serious, but her eyes were dry.

"No." She smiled. "Maybe that was Elizabeth Graham's problem, but I'm glad Rebecca and Bruce found each other."

Eric nodded. "Mrs. Graham likes to get her way. She give you a hard time?"

"She tried."

"And you held your own." It wasn't a question.

"I had other things on my mind." Now her voice wobbled, and the tears threatened. Changing his mind, Fred took her hand. She smiled up at him.

"How can I help?" Eric leaned toward them.

"I don't know what to do next," Joan said. "I suppose we ought to have a funeral, but I don't know what I have to do. It's not like a normal death. And we weren't close. But I'm the only family he had left."

"Have the police released his body?"

"Not yet. But I was thinking of cremation anyway. I don't want his body there."

"So we can hold a service anytime. Before or after."

"I don't even know who'd come. The man he was working for wants to be there. That's all I know. Maybe some of our friends. And gawkers, because it was in the paper. They probably won't stop with one article, either. Not to mention radio or TV."

Fred was glad she'd thought of it. He'd hated to warn her, but he knew it was true.

"You could have a small, private service," Eric said. "Invite the man he worked for, any of the family and friends you want, and stop there."

"Could we do that?" The relief showed on her face. "I suppose Ellen and her gang, too. They might need to come. To find some peace, since it happened in their kitchen."

"It's up to you."

"I doubt Dave ever went to church. And we're not exactly regular."

"That's all right."

"I don't want to drag Rebecca and Bruce back, and Fred's family have enough to deal with."

"You could put 'private service' in the obituary and not say where or when. Then tell the people you want to tell. You can let your distant family know that you don't want them to make the trip."

Fred felt her body relax against his.

"Do you need help with the obituary?" Eric asked.

"Not if I can keep it that simple. I don't know much about him anyway, not that I'd want to see in the paper. The bad stuff will probably be analyzed to death, but I don't want to put it there." Raising her eyes to his, she said, "He served time in prison."

"Uh-huh."

It was in today's paper, Fred thought. She's already blocked it out.

"Can I just put in when and where he was born, who our parents, were, and when he died? Everyone's going to know the rest before long anyway."

"Sure. You could add where he went to school and where he worked. And name yourself and your family. Or just you, and say a niece and nephew also survive him."

"Yes. And then the private service. In the church?"

"If that's what you want."

The frown between her eyebrows almost disappeared.

"What do I have to do about his ashes?" she asked.

"Have to?" Eric said.

"You know, are there any laws in Indiana about them?"

He smiled. "Only one that I know about, and nobody obeys it."

She looked startled.

"There's some form you're supposed to file to tell the state where you've put them. But the only people I knew who tried to follow it came back laughing. They said the official they asked for the form had never heard of such a thing and wouldn't know where to file it if she got it. I wouldn't worry about it. What were you thinking of doing?"

"I don't know. Maybe scatter them on Dave's land? There must be woods, if he was finding out about selling his timber."

"Probably yours by now," Fred said.

"Maybe. Unless he willed it to someone." She shook her head. "I don't know how to find that out, either."

"You have a family lawyer?" Eric asked.

"I haven't talked to a lawyer since my husband died."

"I can recommend one in our church. If you like, I'll be glad to ask her how to find out what you need to know about whether Dave's left a will."

"Thank you. I don't know where to start."

They talked a few minutes more. Eric agreed to keep the service simple and not try to speak about the man he hadn't known. "If you want to say something, you could."

She shook her head.

The simple private service made sense, Fred thought. It also lessened the chance that Dave's killer would attend. He wondered whether Ketcham would want to come. Joan might welcome a police presence as security. He could suggest it to her that way. Or let Ketcham ask her. Not that he wasn't police presence himself.

Eric didn't linger or pray when he left, but Fred thought the visit had done its job. Giving him a brief hug, Joan climbed the stairs to the little desk in what had been Rebecca's room to write Dave's obituary.

———&⚬⚬&———

On Monday morning, she was relieved to get up and go to work, leaving the whole weekend behind her.

"Fine thing," she told Fred. "I ought to be happy for Rebecca, and I am. But the whole weekend feels like a bad dream."

"You sure you're up to working?"

"No, but I don't want to stay here and climb the walls. You'd be just as bad."

He nodded. "Worse. But if you change your mind, you know where to find me."

"Thanks, Fred."

"You want me to walk you there?" He said it casually enough, but his peaked eyebrows gave him away.

"I'll be fine. Don't mother-hen me!" She hadn't meant to snap. Could she make it through a day of even well-meant questions from all sides? Maybe not, but she had to try.

"I know you will." He kissed her and shooed her out the door.

In the park, the untouched beauty she had shared with Fred was now much trampled, rabbit tracks replaced by the trails of kids' sleds, and snow no longer clinging to every twig. Still, the crisp air and almost blinding blue expanse overhead restored her spirits.

But in the senior center, she was bombarded.

First and least offensive was Annie. "Joanie! It's good to have you back. We didn't dare hope to see you this morning." Beaming, she stopped sorting the mail and relinquished Joan's desk chair to her.

"Good to be here, Annie. Anything I ought to know?"

"Pretty quiet this morning. I think people are still leery of driving. Walking, too. It's treacherous on those sidewalks."

Joan sat down and pulled off her snow boots. She slid her feet into the shoes she kept under the desk for such days. "You made it yourself."

"I got a ride. Dropped me off right by the ramp. And my grandson shoveled that for us. And the front walk."

She hadn't even noticed, much less thought of arranging for that essential job to be done. She'd have to line someone up for the rest of the winter—Bert Barnhart probably would be glad of the work. This snowstorm, the first of the season, and coming on the heels of Dave's murder, had sneaked up on her. It might even be the last, but you never knew what to expect in southern Indiana. She'd better be ready for more. "Please thank your grandson for all of us."

"I already did. Told him he didn't have to fuss, but he insisted."

"Good." Joan picked up the letter opener. It was going to be all right, she thought. An ordinary day.

Gradually, the regulars drifted in. Some greeted her with brief, uninquisitive words of sympathy. Just right, Joan thought. Trust old people to understand. But then she began to overhear conversations taking place around her.

"I don't care what you say." Cindy Thickstun's voice rose. "He was a lovely man. So good-looking. And her brother, for goodness sake."

"No smoke without fire," Vernon Pusey told Cindy. "People don't get killed less'n they been doin' something they oughtn't. The man didn't go to prison for nothing."

"That don't mean he deserved killing," Cindy argued.

"You don't know what else he done," Vernon said.

"Shhh!"

Joan couldn't tell who shushed him, but whatever he said next was too soft for her to hear. It didn't last, though.

"Man couldn't keep his hands outta other folks' pockets. I don't care if he was a pretty boy, he was a crook. Once a crook, always a crook."

But he was going straight, Joan wanted to yell. And Cindy's right—even if he wasn't, you don't kill people for the kind of thing Dave did. You don't kill people, period.

"All I can say is, if he done me thataway, I'd go after him, for sure," Vernon was saying.

"With a knife?" Cindy said.

"More like my bare hands."

Now someone really did succeed in shushing him. Joan was so used to hearing Vernon shoot off his mouth that she was surprised at how much it bothered her when he did it about her brother.

She tried to focus on the mail, but it was a lost cause. Putting it down as a bad job, she looked up to see Mabel Dunn standing at her desk.

"Hi, Mabel. Something I can do for you?"

"Oh, no. I just wanted to say how sorry I am about your brother. You mustn't pay old Vern any mind." If Mabel had been wearing an apron, Joan thought, she would have been twisting it.

"Don't worry about Vernon, Mabel. Sit down and tell me how you've been."

"I'm all right." Mabel did sit on her straight visitor's chair, a little uneasily, Joan thought. "You've had such a week, though. I don't know how you hold it together."

"Duct tape, Mabel." Joan suddenly felt better. "I'm one big fake."

"It was the murder that hit the paper." Mabel didn't flinch

from the word, and Joan was grateful to her for it. "But how was your daughter's wedding, with all that?"

"Amazingly okay, would you believe it? But I don't envy her that new mother-in-law."

"If Rebecca's anything like you, she'll give that woman what-for when she needs to."

"Thanks, Mabel. That's one of the nicest things anyone's said to me all week."

Mabel shook it off. "Even so, seems to me you've got more on your plate than you need right now. I hope you'll remember not all of us here think like old Vern. If you need any kind of help, anything at all, I want you to call on me. Even if it's just a shoulder to cry on when you're by yourself, or in the middle of the night. All this is gonna hit you sometime. I'd be proud to listen."

Joan got up and came around the desk to hug Mabel. That this shy woman, usually such a mouse, even after being elected secretary of the board at the center, could offer her such comfort touched her in a way she didn't understand. "Thanks. That means—I can't tell you how much that means to me."

Mabel hugged her back, her brief foray into speech over, and faded back into the woodwork.

Sitting by herself now, Joan couldn't help wondering whether someone hadn't done what Vern said—come after Dave in retribution for something he'd done. Did that mean something he'd done here in Oliver, in the distant past? Or had someone followed him here?

Someone he'd known in prison, maybe. How had he known the man who owned the print shop? She didn't know. There was so much she didn't know about her brother.

Would their parents have known more? But Joan couldn't wish they had lived to see their only son murdered.

Chapter 17

AS THE MORNING wore on, nothing much happened, and Joan began to settle into the routine, at times almost forgetting. But then some new thought would hit her.

Or an old one. Suppose whatever had sent Dave to prison had left someone so bitter as to come after him. Did victims of crime ever do that? Was Vern right? What did Ketcham think? She couldn't bring herself to ask him, but she could feed the thought to Fred, who would know what to do with it.

In a way, it would be a relief. Surely no one that angry at Dave would take it out on his innocent sister. Or was someone who was angry enough to kill rational? As quickly as it arrived, her relief disappeared.

She forced herself to pay attention to her job. Bert Barnhart did indeed welcome snow shoveling when she got around to calling him. "Just put it on your list of things to do," she told him. "Come when it snows."

"And I'll scatter salt, too," he said. "You got some, I know."

She hadn't bothered to look, but Bert probably had put it in an appropriate spot when he'd organized their storage area after painting the railing, back in warmer weather. She and Bert agreed that he'd submit his hours to her and keep them supplied with salt when they ran out. He was good about submitting receipts, she knew.

She'd planned to eat lunch at her desk, but when Fred called, she was glad to escape. He picked her up, and they walked over to Wilma's Café. As usual, Fred chose the booth against the back wall and parked her so he could sit with his back against that wall.

Joan had always figured it came from a cross between wanting to see everything and everyone and not wanting to be surprised from behind.

Wilma poured their coffee. "The usual?" she said.

Fred nodded, but suddenly Joan wished for anything but the usual. "Give me a burger like Fred's," she said.

Wilma raised her eyebrows but didn't say a word.

When the food came, Joan bit into the huge, juicy burger and wondered how she could possibly finish it. Juicy or not, it tasted like sawdust.

"You okay?" Fred asked.

"I don't know." Her eyes filled with sudden tears. Why did this have to happen in a public place? At least nobody but Fred could see her face.

He held out another big handkerchief, and she blew her nose. "Thanks."

"Something happen?"

"Not really. Oh, people talked. But I expected that."

"Say anything?" He asked it oh-so-casually, but she knew better.

"Not really. Vernon Pusey was shooting off his mouth about how Dave was a crook and somebody probably wanted revenge for whatever he'd done that sent him to prison. Then I got scared again. Scared they'd come after me next."

"I wondered when that would hit you."

"It doesn't make sense, does it?"

"Sure. But the odds are in your favor."

"What odds?" Her burger forgotten, Joan stared at him.

"I don't mean whole families don't get killed, but not for that kind of reason."

"So why do they? I mean, the whole world knows we're family. Now they do, anyway."

"I shouldn't have said that. People who go after whole families have all kinds of crazy reasons. It never makes sense."

"Not to you, maybe, but I'll bet it does to them. And I don't want to be on the receiving end, much less Andrew and Rebecca."

"They're adults, Joan. Rebecca's miles away, and Andrew can take care of himself."

"So could Dave, but look where it got him." She chomped down on the burger, taking her anger out on it.

He reached a hand toward her, but hers were fully occupied, and she didn't feel like hand-holding.

"Fred, what would you think of going to see Pete?"

"Who?"

"Pete. I don't even know his last name. The print shop guy Dave worked for. Maybe his only friend."

"I thought you were going to invite him to the funeral."

"I was—I am. But it occurs to me that Pete might know where Dave's will is. He might even have the key to Dave's place. We could look for ourselves."

"You sure?"

"No. But I'm going nuts as it is. You think you could get time off to go with me?"

"Long as I call it looking out for my wife instead of working on this case."

"Call it whatever you need to. Besides, it would be true. We don't know anything about the man really except that he gave Dave a job when he needed one."

"When do you want to go?"

"I'll call Pete after work. But soon, I think. The center will be fine. They weren't expecting to see me back yet anyway."

"And I'll check with Ketcham and Captain Altschuler. We can leave Andrew to hold down the fort."

"Thanks, Fred." On her next bite, juice ran down her chin. "You know, this is good."

"Mm-hmm." His eyes crinkled at her.

"But I'm not going to have the pie with you, too."

"Suit yourself."

Her good humor and appetite restored, Joan finished more lunch than she'd eaten in months. She had no trouble resisting Wilma's flaky apple pie, but drank another cup of coffee while Fred polished off a huge slice topped with vanilla ice cream.

They walked back to the senior center together. Most of downtown Oliver had been shoveled early enough, but here and there the foot traffic had packed the snow into ice before the storekeeper had reached it. Salt and sun would help eventually. For now, Joan was grateful for Fred's arm on the slick spots.

When she walked into her office, the phone was ringing. Shucking her coat, she answered it.

"Mom?"

"Rebecca? Are you all right?"

"Yes, of course. I wanted to see how you're doing."

Joan's shoulders relaxed. She tossed the coat onto her visitor's chair. "What's up? You're supposed to be on your honeymoon, not calling your mother!"

"Oh, Mom, we had to come straight back here. I couldn't take any more time off, so I'm working, and Bruce is moving boxes. So am I, after work."

"Into your new place?"

"Fast as we can. We took possession yesterday, and we can't keep paying for three apartments at once! But we have to leave the old ones spotless. Soon as we empty a room, I clean like you wouldn't believe."

Joan smiled into the phone. "You sound like an old married woman."

"I look like one. A really, really old one." But she sounded happy.

"You want Elizabeth and me to come help?"

"Argh!"

"Just a thought."

"Spare me."

"So you're calling from the bank?"

"No, on my lunch hour. And using my cell phone, not the bank's phone. Actually, that's what made me think of you."

"Oh?"

"The cell phone, I mean. I had a weird call on it awhile ago. A nasty-sounding man climbed down my ear, wanting to know where I got off calling him, anyway, only that's not how he put it."

"What did you do?"

"Told him he had the wrong number, and hung up."

"Good thing I didn't borrow your phone. That guy sounds like someone I reached when I was checking out the calls Dave made from our phone."

"Uncle Dave had some weird friends. You think he met that one in prison?"

"It crossed my mind. But he might just be an impatient jerk. Isn't that what you have a lot of in the big city?"

"You'd be surprised. I've met some of the friendliest people in New York."

"I'm glad to hear it."

"Are you okay, Mom? This has to be hard on you."

"Right now I'm doing fine, thank you. Fred and I may go visit the place where Dave was living—meet his boss, who did sound like a friend."

"You sure you want to do that?"

Joan paused. Was she? "It beats sitting around here waiting for I don't know what."

"You sound…I don't know, scared?"

"I am, a little. I don't have any idea why someone went after Dave. Or what's coming next. You know, Rebecca, it would be a good thing to keep your new address kind of private."

"Really?"

"I don't know, but it couldn't hurt. For a while, anyway."

"Okay. Bruce's agent will have it, and I can give it to you."

"I don't need it yet. Not till you're ready for me to send the wedding gifts."

"More boxes! Not yet, Mom. All I don't need are more boxes."

"Let the post office forward your mail from the old place."

"I already did that. My phone number won't change, so I don't need to tell my boss yet, even. But what about you and Andrew? Everyone knows where you live."

Joan couldn't answer her.

"I'm sorry, Mom. I didn't need to make it worse."

"You didn't. At least we have a cop in the house."

For whatever that's worth, she thought when she hung up. Maybe it was time to put a peephole in her front door. In Oliver, she'd always felt perfectly safe opening the door. But now…

Still, she was glad to have heard from Rebecca. She hadn't wanted to call her daughter, not now, but it was good to feel connected again.

She hung up her coat and dug into the pile of mail on her desk with new energy. How could so much junk accumulate in such a short time? She'd almost finished separating the wheat from the chaff when a light tap on her open door made her look up.

"Margaret!" Of all the center regulars, Margaret Duffy was the one she most welcomed seeing today. Long retired from teaching in Oliver's public schools, Margaret had been Joan's sixth-grade teacher when her family had lived there during her father's sabbatical. When Joan had arrived in Oliver and needed a job, it was Margaret, a member of the center's board, who had recommended Joan for the director's job there. She'd been a staunch friend ever since.

"They told me you were back at work. You holding up all right?" Margaret came in and settled her ample figure on the sturdy visitor chair.

Joan never needed to hide her feelings from Margaret, who probably would have seen right through her if she'd tried. "Some of the time. One minute I'm fine. Then I fall apart."

"Uh-huh."

"I had such mixed feelings about him when he was alive, and now…" She didn't know how she felt now.

"He was a complicated kid, too."

Of course. Margaret was the proverbial elephant. "Tell me what you remember about Dave, would you, Margaret?"

"He took the high school by storm, especially the girls. Broke up a bunch of steady romances, and then of course your family left town, and we were left with the aftermath."

"That bad?"

"Maybe not, but we felt the repercussions all the next year. A lot of parents would have been after his scalp if it'd been around to go after. Not literally, but they weren't happy."

"But you taught my grade, not Dave's."

"Oliver's a small town. I knew those kids. And their parents."

Of course she would have. Come to think of it, Margaret was the person whose brain she should be picking.

"Margaret, was any of that fallout serious enough to lead to what happened to Dave?"

"There were boys all over town with murder in their hearts, but I can't see it lasting this long." Margaret smiled. "They had a better chance once Dave was out of the way."

"Do you remember a big boy named Bud?"

"Bud Snarr? He was closer to your dad's age than Dave's."

"No. This was a boy who bullied me when I was riding my bike home from school. Dave rescued me a few times. I don't know how old he was, but he seemed enormous to me. He yelled anti-Semitic garbage at us—seemed to think Zimmerman was a Jewish name. For all I know, it might be, but I think it's just German. Means carpenter. Oh, and his index finger—part of it was gone."

Margaret sat very still for a moment. Then she said, "That sounds like one of the Fleener boys. There was one they called Bud—I think he was a Junior, named for his father, but I don't remember his father's name. And the boy I'm thinking of had cut the end off his finger. Caught it in a door, he said, but with that family, you never knew for sure."

"Where is he now?" Joan asked.

"Oh, heavens. Could be anywhere. Those kids didn't generally finish school, much less go on. Some of them got in trouble. I wish I could remember Bud better. But from what little I do remember, he might be the one who bothered you."

"Thanks, Margaret." At least she had a last name to suggest to Ketcham.

After Margaret left, she called him, but he was out. She was tempted to ask for Fred, but settled for leaving Ketcham a message. "Tell him Margaret Duffy thinks the Bud I remember might be Bud Fleener."

The woman answering the phone promised to tell him. "You have our sympathy for your loss," she said. "I know they're doing all they can."

Surprised, Joan thanked her.

Chapter 18

AT HOME that night, Joan tried Pete's phone, but it didn't answer. Of course. She had his work number.

It left her twiddling her thumbs, though, because she didn't even know a last name to check his home number. Why hadn't she asked him? Suddenly she wanted in the worst way to know who had killed Dave. Not Fred's mother. No matter how bad it looked, Joan was sure Helga Lundquist hadn't stabbed anyone. She believed what Helga had told Fred, that she had only removed the knife in an attempt, however mistaken, to keep it from killing him.

But someone had stabbed him in that kitchen. Had Helga seen it happen?

She called upstairs to Fred, "I'm going to walk over to Ellen's."

"I'll come along."

Mother-henning again, she thought, but she didn't argue. It was dark outside, and besides, he might come up with something useful. For one thing, he'd been there when Dave died. Or had he? Was Dave already dead when Fred got the call? She didn't know.

They didn't talk much on the way through the park. The dog barked when they came to the gate, and it seemed wise to wait for someone to calm it down before barging into the yard.

Joan was half expecting Laura, but it was Ellen who came out and greeted them. "Hush, dog!" she said, and it did. "He won't bite," she told them.

"That's what Laura told us," Joan said. "But I didn't want to put him to the test."

"A watchdog can be mighty useful," Fred said. Just what Dave had said.

"With no man in the house, I'm glad he's grown up to make so much noise. The neighbors probably don't appreciate him as much as I do, though."

"Far as I know, they haven't complained to the cops."

"That's good. We do our best." Holding the dog's collar, she opened the door and waved them into the living room. "It's not as neat as it was for the wedding, I'm afraid."

"You should see my house," Joan said. In fact, she thought Ellen's always looked neat. Now that it was a bed-and-breakfast, the family things had been moved to their rooms, in the back of the house. What was left looked comfortable, but it was unquestionably an adult space, with no sign of Laura or the other children.

"So, what brings you back?"

"I want to do something, anything, to help figure out what happened to Dave. I mean, I know what, but not how. Or who." She slipped an apologetic look at Fred. "I'm not trying to steal Sergeant Ketcham's thunder. He has resources I can't match. But I can't sit back and wait. It's driving me wild."

"What do you want from me?" For the first time, Ellen sounded prickly.

"Could we talk through what happened in the kitchen? Maybe even go in there again?" The thought still turned her stomach.

"You know I've been through this ad nauseam with the police," Ellen said. "And so have my staff."

"I know. It's not fair to ask you. But I can't stand not knowing more." Joan fought down the shrillness in her own voice.

Ellen looked up at Fred.

"I'm not part of this case," he told her. "Because of Mom, they kicked me off it."

"I wondered why I hadn't seen you with the others. Thought maybe it was because of the wedding."

"No. And tonight is Joan's doing, not mine."

For a long moment, she looked at Joan. Finally, she yielded. Without a word, she led them back to the kitchen.

Even as recently as she'd been in it, Joan had forgotten how industrial the new kitchen looked. Stainless steel sinks and a stainless steel island out in the middle of the room, shining pots hanging above it. No clutter, nothing cutesy, all business. The knives supported by magnetic strips on the wall looked ready for business, too. She shuddered. Which one had killed Dave? Or was it even there?

As if reading her mind, Ellen said, "Don't worry—they took that one away."

"Yes, they would, wouldn't they?" Where to start? What could she ask to learn anything at all? And why did she think she could learn what the police so far had failed to find out? Or had they? Maybe they knew plenty, but they hadn't released the information yet.

"It's so—clean. I mean, I already knew it was clean." She could only imagine how it had looked when Fred had arrived to find Dave dying on the floor. Or dead.

"Where was he when you found him?" she asked Fred.

"Over there, face down." He pointed to a spot on the floor, and she saw that the outside door was only a few feet beyond that spot.

"And that door wasn't locked?" She knew she'd been told, but she was having trouble keeping all of it in her head. Delayed something-or-other, she thought.

"No," Ellen said. "I told the police we needed to be able to go in and out. Take out the garbage, for instance. It's not practical to keep it locked during the day, but you can bet we're doing it now. Means we all have to carry keys and stop to unlock when we come back in from the garbage cans or carry in groceries or whatever. Big nuisance."

"Who was in the room when Dave was attacked?"

Ellen glanced apologetically at Fred before answering. "Only your brother and Mrs. Lundquist. They were getting along swimmingly. He was very sweet with her, and she seemed most at home in the kitchen, so I was happy to let her help with little things. They were putting together the salads for your rehearsal dinner, which we didn't end up using, of course."

"You're very kind," Fred said. "She likes being useful, no matter where she is. Even now."

"Where was everyone else?" Joan asked. She'd heard all this before, but she couldn't seem to keep it straight.

"We were shorthanded that day, even though I'd hired a couple of people who help us out for special occasions like that. Chrissy was helping me set up the dining room, but Patty phoned to say she was feeling puny and would make it in when she could. I'm afraid I wasn't very sympathetic."

No wonder, Joan thought.

"So Dave and Helga really were useful." Ellen looked at Fred again. "I'm sorry. She liked me to first-name her."

"I'm glad you understood that," he said.

Joan was looking around. "Other than being shorthanded, was everything else pretty smooth?"

"That day, yes. I didn't want to worry you about it, but the wedding cake was late arriving at the church the next day. I about had kittens till Catherine finally showed up with it. She wasn't answering her cell phone, and that's hardly the kind of thing you can whip up on the spur of the moment." She smiled.

"It looked beautiful," Joan made herself say, and it had. So Catherine Turner had dragged her heels after all. But if she'd done it to annoy Joan, it hadn't worked, because Ellen had protected her from knowing it.

"I'll try not to hold it against her. And Patty arrived in time to help me clean up in here before the rehearsal dinner."

"I'm so sorry you were put through that," Joan said.

"Oh, I was miffed enough at Patty to make her do most of it," Ellen said. "Once the cops left, of course. They took their sweet time."

"I was surprised they didn't delay us longer," Joan said. "Just as well, though. Elizabeth was fit to be tied."

"Your daughter has my sympathies, with a mother-in-law like that."

"Mine, too. I did a whole lot better." Joan smiled at Fred.

"Helga's a sweetheart," Ellen said. "There's no way in the

world she would have hurt your brother, I don't care what people say."

"I know. She thought she was helping him."

"Is she doing all right?"

"I think so," Fred said. "She's completely forgotten the whole thing—probably even the wedding, by now. But one good thing has come of it. I don't think the family's going to put up any more resistance about getting her diagnosed. Maybe there's treatment that will help for a while, anyway."

On the walk home, he asked whether going had been worth the trouble.

"I probably shouldn't have bothered Ellen at night," Joan said. "But somehow I feel a lot better. Does that make sense?"

"No. Does it need to?"

She laughed. "No. Probably going to see where Dave worked doesn't, either, but I'd really like to do that."

"I'm game," Fred said. "Tomorrow?"

"Or the next day. There's no huge rush about it. But I feel better knowing we're going to make the trip."

"Where is it?"

"I still don't know. In Illinois somewhere—I looked up Pete's area code—it's 815, and that's in Illinois."

"Not the same as Bishop Hill, but not too far away, if you'd like to see my folks."

She checked his face, but couldn't guess what he was thinking. "Not really, if you don't mind. I want to keep my mind on Dave this time."

"Could be in Pontiac," he said. "That's where Dave was in state prison."

"I think his address was Pontiac, now that you say it. I should have looked at my Christmas card list, for heaven's sake. Maybe Pete was the friend who had Dave's post office box key."

"Maybe."

"I wonder how they knew each other. Oh, Fred, you don't think Pete's an ex-con, too, do you? But he could just as well be someone Dave knew from high school. Or the U of M."

"Mm-hmm." His face was straight.

She'd ask Pete, and she'd have to wait till business hours in the morning to do that.

As she might have known it would, Tuesday morning turned out to be particularly busy, with one minor conflict after another brewing at the senior center. Joan wasn't able to close her office door to call Pete until after eleven, but it would be an hour earlier there, with Illinois on Central Time. So why did she feel so anxious?

Pete himself answered.

"This is Joan Spencer, Pete. Dave's sister." She forced calm into her voice.

"Great. Can you hold a minute?" He muffled the phone, but she heard him yell instructions across the room. "Sorry. The new guy—Dave's replacement, but he's not as good—just started a big job I can't afford to have him mess up. Do you know anything more about Dave?"

"Not really. But I'm wondering if you have the key to his place. I'd like to come see where he lived. In fact, do you know, did he have a will?"

"Not that I know of. I never heard him talk about it. But yeah, I have his key. He gave it to me when he left town. Almost like he was expecting trouble, you know?"

"You think?" She'd have to tell Fred. No, Ketcham. Both of them, really.

"I don't know. I don't know what to think. It blows my mind that anyone would kill Dave. Why, for God's sake?"

"That's what we're trying to help them figure out. That's part of why I want to come. And…" She didn't know how to say it. "And I suppose I just want to see where he lived. We'd been out of touch for so long. I hadn't even caught up yet."

"Anything I can do, I'll be glad to. When do you want to come?"

"How about tomorrow?"

"Good enough. I gotta work, but it's easy to find the shop."

She jotted down the directions he gave her. "Thanks, Pete. And…"

"Yeah?"

"Never mind. I'll ask you when I get there." She hung up without asking how he and Dave had known each other. Somehow, it didn't seem right over the phone, with him at work. So was she, for that matter. Remembering, she quickly noted the time of the call. She'd pay for it when the phone bill came.

She could hear Margaret saying, "Oh, that's not necessary," but paying for her personal calls let her make them without a qualm. In the months leading up to the wedding, she'd made more than usual. It had made the whole thing possible. Not for the first time, she was glad to have the kind of job that made it possible to be in charge of her own time. She suspected the center ordinarily came out ahead.

The phone shrilled in her ear. Jolted, she picked it up. Before she could answer properly, Alex Campbell started talking.

"How could you let me read that in the paper?" she raged.

"I'm sorry?" What was she talking about? Had Joan missed something or other about the orchestra in this week of all weeks? It wouldn't surprise her at all.

"You had to know how important your brother was to me! But I had to read—"

Joan quit listening to Alex's tirade even as she could hear that it was continuing. In her own confused emotional response, anger battled with grief and the urge to laugh. Who but Alex could call her, not to sympathize with her on the death of her only brother, but to berate her for not thinking to notify a woman he'd scarcely met? Or had he? Had Dave and Alex actually dated? Hard to imagine, but then, all kinds of things in Dave's life were hard to imagine. He'd certainly been charming to her at the rehearsal.

"Well?" Alex was demanding.

"Alex?"

"Who did you think it was?"

The giggle rose in her throat, and she choked it back. "Oh, Alex. It was terrible."

"Exactly." The demand was still there—I'm waiting, her voice said.

"I still can't talk about it. I'm sorry. I know you'll understand." A bare-faced lie.

It worked, though. "Of course. Now what are you doing about it?"

"Whatever the police tell me to do. I'm not discussing it with people." Lie number two, though at least that one was closer to the truth.

"Not anyone?"

"I've talked a little with the minister."

"Well…" She could hardly argue with that. "You let me know if there's any way I can help." Alex? Offering help? Unheard of.

"Thank you, Alex."

She hung up, limp. It was tempting to ask Alex to take over her managerial chores for the coming concert, but she wasn't about to risk laughing or crying in the woman's ear. She'd be able to do what needed doing, she was sure. Besides, she could imagine the mess Alex would make of her work, if she even made the attempt.

No question about it, getting out of town for a day would be a good move.

Chapter 19

AS IT TURNED out, arranging the short trip took a minimum of fuss. Andrew would be at home to answer the phone and check messages. The last thing Joan wanted was for anyone who mattered to her to worry.

Both the senior center and Captain Altschuler had set them free to take as much time as they needed. There were times, she thought, when playing the sympathy card made good sense.

And now she and Fred were pulling into Pontiac. She was glad he hadn't insisted on visiting his parents up in Bishop Hill afterward. Much as she liked both Oscar and Helga, coping with Helga's problems was more than she felt up to.

They found Pete's small shop on Main Street without difficulty, and a short, balding man met them at the door.

"I'm Pete. I've been watching for you," he said and swallowed both Joan's hands in his surprisingly large ones. "What can I say? I'm sorry for your loss doesn't come close. Dave was my good friend. But he was your brother."

"Thank you, Pete. He was lucky to have a friend like you. This is my husband, Fred Lundquist."

"Peter Vance." Ah, that was his full name. He released Joan's hands to shake the one Fred offered. Then he waved at the machines spewing photocopies behind him. "I miss him here already."

"How did you and Dave first know each other?" She'd been wondering, ever since she knew Pete was in the same town as the prison, whether he, too, had been a prisoner.

"In school, didn't you know?"

She was spared saying how little Dave had told her about

his life when Pete went on. "We were in high school together in Ann Arbor. We kept in touch, and when he moved to Illinois, we renewed our old friendship. Then when..." He looked at her. "When he ended up in Pontiac, I did what I could for him."

"You took our mail to him in prison." She could imagine him carrying it to Dave. What inspection would it have had to pass? She didn't ask.

"He didn't want you to know he was there."

"He told me himself, after he came to Oliver."

"Come in if you want." He stood back. "Trouble is, I can't leave the shop, and there's no good place to sit down."

"Fred and I could go over to Dave's till you're finished here," Joan said. "That's what we need to do anyway."

"Sure, let me find his key. Come on in."

They followed him into the shop, where he went behind the counter and fumbled in a desk drawer before handing her a key.

"I think this is it. Dave was the one who kept my desk in order. It's already a mess." Pulling a piece of scrap paper out of the recycling, he quickly drew a map and held it out to Fred. "You cross the river there."

Fred took it, but didn't show it to her. "Looks clear enough."

He was my brother, not yours! Joan wanted to say, but she kept her mouth shut. This was no time to get on her high horse. "Thanks, Pete," she said instead.

"I'll be done here about five. I can give you a call at Dave's."

On the way back to the car, Fred said, "Lots of time between now and then. Anything else you'd like to do here?"

Joan immediately felt less put upon. And there was something, but she wasn't sure she could face it.

"You all right?"

She looked up at his serious face. "Most of the time. You know."

"I know."

"You think...you think we could go past the prison?"

"Sure." He made a U-turn.

"You know where it is?"

"Yeah."

He probably looked it up before we left home, she thought. Or maybe not. He'd been a cop in Illinois before he came to Oliver. Maybe he'd been to this prison. Delivered someone there, or questioned a prisoner. Or—did they execute people in Illinois? Did he have to witness that? She didn't really want to know. He turned onto a pleasant street of well-kept houses and yards.

"You sure you're in the right place?"

"Look up there." He pointed down the street.

And there it was, smack in the middle of a residential neighborhood. There was no mistaking it for anything else, but she saw people who didn't look like law enforcement out walking nearby. Could Dave have seen such ordinary folks out his cell window? Did cells in that place even have windows? Probably not, but it cheered her to imagine him watching a little boy like that one with a dog almost bigger than he was.

"Okay, that's enough."

Fred found his way back to Main Street without difficulty and then to a street with houses that had seen better days. He slowed down. "We want 176," he said.

Joan watched the house numbers and spotted it, an older frame house that obviously had been divided up. The house, its dirty white paint peeling off, was distinctly grubby, but mature shade trees in the front yard softened it and would make living without air conditioning bearable in summer, she thought.

None of the mailboxes hanging beside the door was marked Zimmerman. He must still have been using his post office box. They could deal with that later. Fred took out the key Pete had given him. "The map says Apartment Two," he said, and the key fit the door with a *2* from which most of the brass was worn off.

Joan hung back when Fred stood aside, but of course there was no smell of death in this place, only the mustiness of a house closed up while Dave had been in Oliver. The door opened into a room with a sagging sofa, an overstuffed chair, and a small table and straight chair. No place for a dinner guest to sit. An old television on a cheap stand with plastic wheels. Through a door she could see an even older sink and refrigerator, both on legs.

She shivered, and Fred found the thermostat and turned it up. Of course. Why would Dave heat the place while he was gone?

"We could find a bite to eat somewhere," Fred said. "It'll warm up by the time we come back."

It made sense, but Joan was reluctant to leave. "In a minute," she said, and he stood back and let her do what she had to do.

So she poked her nose into the kitchen. The fridge was almost bare, but then, he'd been planning to be away for a week or more. In a corner, cans of beans and vegetables and soup, and boxes of noodles and cereal stood on shelves. Above them, a cupboard held a few mismatched dishes, pots, and pans. The old gas stove had a box of matches beside it, but it looked clean enough.

Near the back door, a tiny bathroom with sink, shower, and toilet opened off the kitchen. A bedroom opened off the other side. Single bed, nightstand, small chest of drawers, all with plenty of mars and scars. That was it.

She supposed he might have stored important papers in his chest of drawers. Or in a box or something in the clothes closet. But Fred was right; they might as well eat something and let the heat come up before she did any serious hunting.

They settled on a mom-and-pop place with a clean front window, and Fred aimed for a booth in the back and sat against the back wall, as he always did at Wilma's. A skinny kid with threadbare jeans and pierced eyebrows plopped menus on their table and would have left, but Fred twinkled up at her. "What's good here?" he said. "We're strangers in town."

She looked doubtful. "I dunno. Burger, maybe?"

"How about a BLT?" Joan asked, not wanting to risk much in this place.

"White, whole wheat, or rye?"

"Whole wheat, and toasted." Was that even possible?

"Gotcha." The kid turned to Fred, who was reading the menu.

"Is the soup really homemade, or does it come out of a can?"

"What kind of place do you think this is, mister? We say home-made, we mean homemade."

"The soup, then, and a piece of pie. What are my choices?"

"Apple, cherry, and pecan. I'd choose the pecan, if I was you. Edna's no great shakes on piecrust, but she don't stint on the pecans."

"Pecan, then, and two coffees."

She nodded and left without writing it down.

Fred's shoulders were shaking, but his face was straight when she returned with mugs, spoons, and a pot of steaming coffee.

"Cream?" she asked. They waved it off, and she left.

The coffee burned all the way down, but Joan sipped it grate-fully. She still felt the chill of Dave's empty place.

When she smelled Fred's thick, rich-looking beef vegetable soup, she regretted choosing what would probably be a limp sand-wich. But the BLT surprised her with crisp bacon, dark green let-tuce crinkling at the edges, fresh tomato slices, and three slices of perfect toast.

"I didn't know how much mayo you like, so I put more on the side," the kid said. "Edna don't like to drown you in it."

Joan thanked her, grateful not to have to scrape it off. But when she saw Fred's generous slice of pie, all her virtuous impulses disappeared. The pecans crowded together, and Edna's crust, if not as flaky as Wilma's, looked all right. "I'll take a slice of that, too," she said.

She'd probably waddle back to the car, but once she tasted it, she didn't care. Comfortably filled, she felt up to facing what-ever Dave's place might be hiding. What if they'd made this whole trip, but Dave had carried all his important paperwork with him to Oliver? Still, how likely was that? He had to have expected to come back.

They ate without talking, but not rushing. From time to time their waitress refilled their coffee.

"Had enough?" Fred asked finally.

"And then some." Joan watched him tuck some bills under his plate and then followed him to the cash register, where the same girl rang up their lunch and made change wordlessly. The clock behind her showed only one-thirty, and Joan reminded herself that they'd traveled to Central Time. Part of her wanted to slow down, walk off their lunch, but she resisted suggesting it. They'd lose that hour when they drove back to Indiana tonight.

At least Dave's place had warmed up by the time they opened the door again.

"Whatever he's left here, it has to be in that bedroom," she told Fred.

"You want help?"

He was being so careful not to butt in. "Sure, Fred. Let's go dig."

Tossing their coats on the sofa this time, they went into the bedroom. "You try the closet first," Fred said. "I'll check the dresser. And I can turn the mattress."

"You don't think—"

"People do the oddest things, especially people who live alone. No idea what Dave worried about."

"I suppose." She opened the closet door. Dave had left a few pairs of trousers and some jackets hanging, and only a couple of pairs of shoes on the floor. No file cabinet. An extra pillow and a big suitcase on the shelf above the clothes. But when she pulled the suitcase down, she nearly beaned herself. In the nick of time, she managed to swing it to the floor.

"What on earth does he have in here?" She squatted down to open it.

"Paper's heavy," Fred said, and he heaved the thing up onto the bed.

"It's locked," Joan said.

Fred pulled out his Swiss Army knife and jammed a blade under the lock. "Not anymore."

"Is that legal?" Not that she cared.

"You his only family?"

"Far as I know."

"Well, then, you probably own the thing. If not, if there's a will, let's hope it's in here, and you'll be able to tell someone else the good news about this great inheritance." He waved at the piti-ful room.

"But Fred, he owned property."

"True. Well, then, someone might really get good news. You going to open it?"

Suddenly she wasn't sure she wanted to know. Somehow read-ing words about what he wanted to happen after his death would make it more real than what she already knew. She pulled back her hands. "You do it."

He raised his eyebrows but flipped up the lid and stood back.

Right on top was the family picture that had made her weep when she'd seen it in her own box when she was looking for her parents' wills. There they were again, all four of them, so young. And now she was the only one alive. But this time she was able to smile at her parents and Dave and herself as such a little girl. She leaned the picture against Dave's pillow. Next came his old pass-port. Hadn't he done some kind of overseas travel when he was in school? His passport photo looked to be the right age. She laid it aside, as she did copies of their parents' wills.

A thick stack of tax returns and records accounted for a fair chunk of what had nearly clobbered her. "You think these are all on the up-and-up?" she asked Fred. "Didn't you say his conviction was for fraud?"

He shrugged. "Who knows what he got away with? Let's hope he didn't want to risk messing with the IRS."

"Maybe not. He knew to save his records." She laid them on the bed without reading them. That wasn't the kind of thing she was hunting. Next came a bank statement for a savings account that held $147.38. Not enough to cremate him, much less bury him. If that was all he had, he'd been cutting it mighty close. She set it by the photograph.

"Here's the description of the land." She held it out to Fred. "I know it's in Alcorn County, but I'd hate to try to find it from this."

He flipped through the pages. "Here's a map. You really want to go there, we can."

"Maybe." And there at last was what she'd been hunting. "Here's his will." Two pages, mostly taken up with legalisms.

Fred leaned over her shoulder. "He's left it to you or your heirs, if you die first. So he didn't have any other family tucked away somewhere."

"You thought he did?"

"Crossed my mind."

Handsome and flirty as Dave was, it should have crossed hers, but if it had, she'd blocked it out. "Still, if there were any children, would this will disinherit them?"

"I'm no lawyer, but I think so."

She nodded. Now maybe she was the one who should look into what the timber people wanted to offer for the trees on Dave's land. "I suppose I can afford to deal with his body now."

"We can anyway," Fred said. "Good timber's worth a lot these days—but are you sure you want to sell it?"

She thought of the tree sitters near Oliver, protesting any tree cutting. "I don't know. But Dave must have wanted to. He called those people from our house."

"We can go look at it anyway. What's the rest of the stuff in there?"

She'd found out what she came for, but the suitcase was a long way from empty. "I don't know. Looks like letters." The invitation to Rebecca's wedding sat on top. No surprise. But she recognized her own handwriting on the letter below it, and the one below that. Quickly, she flipped through the stack. "Fred, he saved all my letters. Look, they go way back. And pictures—the kids' school pictures, even their baby pictures." There was Ken, beaming down at his daughter, and there she was with baby Andrew. "Was I ever that skinny?"

"Did he answer them?"

"Not very often. But he kept them. I had no idea." Poor Dave. Living alone, no family, in prison for years. "He missed out on so much."

Fred hugged her to him. "Yeah."

"Oh, look, here's his high school yearbook from Ann Arbor."

The inside front pages were covered with unoriginal sentiments, for the most part, but she wasn't surprised to see what looked like some heartfelt wishes from girlfriends and would-be girlfriends. She flipped to the pictures and found David Zimmerman on the last page of the juniors. On the page before it was a young Peter Vance. A full head of hair made a big difference, but she could recognize his face, even so. No senior yearbook. Maybe he didn't connect with Oliver in the same way—except for some of the girls.

The only other things in the suitcase were a few letters from girls, with little hearts dotting some of the *i*'s. She looked for Patty Chitwood, but whatever Patty might have written to Dave he hadn't saved. What he had kept were Joan's own letters.

"I wish I'd written to him more often."

"You had no idea," Fred said.

"No." She sat on the bed and slid almost everything back into the suitcase, keeping out only his will and the information about his land, now hers.

"What should we do with his stuff?" Not that he had much to mess with.

"We could put it all in the car, if you want," Fred said.

"I suppose. Those few clothes, that suitcase full of papers. We need an empty one."

"Or a trash bag for the clothes."

"I saw some in the kitchen." She looked around the small apartment. "That's about it, unless the TV is Dave's. Or, heaven help us, the furniture is."

"Pete might know. He'll know who owns the place." Fred checked his watch. "Time to ask him about Dave's post office box, too."

The phone shrilled, startling her. "That can't be Pete. It's too early."

Chapter 20

BUT IT WASN'T Pete on the phone. The growl that had scared her before challenged her now: "Who's this? I called Dave."

"Dave's sister." She answered automatically, only then realizing that she hadn't told him Dave was dead.

"Is he there?"

"No. Can I help you?" She waved Fred over, holding the earpiece out for him to listen. He bent his head toward hers.

"Tell him he better call me."

"Let me write down your name and number." She held out her hand to Fred, who pulled Pete's map and a pen out of his pocket.

"He'll know."

"I'm sorry, sir, but I can't very well just say a man called." She tried to sound as put upon as any poor clerk taking a message.

"Hell, lady, say it's Elmer Fudd."

Joan forced a smile into her voice. "That's funny. You must be an old buddy."

Fred nodded and held up a thumb.

"He'll know." The phone clicked in her ear.

Joan hung up the receiver. "Well, I tried."

"It's okay," Fred said. "You have his number on the phone bill at home."

"Yes, with a note beside it to remind me not to call him again. I still don't have any idea who he was to Dave."

"No. But I don't think he knew he was dead. Anyway, he can't hurt him now."

"Fred, let's get out of here. This guy may be in Pontiac for all we know. He can't hurt Dave, but he knows where he lived, and he sure scares me."

The phone rang again. Her hand trembled when she picked it up. But it was only Pete, checking on them.

"Pete! Good you called. We're packing up Dave's personal things. And we need to figure out what to do with his post office box. You still have the key?"

He did, he said. He'd give it to them. He started to give her directions to the post office, but she passed him to Fred. All that food was mellowing her.

They packed Dave's papers in the suitcase, loaded it into the back of the car, and covered it with a green trash bag full of his clothes, looking like nothing. Just in case, though, she tucked his will and the directions to his woods into her shoulder bag with the key to his apartment.

By the time they got back to the print shop, it was hopping again. They had to wait for Pete to find time to hunt through his desk drawer for Dave's other key. Eventually he came up with it.

"Sorry it took so long. Everything takes longer without Dave, you know?"

She could think of worse epitaphs.

In the post office, they had to stand in a long line. No question about it, all the cost-cutting measures were affecting service. A twenty-something clerk missing an arm—a vet? she wondered— was flinging pieces of mail around as swiftly as the man next to him with both sleeves filled. And he was the one who called, "Next!" when they finally reached the front of the line.

Fred stood back, and Joan held the key out to the clerk. "It's my brother's key," she said. "He died, and we need to forward any mail that comes to this box."

He didn't touch it. "You've got the key—you can pick it up."

"I don't live here."

"So you want it sent to you? Don't think I can do that."

"No, to him. The executor of his will can deal with it."

"Right. And you have the court document?"

Oh. "No," she said. "We just found his will."

"Sorry," he said. "If he's not here to do it himself, the court has to authorize you. We can't have just anybody messing with people's mail. Even dead people's."

Joan's shoulders sagged. She should have known better. "But can we close the box?"

"Sure, but you'll want to check it first."

She sighed. He was right, she thought, but the line was as long as when they'd come in.

"Let's go do it," Fred said, and she followed him out to the row of boxes in the lobby.

Dave's key fit one of the smallest size, and inside they found an envelope and an oversized postcard from a car dealer with a car key attached to it. She handed the card to Fred, who smiled.

"Care to try your luck?" he said. "We still have a little time to kill. There's a car we can drive off in if this key fits." For a moment she thought he might be serious, but his eyes gave him away. "What's the letter?" he asked.

"Something from a timber company. I'd better keep that." Feeling awkward about opening it right there in the post office, she tucked it into her shoulder bag and was amused to see Fred tuck the card with the key into his coat pocket.

"You sure you want to close it?" he said.

"We can't, can we? Not if they won't forward his mail. We'll have to ask Pete to keep the key for now." At least they could turn their backs on that line, which was still growing.

Finally finished at the post office, they went back to the print shop. It was close enough to five.

Pete came out from behind the counter to meet them, looking less harried than before. "You like pizza?"

"Oh, sure," Joan said. On top of pecan pie, no less. Following his directions, they waited for him in the pizza place, which turned out to be surprisingly peaceful.

Over a vegetarian pizza and a crisp green salad, they returned the key to Pete, who promised to keep checking the box.

"I go there every day anyway, for the business."

Joan offered to reimburse him for forwarding Dave's mail to her, but he wouldn't hear of it. Then they asked him about the apartment and the furniture.

"It's his stuff, except the stove and icebox. When he got out, he bunked with me a week or so. Then he found that place. Bought secondhand stuff—at best. From junk shops or wherever. He picked up some things off the street."

"You know anyone else who could use it?" Joan asked.

"Matter of fact, the guy who took Dave's job is looking for a furnished place in town. I know it's cheap enough for him, and if you don't want the furniture…"

"Call it Dave's legacy."

"I know the landlord. And you'll get some rent money back. Dave paid January, just in case he wasn't back in time."

"Then he could move right in. Dave's treat."

"You sure?"

"I'm sure."

"That's great. We'll fix it after supper."

Pete was right about Howard, Dave's replacement, who was delighted with the whole arrangement. When Joan called the landlord, he dredged up a couple of words of sympathy, but mostly he was worried about finding a new tenant in January and coping with the junk his dead tenant would have left behind. She put his mind at rest by providing one who would take the place as it was.

"He'll be Dave's guest in January and take over the rent himself the next month," she said. "So you won't have to refund January."

"You know this guy?" the landlord asked, though he didn't sound particularly worried.

"No, but his employer can recommend him. I'll put him on the line." She passed the phone to Pete, who took care of the rest.

Still sitting in the restaurant, she had to ask again. "Pete, when I phoned, you sounded as if you couldn't think of anyone who'd want to kill Dave. Are you sure about that? You knew him from way back, and he must have talked to you about things that happened in prison."

His eyes filled with tears. "Not much. He hated the place. And it's not like you couldn't hear the other people talking when I visited. That means they could hear everything we said, too."

Fred was nodding.

"But after he got out? After he came to work for you? When no one was listening?"

He shook his head. "I don't think he trusted anyone enough to tell that—stuff. Not even me. Not that he thought I'd tell. But if someone came after me, the less I knew, the safer he'd be. I didn't argue."

"Oh, Pete." Now her own eyes were stinging. She reached for his hand.

"Sorry."

"And nobody you knew in Ann Arbor?"

"We were just kids back then. Who'd want to do that to a kid?"

Joan looked at Fred. She was sure he knew plenty of answers to that question, but none he'd say now.

Nothing else to hold them in Pontiac. They thanked Pete, handed Dave's key to him, and were in the car, ready to leave, when Joan remembered the phone message.

"We'd better cancel Dave's phone," she said. "Not only to clear up their records, but so old Elmer Fudd won't bug the new guy."

Pete laughed. "Scared you, did he? I'll tell him about Dave. I'll get the electricity changed to the new guy, too."

"You know him?"

"Yeah. 'Elmer' used to work for me, too. A souse and nothing like Dave, but they hit it off. And he's a softie. One of the good guys."

"It's not really Elmer Fudd."

"Well, no, it's Jeff, Jeff Axsom. He's a big kidder. He'll be sorry about Dave, though. Might show up at the funeral."

She shivered.

"He won't hurt a fly. I'd trust my life to him."

"If you say so." She wasn't reassured. She'd still be sure to cancel the phone. "I'd just as soon you didn't tell him how to reach me."

She saw the look Pete swapped with Fred. That was all right. Let him think she was a wimp.

"I won't," he promised.

It was late by the time they made it home. They hadn't talked much on the trip back. Joan had tried to nap, but sleep had eluded her. She would be tired at work the next day. Or maybe she'd take another day off.

Fred insisted on carrying the suitcase full of Dave's papers and the bag holding his clothes into the house. "Where do you want this stuff?" he asked.

"Up in Rebecca's room. I'll worry about it tomorrow. And I ought to ask Ellen for the things he left at her house. Should have done it when we were there before." She'd sort through his clothes. Check out what Andrew could use.

So little, for a whole life. She sighed.

"You okay?" Fred asked.

"I will be."

He didn't tell her she found what she went for, and she blessed him for that.

"Come to bed, woman," he said instead, and she crawled gratefully into his arms.

———

In the morning she checked the phone messages. Nothing that couldn't wait. She called the senior center and told them she was taking another day, or part of it, anyway.

For a change, it wasn't Annie Jordan who answered, but Margaret Duffy, her old teacher.

"How're you doing?" Margaret asked.

"Okay—sometimes," she said. "We drove to Illinois yesterday to bring back Dave's things. Found his will, which simplified life."

"That's good."

"Only I kept feeling so sad."

"Yes."

"I didn't expect to feel like this."

"Oh?" Margaret waited. She always had listened well. It was part of what had made her such a good teacher. And what made her a good friend now.

"I hardly knew him. My own brother."

"Uh-huh."

"Margaret, he'd saved all my letters. I mean, all of them."

"Well."

"And practically nothing else, except tax junk. I had no idea. If I'd known, I would have written more often. Invited him to visit. Maybe made a difference in his life."

"Sounds as if you already had."

"But look how he ended."

"And that was your fault?"

"Oh. Well, no." Was that how she'd been feeling? That it was somehow her fault that he'd been killed because he came to Rebecca's wedding? "So why does it feel that way? He had nothing, Margaret, and I have everything."

"Uh-huh. And you could have done what to change that?"

"I don't know."

Margaret waited while she thought about it.

After a bit, she said, "Thanks, Margaret."

She still didn't want to go to work, but she could face her day now. If it weren't for the snow, she'd like to try going out to Dave's land. Could she anyway? She had no idea how rough the roads would be out there.

She proposed it to Fred.

"Why not?" he said.

"You sure?"

"If you'll let me drive." His eyes smiled down at her.

"You're on." She'd counted on his driving, as she knew he knew.

She packed a survival kit anyway—hot coffee, sandwiches, matches, and toilet paper, just in case they got stuck out there. Fred always had blankets in his Chevy, she knew. And she dug a couple of stout walking sticks out of the mess in the hall closet, as much for checking what was hidden under the snow as for support.

"How far do you think we're going, anyhow?" Fred asked when he saw her preparations.

"You're the one who looked at the map. Where'd you put it?"

He patted his jacket pocket. "You want to take Andrew?"

"Oh." Andrew might like that. Maybe he and Fred both would. So why was she dragging her feet? "I suppose."

"But?"

"I don't even know but what. Sure, ask him."

He gave her a dubious look. "Maybe you'd better do it. If you're sure."

Had she been that touchy? Probably. It wasn't that she didn't want Andrew around. More that sharing her emotions with one person at a time was about all she could handle today.

It didn't matter. Andrew wasn't in the house. For all she knew, he might not have been there when they arrived home from Illinois. She wouldn't worry about him.

"Not here," she told Fred.

"Okay, then." And they were off.

Joan's spirits lifted when the sun made the snow crystals glisten. With very little wind, even branches and twigs were still coated with the dusting of fresh snow they'd had overnight. She soaked in the beauty.

On this unfamiliar back road, they passed ramshackle frame houses, mostly small, and elderly trailers. The snow gentled them and hid the trash likely scattered around them. Watching for animals, she felt vaguely disappointed at not seeing so much as a line of deer tracks. Beside one house, a long line of laundry was freeze-drying. Much as she loved the smell of sun-dried, wind-blown bedding, she didn't envy the poor woman who would have to break these frozen sheets into folds she could carry.

Fred didn't even look at the map before turning off to the south and crossing a little bridge. About a mile farther, he turned again, and the road narrowed to a one-lane track untouched by plows or vehicles since the recent snow.

"You sure?" Joan asked.

He nodded. "Almost there." Soon he pulled over to the side of the road, such as it was. "This is it."

"Nobody will be able to get past us."

"Doesn't matter. This road is almost your driveway. It dead-ends into your land."

It was her land, she reminded herself, or would be as soon as the will was probated. "How big is it?"

"On the map it looks like almost a quarter section."

A fragment of junior-high math came back to her. "A section is a square mile?" She couldn't remember it in acres.

"Uh-huh."

"So this could have a lot of timber…if it has timber at all." What she saw at this point hardly looked like anything to excite timber buyers.

"Let's take a look."

Joan pulled the backpack and walking sticks out of the car and smiled when Fred automatically shouldered the backpack. A path of sorts led into the scrub. As they climbed over a rise, the scrub gave way to trees of a size that explained the phone calls.

"Uh-oh." Fred was pointing at one of them.

"What?"

"The paint."

She followed his pointing finger. Sure enough, the tree was marked with a line of paint at about shoulder height and another down near the ground. Ahead, she saw another marked tree, and then another. In the winter woods, with trees bare of leaves and the sun behind them, it was easy to see a long way ahead. "What does that mean?"

"Someone's marked those trees for harvesting. The paint down near the ground is so they can check the stumps afterward, to be sure the right ones were cut."

"You mean Dave already sold them?"

"That, or it's timber thieves."

"People steal trees?"

"You bet they do. But if he was looking into selling timber, he may have paid someone to mark the ones he wanted timber buy- ers to bid on. These have certainly been marked systematically, stumps and all. Timber thieves would be more likely to come in and clear-cut everything. You can't tell by looking whether he's signed a contract with a consultant to mark them, or he's actually sold them."

"We didn't find anything like that in his papers, but I wasn't looking for that kind of thing." Without a contract, how would she ever know?

"No."

"I'll have to look when we get back home."

They trudged on. Joan stumbled on the uneven ground as her feet gradually lost sensation in spite of her warm boots. Even though her nostrils were sticking almost closed in the cold, she could smell the promise of more snow in the air.

Fred pointed out some marked trees he said were particularly valuable. Huge white oaks he said were veneer oaks. And black walnut and cherry, all big trees, all very straight. It made sense. In these woods, side branches would have been shaded out by nearby trees. She supposed straight trees like these would be worth more.

"Fred?"

"Mmm?"

"I was thinking of Andrew. What will he say if I let them cut down trees?" Andrew, who'd risked his life sitting seventy feet above the ground to protest just such tree cutting.

"It would wipe out his college loan."

Somehow she didn't think that would cut any ice with An- drew. "Would he have to know?"

Fred raised his eyebrows at her. "I suppose you could let him think you robbed a bank."

"I wonder how much it would come to."

"Depends. So far, I'd guesstimate they've marked about ten trees an acre. Maybe a little more, or less, depending on how much of the area is this good. If you have a quarter section and they're planning to cut that many on the whole property, that's 160 acres, so say 1600 trees. I can't turn that into board feet, and of course it depends on what kind they are, but half that many trees worth marking would be a goodly pile of change."

"How do you know all this?"

"Oh, even Illinois has timber. Not so much, up where I grew up, but I dealt with timber thieves years ago. People who know can look at the stumps and estimate the value of what's been stolen."

"What do we do now?" Go home, she hoped. Her numb feet were screaming for relief.

"Wienie roast?"

She laughed. In fact, with all this snow on the ground, it would be safe to risk a fire, and there was certainly no lack of twigs and dead branches to burn. "You want to stay awhile?"

"Up to you."

It held a certain appeal, especially with a fire. "Maybe another day soon. We could invite Andrew."

"You're going to let him see it."

"Oh, sure. I couldn't really keep it from him. But Fred, if these trees are as valuable as you say, we know Dave didn't sell them. Not yet, anyway. He was almost broke."

Chapter 21

ON THE WAY home, she said little, mostly welcoming the gradual return of warmth to her feet.

"How do you guys do this?" she finally asked Fred. "You cops."

"Do what?"

"Figure out what happened."

He was silent for a few moments, his eyes on the road ahead. "We don't always," he said. "Sometimes we never know. Other times it falls into our laps. And sometimes our honest-to-God detective work bears fruit. Even when we use all the tools we have, though, they aren't always enough."

She digested that thought in silence. Never mind the trees, which were at least still standing. How would she feel if she never knew who had killed her brother, and why? Angry? Afraid? Mostly sad, she decided. Even if I do know, I'll be sad. What a wasted life, for a man who could have been much more than he was. How had her parents faced the way his life had turned out? They had to have known enough, if not how he died. Suppose it were Andrew? She couldn't imagine coping with that.

Big tears rolled down her cheeks. Fred held still another clean handkerchief out to her. He seemed to have an endless supply. She supposed she must have ironed them.

"Thanks." She wiped her eyes and blew hard before tucking it into her own pocket.

He was pulling into Oliver now. "Anyplace else you want to go?"

"Ellen's, I guess. I can take his things home."

"Okay. Good thing I have the car."

"Oh, he didn't bring much." She remembered the case he'd carried when he first arrived.

"That's all right. I'll stick around."

Still mother-henning me, she thought. "Thanks, Fred."

This time they didn't stay. Ellen gave her Dave's suitcase right away. It matched the large one they'd brought home full of his papers, Joan noticed now. Leather, both of them, though they'd both seen better days. Must have been a set, back when he had money; who knew how he got it?

"I packed all his things in it," Ellen said. "Should have given it to you when you were here before."

"Thanks."

"Hope you don't mind. I tossed the ones in his laundry bag in when I did the rest of the laundry—mostly underwear. I did check his pockets, but didn't find anything. Chrissy ironed his shirts. I think she was beginning to be kind of sweet on him."

Touched, Joan hugged her. "Thank you. And tell Chrissy thanks for me."

"You come back when all this dies down. Just to visit."

"I owe you money, too." For Dave's stay, and for the Lundquists. Thank heaven, Bruce's family had found their own housing. Not only did it save her money, but it spared the rest of them even more of Elizabeth's company.

Ellen wasn't coy. "I'll work up a bill. You want me to mail it to you?"

"Any way you choose. That's business."

Ellen nodded and saw them out. With her straightforwardness, Joan wasn't tempted to descend again into tears.

Fred took the case from her and carried it out to the car. "You think Andrew will be able to wear any of Dave's things?"

"Maybe. Andrew's as tall as he was." Would he feel peculiar about it?

He was home when they arrived, and he had no qualms. "Yeah," he said. "I could use some new clothes."

"Not new," Joan warned him.

"New to me. He probably had a suit, too, for the wedding."

"Probably, and we have the rest of his clothes, from his apartment. They're in a plastic bag up in Rebecca's room. You can take whatever clothes you want. Save anything else for me."

He held out his hand for the suitcase. "Thanks." And he took the stairs two at a time.

When he came back down, he was dressed in a beautifully tailored black wool suit Joan didn't remember having found in Dave's closet. It must be what he brought to wear to the wedding, she thought. White shirt, gold cufflinks, and a silk tie. The suit fit Andrew as if he'd been measured for it.

"Everything but the shoes," he said. He was wearing his own black dress shoes, which he'd polished to a high shine for the wedding. "My feet are wider than his."

"You do look good in it," Joan said.

"I think it's new. About the only new clothes he had. The rest of his stuff is okay, but this is great."

"I'm glad you can wear his things. I think Dave would be, too." Had he bought a new suit especially for Rebecca's wedding? It was possible. Another sign that she'd meant more to him than she'd known.

Fred put his arm around her shoulders, but she wasn't feeling at all tearful. "Looking good, son," he said.

"Thanks." Andrew looked down at his new splendor. "Guess I'd better hang this up till I need it. Too bad graduation's in warm weather."

"You'll think of something," Fred said.

Andrew grinned at him and took off up the stairs again.

No wonder, Joan thought. Andrew's wardrobe was on the skimpy side. He didn't complain much, but as tight as their finances had been and as fast as he'd grown, he'd been making do for a long time. If Fred was right about the value of Dave's timber, she'd be able to do better by Andrew. Maybe even herself. How long was it since she'd blown money on new clothes? She couldn't remember. Come to think about it, she'd expected to buy something for the wedding, and then Rebecca had surprised her by making that lovely dress.

"You okay?" Fred asked.

"Just thinking. Are those trees really worth a lot, Fred?"

"Yes."

"College money for Andrew? You really think it's that much?"

"Unless what we saw wasn't typical of the rest of the land."

"Amazing," she said. "I think I'd better track down who made those marks on them."

"How do you plan to do that?"

"I can start with the list of numbers Dave called. Some of them were timber buyers."

Fred lifted an eyebrow. "Those people didn't have time to mark the trees."

"Not unless he'd been in touch before he came here, but they might know who did. It's a place to start. And there's that letter from his box. I haven't even opened it."

He nodded slowly. "I can ask around, too, in case they don't."

"Sure."

"I'll see you later. You're staying home for the rest of the day?"

"I think so." She waved her hand at the phone.

He gave her a quick kiss. "Holler if you need me."

"I'll be fine, Fred." And he left.

It was almost a relief not to have him hanging over her every move. For right now, she didn't feel much like trying to track what Dave had done. She was grateful just to be home again. It even smelled like home. Poor Dave, living in that musty old place, bereft of so many ordinary comforts of life. No wonder he'd wanted to stay here so long.

No, I'm not getting into *poor Dave* again.

The phone rang, interrupting her maudlin thoughts. Picking it up was so automatic that she didn't even consider letting the message machine take over.

"Dave Zimmerman, please," a pleasant woman's voice said.

"He's not here," she answered automatically. "This is his sister, Joan. Can I take a message?" This woman obviously wasn't local—anyone in Oliver knew what had happened to Dave.

"We've marked the timber as we agreed with him, and we're asking for sealed bids on or before the first of February. That should give all the buyers time to compare the board footage we estimate with the trees that are marked."

"I see. And who's calling, please?" She scrabbled for a pen and scrap paper to write it down.

"Kelley's Consulting Forestry, Dawn speaking." The woman gave a 988 phone number that had to be Nashville. No wonder it hadn't been listed on her long-distance charges. Nashville, Indiana, was a local call, even though it was in Brown County. Still, it was close enough that she was surprised they hadn't heard about Dave.

"Dawn, I'm afraid I have some bad news."

"He changed his mind? He can't do that now."

"Worse. He's dead." She hoped the police wouldn't be upset at her, but it was, after all, public information.

"Dead! Oh, my dear, I had no idea he was even ill. I'm so sorry for your loss."

"Thank you. He wasn't ill, though. He was murdered."

There was dead silence on the other end of the line. Joan waited her out. Would she put it together with the press coverage, after all?

If she did, she didn't let on. "I—I suppose we should have had him sign a contract, seeing as how he wasn't from around here. But we've always operated on a handshake. It's never let us down before."

Joan took pity on her. "What is your usual financial agreement?"

Dawn pulled herself together to answer briskly. "Ten percent of the purchase price. That's always paid on the spot when the bid is accepted."

"I see. His heir may want to honor that. But it's also possible that there won't be any sale at all. What happens in that case?"

"I don't know. It's never come up."

"Are you in charge?"

"No, that would be Mr. Kelley. He's the one your brother was

working with. Shall I put you through to him?" She sounded eager
to pass the buck.

"Not yet. But give me his phone number, and I'll call him
when I know something more."

She did. "And your full name?"

"Joan Spencer. Dave was visiting here, which is why you have
my phone number."

"You have my sincere sympathy, Joan. And Mr. Kelley will be
as shocked as I am. We hope to be able to work this out."

"Thank you."

Well, that explained why she hadn't found anything like a contract. There hadn't been one with the forester, much less a timber
buyer. She'd played it close to her chest and hadn't admitted to
Dawn that she was Dave's elusive heir. Anyhow, first she would
have to consult a lawyer about the will. Might as well try the woman the minister knew.

The church secretary put her through immediately.

"Eric, I hope I didn't hit you at a bad time. But I think I do
need the name of that lawyer."

"Sure. I did ask her, and she said she'd be more than happy to
help you. Her name is Megan Wylie. She really knows her stuff. I
spoke to her not long ago, so you might be able to reach her." He
gave her the phone number.

"Oh, thank you. We found Dave's will, and I do have some
questions."

"Try her. If she doesn't know, she'll know how to find out."

She thanked him again and dialed the number he'd given her.
Sure enough, it was answered on the first ring.

"Wylie's law office."

"This is Joan Spencer. I have a legal question, and—"

"Joan, this is Megan Wylie. Eric said he'd refer you to me. I
could see you at three this afternoon, if you'd like to come in."

Glad to get off the phone, Joan agreed. She was more tired
than she'd expected. The emergency food and hot coffee she'd
carried to the woods took care of her lunch. Andrew would fend
for himself, she knew. She lay down on the sofa for a quick nap

and woke surprisingly refreshed, relieved to have nothing hanging over her.

Amazing what a few minutes will do, she thought. But the time on her watch shocked her. How could it be almost a quarter to three?

Even so, she was sure she could make it on foot. It wasn't hard, in little Oliver. By the time the courthouse clock chimed three, she was sitting at a table in a small, businesslike office near the courthouse. Megan Wylie's voice had sounded young, but she looked to be comfortably middle-aged, a little on the plump side and with a fair amount of salt in her dark hair. "So, how can I help you?"

Joan pulled Dave's will out of her bag. "You probably know that my brother was murdered."

"Yes." How could she not? If nothing else, the minister would have told her who Joan was to the man whose murder had made the Oliver news in a big way.

"He made this will, in which he left everything to me." She passed it over, and Megan quickly scanned it.

"You mind if I make a copy?" she asked.

"Go ahead."

"I'll do it before you leave. But it seems very straightforward. So how can I help you?"

"If I'm his only heir…"

"As you appear to be." Megan peered at her over the tops of her glasses.

"Yes. Not that he had any children."

"Even if he did, unless a later will surfaced, it won't change this one."

"So when can I do anything with what he's left?"

Megan looked her in the eye. "Is there some particular hurry?"

"I'm not short of funds, if that's what you mean. In fact, Dave had almost no money." She held out his bank statement. "But he inherited some wooded land from our parents."

"Uh-huh." Megan glanced at the statement and wrote on the pad.

"My husband and I went out to look at it, and we found a lot of the trees marked for cutting."

"I see."

"We didn't know who marked them, except that Dave hadn't been here long enough to do it himself, if he even knew how."

"Sounds as if you need a detective, not a lawyer."

Joan smiled. "My husband's a police detective. But I got lucky. A woman phoned for my brother. Turns out she was from the consulting forester he'd hooked up with before he even came here. That's who marked the trees. She said they did it on a hand-shake—only I suppose it must have been a phone call—but they expected Dave to sell the trees soon, and then they'd get their cut. So he hadn't signed anything. She knows I'm his sister, and I told her he was dead. I didn't tell her I was his heir. Anyhow, what do I do now?"

"What do you want to do?" Megan leaned back in her chair and steepled her hands.

Joan thought she knew. "Probably sell the trees. But can I?"

"Not yet. Not till the will's probated. And much as I hate to say so, until you're cleared of having anything to do with his death."

"Oh." Of course, but it hadn't occurred to her.

"There's no chance you won't be, is there?" Megan's eyebrows rose, but her voice didn't.

"I think they may already have done it." Joan explained how the police had questioned the people at the wedding rehearsal. "Dr. Graham, the father of the groom, vouched for me to Sergeant Ketcham. I mean, he said he heard the clock chime five o'clock when I walked into the church. Before that, I was home. Dave was over at Ellen Putnam's, where he and some other relatives were staying. They say he was in the kitchen with my husband's elderly mother." No point in mentioning the knife Helga was holding. She wasn't in Dave's will, and this woman wasn't a cop.

"But you don't know exactly when he was killed?"

"No."

"They may still be sorting it out then. I take it they aren't treat-ing you as a suspect, though." She raised her eyebrows.

Joan shook her head. "Not at all."

"Good. It may still be a slow process. And even if they weren't dealing with a murder, probating a will can take a year, or even two."

"Good heavens, why?"

"Sometimes because the estate itself is complicated. Sometimes because the law drags its feet. Once your name is cleared, though, we could have you named his personal representative, as he's named you in his will—that's the same as an executor. If you're willing to do all the paperwork, it could speed things up and save you some money. Did you know your brother's lawyer?"

"No."

"That's all right. Would you like me to act for you in this matter?"

"Yes, if you would. I trust Eric's recommendation." The woman seemed cool, but she had sensible enough questions.

"Then if you'd leave me a small retainer now, we could deal with the rest later."

"How much?" Joan hoped it wouldn't be more than she could swing.

"A hundred now. Then we'll see. It depends on how much time is involved and how many things you want to do yourself. My hourly rates are on this sheet." She passed it across the table.

Joan wrote the check, glad she could. "I've already given his junky secondhand furniture away, and I've brought his clothes home for my son. Some of them are pretty nice. I suppose I didn't have the right to do that, either."

"Maybe not technically, but I wouldn't worry about that kind of stuff. Selling land or timber, though, is another business, and you can't touch his bank account yet. For right now, you'd better tell that consulting forester that their agreement needs to be on hold till the will is probated, or at least until an executor is appointed. As executor you'll be able to pay his bills, if he left any. You could sell the timber to pay bills of the estate."

"I can do that. But not until I'm named executor, right? I mean personal representative?"

Megan nodded. "People are used to having to wait for their money in cases like this. Meanwhile, if you spend any money of your own—to bury him, for instance, and that check you just wrote me—you can bill his estate for it and later be reimbursed, by whoever is named to execute it. You, in all probability. So you'll want to keep good records."

"When I asked about forwarding his mail here, the post office said I'd need something from the court. So I left his post office box key with his friend."

"Yes, that has to wait, too."

Chapter 22

BY THE TIME she left the building with the copy Megan Wylie had made of Dave's will, which she'd left with her for safekeeping, Joan had the odd sensation of plunging more deeply into her brother's affairs than she wanted to. But she also felt relief at having turned the problem over to someone who could deal with it. She could start a file folder on the estate and begin keeping those records right now.

Who had been the executor, if that's what they'd called it then, of her parents' wills? She had no memory of having done it herself after the accident that killed them both. Maybe Dave? From what she'd been learning, she doubted it had been Dave. Maybe Ken had done it. Her children's father had been a careful man, with an eye for detail, who hadn't minded tedious paperwork. Whoever was named in the wills, it might have been Ken who followed through.

Come to think of it, her parents would have had a lawyer who might have taken care of the actual work. What came back to her from that time was her shock and sadness, not the details of closing up their house, disposing of their possessions, or any of the many practical things she knew she had coped with.

Fred opened the door to her when she arrived home. "Where've you been?"

"Is it that late?"

"Not really." He looked a bit lost, and she could understand why. This whole mess—and he couldn't even go to work and dig into it. He reached out his arms, and she walked into his embrace.

She told him about her visit to the lawyer. "And oh, Fred, I found out about the trees! It's not timber thieves at all. Dave had arranged for a forester to mark them for sale. They were ready to open the bidding. I told them they'd have to wait and why. So now it's just routine. I need to be cleared of suspicion and appointed his personal representative, so I can pay his bills and deal with his estate even before I inherit it. I am cleared, aren't I, Fred?"

"I think so. But officially I don't know a thing."

She laughed, and it felt good. "So how do I find out officially?"

"You could ask Ketcham yourself. But in fact, even if he says your alibi holds up, being in the church and all, I don't know that the courts would consider it official when it comes to inheriting from a murder victim. Not till someone else is convicted. Did you ask the lawyer that?"

No, she hadn't. "Guess I'll start with Sergeant Ketcham."

"Any chance you'd start supper first?"

Two hours later, her hands sunk in a sinkful of supper dishes and suds, she was feeling cheerful. After all, she knew she hadn't killed her brother. It was only a matter of time before she'd be cleared of suspicion.

But someone else had, and knowing that Dave had arranged for the trees to be marked didn't mean the real killer was no danger to her or her children.

"Are you all right?" Fred came up behind her.

She gulped. "No."

"Sad again?"

"Scared. Whoever killed Dave is out there." She didn't want to say the rest of it out loud.

He held her tight. "You talk to Ketcham. Go ahead, call him tonight."

"I don't want to be a bother."

"Believe me, compared to the people we deal with day in and day out, you don't even come close." He kissed the tears off her eyelashes.

She could imagine. That didn't mean Ketcham would want to hear from her when he was home putting his feet up.

"Go on," Fred said. "He'll probably be glad to have a legitimate excuse to question you again."

She hadn't thought of it that way, even if she couldn't think of anything useful she could tell him. "Okay, I'll call him."

As it turned out, she didn't have to bother him at home. When she called his number at the police station, he picked up right away. "Ketcham."

"Sergeant Ketcham, this is Joan Spencer. Do you have a minute?"

"I'll be right there."

"See?" Fred said when she told him.

"I'll make some fresh coffee."

"You do that, but he'd probably rather have some of your apple pie."

She'd frozen it weeks ago, but that hadn't seemed to matter when she'd finally baked it. Fred was right. Ketcham sat willingly at the old kitchen table and dug into a big slice as if he were starving.

"So," he said. "You wanted to ask me something?"

"Well, yes, but I don't know how much you can tell me when you're still investigating."

"Can't hurt to ask." He licked his upper lip and washed his pie down with some of the coffee.

"First, am I on your list of suspects?" She had to ask, even if he couldn't tell her.

"You? Of course not. Even if I didn't know you better than that, you were stuck in the church at the time that matters."

That took care of one problem, but it didn't touch her real concern. "That's good. But I can't help being afraid. Somebody did kill him, and whoever did it knows I'm here. Andrew, too, and it wouldn't take much to track Rebecca down if you were really determined."

"You think someone has it in for your whole family."

"Wouldn't you? Or do you know something?"

"Not as much as I wish." He passed a napkin across his mouth. "But we've checked out a few things. Bud Fleener, for instance, hasn't been seen around Oliver for years. But he never quit being a bully. Did some real damage to a few guys, got in trouble for it. If he found a chance to get back at someone who showed him up, even that long ago…well, it's possible. We're looking for him."

He waited, and she thought. She'd have to trust him to keep looking. "When Fred and I found Dave's trees marked—you know about that?" He nodded. Of course Fred had told him. "Well, that worried me till I found out Dave had arranged to have it done. I suppose someone could still have wanted his land, but that seems pretty far-fetched."

Ketcham was nodding again.

"So why am I still so scared?"

"I could say something dumb like you've got a cop in the house and shouldn't worry, but that's not going to help, is it?"

She smiled at Fred. "Not much, even as big as he is."

"We'll do our best. Nothing we've come across yet suggests anyone who's got it in for the rest of you. After all, you've been in town for some years now, and until Dave showed up, you didn't have any trouble. We're checking out the people he ran into in prison. I gather he did have some run-ins there—the warden's cooperating, but I can't tell you anything at this point."

"Oh." She thought of that fierce voice on the phone. No matter what Pete said about "Elmer Fudd," the guy was scary.

"And there are always the people he defrauded. They had legitimate reasons to be angry, especially once he was out. And some of them said things back then that sounded pretty threatening. Trouble is, we're going back awhile, and it takes time."

She nodded.

"We're not giving up. There's no question about the means— that knife was in the kitchen already. As for opportunity, they'd left the back door open and anyone could have walked in. There were plenty of tracks to and from the garbage cans and beyond them, so that's no help. With just the two of them in the room when they found your brother, it's only too bad Fred's mother can't tell us anything."

"You don't think she killed him, do you?" If Helga's dementia was changing in that direction, that was scary in a different way.

"No. The autopsy showed he would have died even if she hadn't pulled out the knife. And no one suspects her of doing anything worse than that."

"I wonder why the killer didn't hurt her, too." A new concern.

"That's what makes us think it was aimed at Dave personally. She's just lucky the killer didn't turn on her as a witness. Maybe he got out fast enough that she didn't get a good look."

"Or he knew her?" Joan wondered. "Knew she wouldn't remember?"

"Seems unlikely. She'd just arrived, and unless they had time to talk, how would anyone know? Fred's brother says she still has pretty good social manners."

"Hardly a social occasion." But Helga might have welcomed anyone into the kitchen as if it were.

"I don't think we're going to know how she acted," Ketcham said. "Or even whether she actually saw it happen."

"Maybe he didn't even see her," Joan said. Was that possible? Fred's face was stony. Time to stop talking about his mother. He had reason to be worried, too. At least Helga was safely out of town.

She turned to Ketcham. "Thanks for coming over."

He brushed the last crumbs from his lips and stood. "Thanks for the pie. Sorry I can't tell you more."

She didn't think it was because he wasn't supposed to talk to Fred.

After he left, Fred asked her whether she'd found it helpful to have him come.

"Kind of. He didn't tell me much, but I'm glad he took me seriously about old Bud. And he did tell me I wasn't an official suspect."

"You knew that."

"I didn't think I was, but I was glad to hear him say so."

He put his arm around her. "You going to be okay?"

"For now. I can't seem to think very far ahead."

"I know the feeling."

They were still standing in the living room when she heard someone outside stomping on the porch. More than stomping, pounding.

"What on earth?"

Fred threw the door open, and there was Andrew, pounding the bottom of a fresh Christmas tree on the porch and leaving a mess where it hit.

"I wanted to shake the needles off before I brought it in. We are going to celebrate Christmas, aren't we? I mean, I wasn't sure, but I wanted a tree."

"Oh, Andrew!" She hugged him, ignoring the cold and the tree's prickles. "I'd just about forgotten Christmas." She'd taken care of family gifts before all the wedding shenanigans started, but since then all her attention had been taken up with Dave's murder.

"Well, are we? I could leave it on the porch if you don't feel like it."

"Bring it in. If you'll help, of course we can have a tree."

This was the first year she could remember not having gone out with him, and Rebecca, too, when she still lived at home, to choose a tree. And now he'd done it himself.

They spent the rest of the evening setting up the tree. Andrew and Fred got it standing firm and put on the lights. Joan helped hang the decorations, some from her childhood, some from Andrew's and Rebecca's, and some beautiful handmade glass ones she'd brought back from a gift shop in Bishop Hill. It was good for her spirits, even though it didn't change a thing.

But with Christmas that close, it was time to deal with the arrangements for Dave's funeral. Pete wanted to come, and he could invite anyone else Dave knew there.

"Do you think I ought to invite Ellen?"

"Huh?" Andrew asked.

"I'm just thinking out loud. Invite her to the funeral, I mean. The only people who knew Dave here were Ellen Putnam and her crew."

"Didn't you say Alex Campbell was mad when you didn't tell her what happened to him?" Fred said.

"Oh. I suppose I could stand having Alex there. It would save me a lot of grief, wouldn't it?"

"And maybe Margaret Duffy? You told me she was support-ive."

"She sure was. And Annie Jordan. Thanks." She sat down and started making a list. "I think we ought to do it before Christmas."

"Sure, if that's okay with the minister."

Joan thought back to the many times her family life with Ken had been interrupted by funerals. "I'll ask him, of course, and we'll have to work around the church schedule, but it probably will be easier before Christmas than afterwards. A lot of ministers take that next week off, get a guest preacher in."

She glanced at the phone, but it was too late to call for anything but an emergency.

"How about Johnny?" Fred said.

"Sergeant Ketcham? Sure, if he wants to come. But I don't think he'd learn much."

"I meant as our friend."

"Why, Fred, of course. I wasn't thinking."

"Then when you've set a time, I could call him."

Andrew spoke up. "And Rebecca."

Joan and Fred exchanged the kind of look that drove Andrew wild. "I'll tell her, Andrew. But this is not the kind of thing she should take time off work for. It's not as if it were your funeral. And weird as it is, what with the murder and their packing and moving, she's on her honeymoon."

"Give her a choice, that's all."

"I will." Just barely, she thought. I certainly do not want Re-becca to tear up her life for this little observance of Dave's.

At least she knew what she needed to do in the morning. And the way she felt now, there was no reason not to do it from work.

Chapter 23

JOAN ARRIVED at work on Friday to minimal fuss. The excitement over Dave's murder had died down; even Vernon Pusey had other things on his mind. Fine with me, she thought. She dealt with the mail, returned calls she had missed, and settled quietly into the routine of the center.

It was midmorning before she had time to call the church. Eric Young answered the phone himself. The secretary was off sick, he explained.

"Then it's not fair to load one more thing on you," Joan said.

"I've been waiting to hear from you. Was Megan helpful?"

"Yes, and thank you for getting me right in. But what I'm calling about now is a small, private service for my brother, as you suggested."

"Of course. When would you like to have it?"

"Soon, if that's possible. Would before or after Christmas be easier for you and the church?"

"Joan, it will hardly matter. You're not asking for a big affair with many ushers and a luncheon afterwards."

"Heavens, no. Just a quiet service for the people who need to say good-bye to be able to."

"Do you want me to say anything personal about him?" He'd already asked that, but she was glad he was giving her a chance to change her mind.

"I hardly know anything personal. He was a good big brother—rescued me from bullies when I was little, and he was kind to Fred's mother before he died. His employer in Illinois will be there. He says Dave was a good worker who organized the whole print shop. They miss him there. Pete knew him much better than I did. That's not much to know about his whole life, except that he was a swindler who spent years in prison for it." Her eyes stayed dry. I'm making progress, she thought.

"Then I'll stick to the basics. Read Ecclesiastes and such."

"Yes."

"How about music?"

"Dave stuck his nose into the orchestra rehearsal when he first arrived. We were playing Mozart, and he admired it—I have no idea whether he meant what he said or was just flattering our conductor. He did that kind of thing. But he did name the composer."

"I could ask the organist to play some Mozart."

She nodded, even though he couldn't see her over the phone. "Good. There won't be enough of us to sing hymns."

They agreed on holding the service the very next day, Saturday, at one o'clock, to give Pete time to come and return home in the same day. That meant making more calls from work today to give people any notice at all, and it wiped out any possibility of Rebecca's coming. Good, Joan thought. I'll call her from home— right now she'll be at work herself. At least the senior center is closed on Saturday. I've missed enough work.

"Sure," Pete said, when she called him. "You bet I'll be there. The guy who's taking over Dave's apartment can hold down the fort for that long. And you'll get to meet old Elmer and see he isn't so bad after all."

Joan hoped he knew what he was talking about.

Ellen was next. "Thank you for thinking of us," she said. "I'll come, and I won't be surprised if Patty and Chrissy do, too. I don't know about Laura—but she managed to go to her dad's funeral, and she liked your brother. The big kids didn't know him, but he was sweet to her."

"It's hard to decide things like that, I know," Joan said. "But it will be a brief, simple service, and there won't be a casket." For that matter, she didn't know when his body would be released.

"That might help. I'll leave it up to Laura. If she doesn't want to come, she can visit a friend."

Joan took a break from the phone calls to tell Annie she'd be welcome. "You're so much a part of my life, you're almost family."

"I'll be proud to come," Annie told her, and squeezed her hand. "Have you asked Mabel?"

"No, but you're right, I should. And I want to invite Margaret Duffy." Not because of Dave, but for my own sake.

"Good. They'll both be here this afternoon—maybe they're already here." Annie would know. "Can I do anything to help?"

"Thank you, Annie, but there's nothing to help with. The minister will say a few words and the organist will play. That's all."

Annie nodded and left the office, her back straight.

Once in a while I get it right, Joan thought, watching her go.

She'd told Annie the truth. There wouldn't be much to do. She'd leave a check for the organist and give one to Eric, if he'd accept it. Ken never had taken money for funerals, but times were harder now. And of course he'd accept a donation to the church, even if he wouldn't take money for himself.

Only one more call. She girded herself. But when Alex answered, Joan hardly recognized the tyrant she knew. "Thank you, dear." Joan sat back on her mental heels. Unheard of, for Alex to call anyone *dear*. "I knew you'd remember me." Translated, that had to mean she was afraid she'd be left out. "I'll be there. Would you like me to arrange some music?"

"Thank you, Alex. That's very thoughtful of you. But this will be such a brief service that the church organist will play only a little. The minister will ask the organist to play some Mozart. I told him Dave liked our Mozart."

"He did, didn't he?" Alex glowed through the wires. "And he told me he liked Schubert. Your brother had taste."

So they had at least talked again. Amazing.

After Joan hung up, she turned to planning a winter program for the center, for the letdown that followed major holidays. She was concentrating so hard that at first she hardly heard the strident voice that broke into the peace of the morning. Silence fell among the card players and people at the craft tables. Then Elizabeth Graham marched into her office without so much as tapping on the door.

"Where are they?" she demanded, her face a thunderstorm.

"Elizabeth!" was all Joan could manage, but she stood to defend her turf.

"Where have they moved? I'm sure you know."

Oh. She was mad because Bruce and Rebecca wouldn't tell her where their new apartment was. "Please, sit down, and I'll tell you all I do know."

Her face still tight, Elizabeth perched on the edge of the straight chair opposite Joan, who sank onto her own desk chair.

"Well?"

"I know they've been closing up both their apartments and moving into a new one. Rebecca told me they were spending every spare moment packing and cleaning. She's getting her first taste of real married life."

Elizabeth wasn't buying it. "And? Where are they?"

"That's what they haven't told me. Where the new place is, I mean." For the first time, she was glad she'd worried enough about danger to Rebecca that she hadn't wanted to know.

"Your daughter hasn't told you?" Elizabeth's voice rose with her eyebrows. "As close to you as she seems? Your family is nothing like mine."

And whose fault is that? Joan thought, but not entirely without sympathy. What made Elizabeth the way she was? She demanded closeness at the same time she drove her family—and everyone else—away.

"I'm afraid this is my brother's fault."

"Your brother? I don't think I remember your brother."

You insensitive… Joan stopped herself before she said it aloud. "You never had a chance to meet him," she said between her teeth. "My brother is the man who was murdered at the bed-and-breakfast, while we were all at the wedding rehearsal." Might as well make it clear where I was, in case she's still blaming me for coming late. "We still don't know who killed him, or why." She gulped. "Or if any of us are in danger, too. So I warned Rebecca and Bruce to keep their distance from us. My husband is a policeman, but even he couldn't protect my brother. And no New York cops will be watching out for your son and my daughter. I didn't want anything to happen to them because of my brother."

"How could your brother do anything, if he's dead?"

Dead and gone, he's more of a comfort than you'll ever be to anybody. "He couldn't, of course, but whoever killed him might have some twisted reason to want to harm the rest of us, too. Maybe I'm borrowing trouble, but that's why I didn't want to know where our children were moving. And I don't know when I will." She drew a shaky breath.

Elizabeth stared at her. "How can you bear it?" Her voice softened, and for the first time she seemed almost human. She leaned forward. "Not knowing. And worrying about something so terrible. But here you are, back at work."

"Thank you, Elizabeth. You're right—I almost can't bear it, but staying home is just as bad as coming here. Maybe worse."

"Is there anything we can do to help?"

This is Elizabeth? For the first time, Joan had the barest inkling of why the doctor had married her in the first place.

"I don't think so, but thank you for asking. And I promise, I understand why you feel so bad being out of touch with our children."

"You'll tell me where they are when you know?" It was a far cry from her original demands.

"I'll tell you when I can, but I'm sure you'll know as soon as I do." It might even be true. Bruce did seem to share his father's devotion to her, in spite of not letting her attend his concerts. "So far as I know, they haven't changed their phone numbers, so you ought to be able to reach them." If they answer, of course, she thought. They surely had caller ID.

Elizabeth stood gracefully. "I'm sorry you're going through this terrible time. I'll try not to make it worse for you."

"Thank you."

She turned and left as suddenly as she'd barged in, not even glancing at the people around her, most of whom probably hadn't missed a word.

Joan sat, stunned. Hadn't Elizabeth understood about Dave when it happened? Had she been so stressed by losing her son, as she clearly was at the wedding, that she couldn't take in anyone else's troubles? It was a relief to see any part of her that might not poison Rebecca's future, even if it wasn't realistic to trust it.

Should she call her daughter? Surely Rebecca must already know that Elizabeth was after them. It could wait. Time enough to call her after working hours and tell her about the service for Dave, for that matter.

Shelving her personal life for a little while, Joan tried to dig back into the planning Elizabeth had interrupted, but it was no use. Her shattered concentration refused.

She was relieved to see Mabel at her door. Annie must have sent her. Mabel, too, was pleased to be invited to Dave's service and offered to help. No help needed, Joan told her.

Time to look for Margaret. Then maybe it would be all right to call it a day. At least she had put in an appearance at the center.

But Margaret, like Mabel, tapped on the door.

"Annie sent me," she said.

"I thought she was doing that. Nice to have an unpaid personal secretary. And it's especially good to see you, Margaret." She hugged her before they both sat down. Somehow, with the murder and the wedding, she'd been doing a lot of hugging lately. But it felt right.

"You doing any better?"

"About Dave? I think so, but Elizabeth Graham just roared in here and shook me up."

"So I heard," Margaret said.

"I imagine the whole place heard her."

"She does put on a show, doesn't she?" Margaret smiled.

Joan managed to smile back. "That's one way to look at it. At the end, she actually dredged up a little sympathy. I didn't know she had it in her."

"And you're not sure you believe it."

"Exactly."

They sat in silence for a bit, and then Margaret got up to leave. "Annie said you wanted to ask me to Dave's funeral."

"Did Elizabeth make me forget that, too? Yes, of course I want you. Thanks, Margaret. Don't feel obligated, but I hope you can come. Did Annie tell you when and where?"

"Yes," Margaret said. "And I'll be there."

Was that everyone? She thought so, when Margaret left.

Time to go home. She dragged herself out of her chair, said her good-byes, and braved the cold.

Chapter 24

THIS TIME, Joan avoided the park. Walking home through the familiar streets, she wondered why. Had she done it out of boredom, or because she didn't want to walk past the house where Dave had died? Been murdered, she reminded herself. Don't forget that part.

But right now she wanted to forget. Blot it out of her mind. Pretend it hadn't happened. As if he'd never agreed to come to the wedding at all. And Rebecca and Bruce had been married in a cloud of joy, not the black sorrow that surrounded her if she let the pretense slip away from her.

She focused on the snow crystals shining beneath her feet and beside the properly shoveled sidewalks. Looked at the wreaths hanging on front doors and the decorated trees standing in windows. A few were already glowing with colored lights, even though it wasn't dark yet.

That was dear of Andrew, to bring home a tree. She wasn't surprised when she saw the tree lights already lit in their own front window. He must be home.

She hadn't told him or Fred yet when the funeral would be. Fred wanted to call Johnny Ketcham. And Andrew would be all over her to call Rebecca. She might as well beat him to it.

Pulling her cell phone out of her pocket, she paused and leaned against a sidewalk tree while she punched in the familiar number. She'd never caught the knack of talking on a cell phone while crossing streets. Besides, she didn't want to be in the middle of calling when she arrived home and faced Andrew. And who knew how long Rebecca would want to talk? If she would even be home. But she was.

"Hi, Mom. What's up?"

"Are you okay? You're home early."

"I took a few personal hours to work on moving in."

"How's it going? Oh, and I should warn you that Elizabeth is on the warpath again."

Rebecca sighed. "Tell me something I don't know. She's been wearing us out, trying to track us down."

"I tried to explain why you were keeping your location secret."

"Thanks, but you know her. Everything is about her, no matter what's going on. Fortunately, Bruce mostly keeps her off my back, but she's hard on him, too."

"I can imagine. She actually showed up here today. All the way to southern Indiana, can you imagine? Oddly, though, she finally seemed to hear it about Dave. Even said something that sounded like sympathy."

"It won't last."

"You may be right."

"So, Mom, I hope you didn't call about Elizabeth. She's not worth it."

What a thing to say about someone in your family. What a thing to have anyone say about you. But Joan didn't argue.

"You okay, Mom?" Rebecca said in her ear.

"Oh, sure. I'm only sorry you have to put up with her. But you're right, I didn't call about her. I called to tell you we're having a brief service for Dave tomorrow at one."

"Oh, Mom, we can't possibly come. I'm so sorry."

"Don't be. I didn't even want to tell you about it, but Andrew made me."

Rebecca giggled and sounded like a teenager. "He made you? My little brother?"

"You and Bruce aren't the only members of the family who can push mothers around." Joan smiled. "Oh, Rebecca, he was so sweet last night." She told her how he'd shown up with the tree and how they'd put it up and decorated it.

"I wish I could have been there. Bruce and I haven't even thought about a tree yet, if we'll do it at all. We're still moving stuff into the kitchen. And painting. This new landlord doesn't mind, thank goodness, because the colors the last people used about blinded us. But it's a job. And we need curtains. At this point we're still using bed sheets."

"I could...if you'd send me the measurements of your windows." She'd managed to make halfway decent curtains when they'd moved to Oliver.

"Oh, Mom, I can make curtains! And I know exactly what I want. It isn't making them, it's finding time to do everything." Of course she could make mere curtains. This was Rebecca, who'd made her own wedding dress, plus dressing her mother and bridesmaid.

"Exactly. And you'll want to have something that's just right for the two of you when you finally do get around to it."

"Whew. Elizabeth would have given me a hard time about not letting her do anything for her son. Never me or even her children, you understand, but her son."

What a burden to put on any son, Joan thought after they hung up. She hoped she hadn't done that to Andrew, but she wondered what kind of pressures Dave had felt. What had made him turn into the person he was as an adult? Could it have had anything to do with why he was killed? Or was he only in the wrong place at the wrong time? Someone could have broken into that kitchen with who knew what motive. Had Dave possibly protected Fred's mother from an intruder? Had the police checked the door? Wait a minute—they hadn't been locking that door—no one needed to break in, and there wouldn't be any evidence of an intruder. If only Helga could tell them anything useful. No use wishing. While she was at it, she might as well wish there hadn't been an intruder at all.

But then they'd be left with Helga. And Ellen, Chrissy, Laura, and the dog. Now I'm getting ridiculous, she told herself.

Fred met her at the door. "You all right?"

"That's what Rebecca asked on the phone just now. Am I giving off not-all-right vibes?" She reached up for his kiss.

"You looked mighty serious, that's all."

"Suppose I was." She stomped the snow off her feet. Funny, she hadn't even remembered walking through snow. Inside the living room, she pulled off her boots and hung up her coat.

"Well?" He was still waiting. "Is something wrong?"

"Only Dave. I've been calling people about his service. Tomorrow at one—Ketcham's welcome, if he wants to be there. And Elizabeth invaded us this afternoon."

"Tell me she's not planning to come." He followed her into the kitchen.

"Come! She couldn't even remember about Dave. Squeezed out a couple of words of sympathy when she finally got it."

"So why was she here?"

Joan started washing and chopping vegetables for stir-fry. "She wanted me to tell her where Bruce and Rebecca have moved."

"Did you?" He pulled out the wok and set it on the stove.

"Couldn't. I don't know either. That's when I told her about Dave and why I was worried for them. I called and warned Rebecca she was it again, but of course she'd already had an earful from Elizabeth."

"I can believe it."

"Oh, Fred, I wish I'd known Helga earlier. She's such a dear."

"What brought that on?"

"I was feeling sorry for Rebecca and thinking how much luckier I'd been with my mother-in-law. Even considering the shape your mom is in. How much I would have enjoyed her when she was herself."

"Yeah." He put his arms around her and nuzzled the back of her neck. "Dad and I both got lucky."

"Aw, g'wan." But she couldn't help responding, and chopping vegetables gave way to something more interesting.

Till the back door slammed.

"Mom? Fred? What's going on here, anyway?" Andrew demanded.

"Caught in the act," Fred said. "Back to your chopping, woman."

Joan laughed and picked up her knife. "You guys better watch it. I'm holding a lethal weapon." But she wasn't thinking of Dave when she said it. Only when she intercepted the look Andrew gave Fred did her brother occur to her. And even then, the sadness didn't return to wipe out the lighthearted nonsense. "I'm okay, Andrew. It's safe to laugh."

He didn't, but he shed his boots and came over to give her a hug. "Welcome back, Mom. I've missed you."

"Me, too. It's going to keep happening, but right now I'm grateful to feel darn near normal. Oh, and Andrew, there will be a service at the church tomorrow at one. Nothing fancy, just a brief memorial service with a few people."

"I'll be there."

She nodded and peeled the onions she'd set out. If I cry now, she thought, it won't count.

Chapter 25

WAITING IN the narthex of the church with Fred on Saturday, Joan could hardly remember having been there for Rebecca's wedding. Would it come back to her? Or had Dave's murderer wiped out that day as well as his life?

People trickled in a few at a time, not that there would be many when they were all there. Ketcham was already there, in a dark blue suit, looking like the friend he was rather than a cop. After shaking hands warmly with Joan and Fred, he'd chosen to sit on the end of a back pew. Probably so he could see everyone else come in without having to turn around, she thought.

Alex arrived before the organist began playing. "I don't want to miss any of the music," she whispered to Joan.

Ellen came alone. "Laura decided she wanted to remember him playing with the dog," she said. "I told her that was just fine."

"Good for Laura," Joan said. She hoped she'd be able to remember his better moments, too.

Not far behind Ellen were Chrissy and her mother, Patty. Chrissy was weeping openly, and Patty's face was appropriately solemn. They sat down without speaking.

Mostly, though, it felt like a reception line. Joan was ready to go in, but she wanted to be sure to welcome Pete and whoever drove over with him from Pontiac. First came several people from the senior center.

Andrew came to stand with her and Fred. He had polished his shoes and was wearing Dave's black suit. A thoughtful gesture, Joan thought. And it did look elegant on him. She herself wore her favorite blue wool, if she didn't count the mother-of-the-bride dress Rebecca had created for her, and most of the other women were wearing colors, too.

Finally she recognized Pete's bald head emerging from a van with two men she didn't know. She girded herself for the one who'd been scaring her.

Pete's big hands surrounded hers. "Thank you for including us." He turned to the other two. "This is Jeff. He's the one who had the Elmer Fudd joke going with Dave."

"I'm sorry I worried you," the familiar gravelly voice said. "But not half as sorry as I am about what happened to Dave." The sweet face of the little bald man with the big eyes matched his words, if not his voice.

"Thank you for coming, Jeff," she said.

Then Pete introduced the other, a tall, skinny fellow. "This is Howard. You let him take over Dave's apartment."

"But I thought you said he was holding down the store today."

"He wanted to be here, so I closed the print shop. It was the least I could do."

"Oh, Pete." It touched her.

After the three men entered the church, Fred took her arm. "Time to go up front." She nodded and went. Andrew followed them.

They'd said nothing about flowers, but someone had set a modest bouquet of white roses on the flower stand. Joan nudged Fred, who shook his head no. Maybe the flowers had arrived early for Sunday's morning service. She would have to ask and be sure to thank whoever was responsible. Otherwise, the church was decorated only with evergreens and candles, not lit at this hour of the day.

Except for Johnny Ketcham, everyone had clustered in the middle of the church.

"Let's don't sit in the very front," Joan said. So they settled in the fifth row on the pulpit side.

Eric Young came into the chancel. When the organist stopped playing, he climbed into the pulpit and began by inviting the congregation to join him in reciting the Twenty-third Psalm. Ignoring the new translation that was almost certainly in the pew Bible, he was saying the familiar King James words, and Joan rejoiced silently. Aloud, she was glad to find her voice steady enough to recite with him and to hear the small chorus behind her stumble through it. For a moment, there was silence. When he began speaking, she held her breath, but it was all right.

"Our little town has been shocked by the death of David Zimmerman, a man most of us didn't know until he arrived for what was to have been a joyous occasion, the marriage of his niece, Rebecca. We learned in the newspaper account about his failings, all most of us ever knew about him. But as a boy, he'd rescued his sister from bullies. In recent times, he was a dependable and valued worker to his employer. We'll never know what would have happened in the rest of his life.

"Was it his time to die? We don't know that, either. But let the words of Ecclesiastes bring you comfort." And he read the familiar passage about a time for every purpose under heaven. Well as she knew the words, Joan almost couldn't hear them anymore without hearing the song they had become.

From there he moved to words about the love of God and the importance of love. Her mind wandered, but she was able to join in again to recite the Lord's Prayer.

The organist ended the brief service with more Mozart. Joan assumed it was more, but in fact she hadn't heard a thing before the service. Now she was listening. After the beginning of the *Requiem*, he broke into the "Alleluia" from *Exsultate, Jubilate*. It seemed an odd choice, in the circumstances. Had anyone warned this man that he was playing a service for a murder victim? But maybe it didn't matter. In any case, it should make Alex happy.

"You have my check?" Joan asked Fred. He patted his pocket and promised to take it up to the organ loft.

What next? It wasn't like a wedding, with a cake to celebrate the occasion, or even a funeral for someone beloved in the community, possibly with a meal afterward prepared by friends and family. For Dave, this was the extent of it. Joan felt at loose ends. She'd already greeted most of the people. She was glad to see Eric trot down the chancel steps toward them, his robe flapping around his legs.

"Thank you," she told him. "Thank you for keeping it so simple. You really heard me."

"I not only heard you, but agreed with you. Now be gentle to yourself. You did all you could."

"I'd better thank the people for coming."

"Sure, if you want to. But don't put more pressure on yourself."

She smiled gratefully. "Oh, maybe you'll know. The roses—did someone donate them for this service? Or are they for Sunday?"

He glanced over at the flower stand. "No idea. Maybe there's a card."

"Of course." She'd have to check. But Andrew appeared at her elbow. "Andrew, would you take a look at the flowers up there? Look for a card?"

He nodded and loped off. She saw him look, but rather than bringing anything back, he raised his hands and shrugged.

She'd have to wonder. She turned back to find Pete and the others waiting.

"We hate to rush off like this," Pete said. "Is there anything we could do for you while we're here?"

She thanked him and told him how much it meant to her that he'd closed the shop.

Jeff hugged her hard. "You find the jerk who done this to Dave, I'll break his neck with my own hands," he growled.

Not the kind of thing she could very well thank him for. "I know you cared."

"You better believe it!"

She hoped he would never hear that Helga was holding the bloody knife in her hand.

"I don't suppose those flowers came from you?" she asked Pete. He'd hardly had time. But he shook his head, as did the other two.

"Nice touch," Howard said.

For a murder, Joan thought. "Have a good trip home. And thank you again."

After they left, Joan looked back and realized that Eric had left, too. And she hadn't given him the check she'd written for him. She'd have to mail it to him. Probably just as well. A lot less awkward all the way around. She could put in a note about using it for the church if he preferred. But maybe not. The man could use a new pair of shoes for himself, she thought.

"Aren't you going to take the flowers home?" It was Chrissy, waiting near the door.

"I don't know that I can. They might be for the church. For tomorrow."

"No," Chrissy said firmly. "They're for Dave."

"Chrissy, you didn't!"

"I had to. I didn't just like him. I loved him." The tears spilled.

"Oh, Chrissy." Joan held out her arms, but Chrissy kept her distance. "I had no idea it was like that."

"We weren't ready to announce it yet, but…"

"I see. I'm so very sorry for your loss."

Chrissy wiped her eyes. "Thank you."

"Chrissy, you should take the flowers."

"No, they're for his family." Her jaw was set.

"Thank you. It means a great deal. But wait just a moment." Joan went up to the flower stand and brought back the simple vase. She pulled out one white rose. "You keep this one, okay? To remember him by. And we'll think of both of you when we look at the rest."

Chrissy nodded, tears welling up again. She accepted the rose and left, alone. Patty seemed to have disappeared.

But maybe they don't even live together. I know so little about these people, Joan thought. How could I have missed what was going on between Chrissy and Dave? Or was Chrissy imagining it? Alex could blow up his kind of flirting into more than it meant. Could Chrissy have done the same thing?

She looked over at the corner where Ketcham had been sitting, but he was gone. Had he missed that whole exchange?

Chapter 26

AT HOME, Joan set the flowers on Grandma Zimmerman's old table. She wondered again whether Dave had even known he'd won this girl's heart.

And how had Patty reacted? She and Dave had been dating by the end of the year they'd spent in Oliver. Was she jealous of her daughter? Or was it only natural to look sad when an old boyfriend had been murdered? Not to mention the man her daughter had considered herself engaged to.

She felt Fred's touch on her shoulder and turned toward him. "You okay?"

"I guess. The whole thing felt so weird."

"Yeah. Was that Jeff the guy who scared you on the phone?"

Jeff. She'd almost forgotten Jeff. One look at him and she'd understood why he and Dave had the Elmer Fudd joke between them. Though the last thing he'd said had sounded more like the kind of threat that worried her. "You hear what he said?"

"Yeah. I wouldn't want to cross him in a dark alley, would you? But in the daytime, he's all bluster."

She nodded slowly. "Maybe. Or maybe the sweet face is a front. Still, there's no way Jeff hurt Dave." Why couldn't she just say murdered him? Or stabbed him? But the words stuck in her throat.

Fred nodded. Maybe he even understood her problem. He seemed to see right through her at the oddest times.

Andrew poked his head into the kitchen. "Okay if I come in?" He'd changed back to jeans. Joan hoped he'd hung up the elegant suit, but she didn't ask. Aside from wanting to treat him like the adult he was becoming, she knew it must have been hanging since he first tried it on. Not a crease on it this afternoon.

"Come ahead," Fred said, and started the coffeepot.

Andrew pulled mugs out of the cupboard without being asked. "Did I hear right?" he asked. "Was Chrissy telling us she and Uncle Dave were kind of engaged? She's not all that much older than I am." And he was older than you, he didn't say.

Joan nodded. "I think so. She thought so, anyway."

He gave her a funny look. "She oughta know."

Joan's eyes met Fred's. "People can fool themselves sometimes," he said.

"You think she was making it up?"

"Not making it up," Fred said. "But he came on strong to some people."

Especially women, Joan thought.

"Maybe she got it wrong," Fred said. "Or took him more seriously than he meant."

"Maybe." Andrew clearly wasn't buying it.

"We'll never know," Joan said. And that was the worst of it. There was so much they'd never know now about her brother.

"I wish I'd known him better." Andrew was reading her mind. "Don't you have some pictures of him when he was younger?"

"Some, if I can remember where."

"Let's look at 'em. To remember him by."

He was reading her mind. "Okay. I think I even know where to look."

She did. Fred's coffee was still perking when they spread out the family albums on the big table. In fact, her parents had taken plenty of pictures of their firstborn as a baby and small boy. By the time she'd come along, their enthusiasm (and probably their available time) had shrunk. Her own small self was represented by far fewer baby pictures, but she thought Dave looked protective of her even in those.

"He really loved you, didn't he, Mom?" Andrew pointed to one in which Dave was supporting her on a playground horse that rocked on a spring.

She smiled. They were sweet pictures. From before she could remember, but good to see anyway. And later came the big brother who soon would have done his best to protect her from the bullies. The only pictures of him doing that were in her own mind, but they were vivid.

Fewer and fewer pictures as they grew older. It was true of her own children as well. Here, widely separated by their ages, were portraits of their first formal dances. A few pages later, Andrew exclaimed, "There's Chrissy! How'd she get in here?"

Joan looked. "She didn't. That's her mother, when she and Dave were dating." But he was right. Chrissy was a dead ringer for Patty in her younger years.

"She's blonder than Chrissy."

"Yes." Patty had always been a natural blonde. Was she still, or was she helping it along by now? It didn't seem to matter. Maybe Dave had fallen for the girl he once knew when he saw her daughter, and Chrissy's darker hair hadn't mattered.

"You think she was jealous?" He was still reading her mind.

"Maybe. But that was a long time ago."

"Was she his first love?"

"Would I know?"

He laughed. "You mean, like does Rebecca know my secrets?"

"Something like that. And you've got to remember how much younger I was. Dave sure didn't confide in his kid sister."

"Any more than Rebecca told me anything. First I heard about Bruce was when you did."

"I told you as soon as I knew." She smiled at him.

"Yeah." He flipped some more pages, but there were no more pictures of Dave after the last high school dance. Her own continued, though. A few during college, then graduation, then a couple of Ken. Their wedding pictures were in a separate scrapbook, she knew, but here were baby pictures of Rebecca and Andrew. And the last family portrait before their father's death. Alone, she'd taken very few.

"You two got shortchanged," she told him. "There's Rebecca's college graduation, and yours from high school."

"Yeah. And the ones I took of you and Fred when you got married. We don't have Rebecca's wedding yet."

Had they even taken any? She'd blanked that out, too. She hoped someone had done it.

He must have seen her face. "They took some ahead of time. Bruce's mom hired a photographer, remember?"

"No," she confessed. "I hardly remember the wedding. You think they'll give us any?"

He laughed. "Rebecca will, but even Bruce's mom would… well, his dad would, anyway."

"His dad's a sweetie."

"Hey," Fred objected. "What am I?"

She stood up and kissed him. "You're mine."

"All right then." He poured her a mug of his potent brew.

Andrew pulled another package of Fred's sweet rolls out of the freezer. "Okay to heat these up?"

Calories again. But his timing was great. She nodded, and he stuck them in the microwave.

Sitting at the table with her men drinking Fred's coffee and not even trying to resist his rolls, Joan felt sad again for Dave. Except for that old one of his childhood family, she hadn't found any pictures among the papers they'd brought back from Pontiac. It was as if he'd never had a life. And now he never would.

"You all right, Mom?"

"No, but I will be." She managed a smile. "Someday I'll remember more about the wedding than the murder."

"At least you saw the wedding."

More or less. "And I heard Bruce play for Rebecca." That she did remember. That and the murderous look it evoked from his mother. If that woman ever had any reason to go after anyone, Joan wouldn't have put murder past her. "Did you know he was going to do that?"

"Well, sure. I had to give him the violin."

"That's right." It came back to her now. "How did you keep it from the rest of us?"

"The minister helped us hide the fiddle. Honest, Mom, that's what Bruce calls it."

He would, of course. But it was a pretty ritzy fiddle. "I don't remember seeing it after the wedding."

"Oh, the minister took charge of it then. Locked it in his study. I was glad I didn't have to worry about it."

Me, too, Joan thought. Andrew had been too distracted by Sally and Kierstin to be trusted with a valuable instrument.

"You two mind if I take off for a while?" Fred asked.

"Go right ahead," Joan told him, knowing he didn't really mean Andrew. "I'll be fine." The sadness had faded. Andrew was helping, of course.

"If you're sure." He pulled on his coat and gloves and wrapped his scarf around his neck.

"I'm sure." And he was gone.

"C'mon, Mom," Andrew said. "You've still got me."

She plastered a smile on her face for his benefit, but in fact, she felt encouraged. Even if she never found out who killed her brother, she had a family. And now Bruce had joined it, and so far, she'd managed to tolerate his mother, for whom there might yet be hope.

Chapter 27

FRED PULLED out his cell to call Ketcham. "Okay if I come to the station?"

"We're pretty busy here," Ketcham said. That almost certainly meant Altschuler was at his elbow and would have kept them from talking. For that matter, if Fred had gone in, Altschuler might have rooked him into some kind of boring routine, even while preventing him from learning anything about the one case he cared about. "But I need to take a late lunch."

"I'm on my way." He didn't need to ask where. When he reached Wilma's, he headed for the back booth. By the time Ketcham arrived, he'd buried his face in a handy newspaper, just in case he was spotted. No point in getting Ketcham in Dutch. Not that there was much of anybody to notice them at this time of day. The place was mostly empty, except for a few college kids who'd found it served better food than the dorms and was a good place to hang out on a boring Saturday afternoon when school wasn't in session.

Fred settled for a cup of Wilma's coffee, but Ketcham nodded when she suggested his usual burger and fries.

Once the food had arrived and he could be sure they wouldn't be interrupted, Fred raised his eyebrows. "Any news?"

"Not so's you'd notice. We've gone though every last bit of evidence and talked to everyone but your mom. I'm not about to drag her back."

"For all the good it would do."

"Exactly. Even Altschuler knows that." Ketcham dunked another fry in his ketchup. "I have to tell you, Fred, at this point

I don't know where to turn. It's as if someone walked in there, stabbed him, and walked out again without anyone noticing."

"The dog didn't bark?"

"Nope. It was out back, playing with Laura."

"Out back? I thought she was answering the front door."

"Not by then. Once you were all over at the church, she took the dog out to play Frisbee in the park. That park is their backyard. All kinds of people go through it, and the dog doesn't bother barking except if it thinks it's guarding the house. Laura wouldn't think anything of strangers there, either. But she couldn't describe anyone except a mom with some little kids heading for the playground. They wanted to pet the dog, and she was making sure it didn't bite them."

"And that distracted her."

"Sure, but she didn't have anything to be distracted from. She was just out playing."

"So she didn't see anyone come in that back door, either?"

Ketcham shook his head. "From what I could tell, a herd of elephants could have walked in. All she had to worry about was keeping out of the way while the grown-ups fixed that rehearsal dinner. How was it, by the way?"

"Miserable. Not the food—but some of the people."

"Yeah. I met her, too. And your mother? Had she recovered?"

Fred shrugged. "She'd lost the whole business. Was perfectly happy, especially when people started telling her what a good cook she was."

"She thought she'd cooked dinner?" Ketcham's eyes lit up, and Fred could see where he was going.

"No, they were buttering her up about her cooking at home. She's not going to remember anything here."

Ketcham subsided. "Yeah."

"You get a chance to check out any of the Pontiac people?"

"The warden's not coming up with much. A few altercations. Dave spent some time in solitary after one of those fights. Warden did it as much to protect him as to punish him, though that's not the official version." He stopped to chew.

"That guy out yet?"

"Nope. A couple of others are, and they've done a pretty good job of disappearing. We're still looking for them."

"How about Dave's friends in town?"

"Not so much as a parking ticket, even the one who scared Joan on the phone. I'd kind of thought they might have been in prison with him, but they just worked for Pete. And the only reason he knew Dave was their years in school together in Ann Arbor."

"College, too?" Fred asked. He knew about the high school.

"No, they neither one finished college. Pete served three years in the army—never was sent overseas, though, and Dave flunked out at the end of his sophomore year at the U of M. Just high school buddies."

"Handy for Dave, when he ended up there. They must have kept in touch. Dave gave him the key to his post office box for Pete to take him mail in prison."

"Yeah, you told me." Ketcham sighed.

"So what else do you know?"

"Not much. No physical evidence that wasn't obvious. The rest of the calls he made besides the one to his buddies in Pontiac all make sense in the light of the timber he'd planned to sell."

"Yeah."

"He was always a ladies' man, but we didn't find any evidence of a wife or even a long-term partner. One of the people he pulled a scam on was expecting him to marry her and take her away to a life of leisure, but that comes under the category of business, I'm afraid. She was still mad enough to be worth a little more checking, and not smart enough to hide it. No idea how she'd've known where he was, though, and we found her at home. Doesn't mean she's the only one, of course. But the warden says he hardly got any mail or phone calls in prison, and only Pete visited."

"So you're up a creek."

"Altschuler's tearing what's left of his hair. I tell you, Fred, I don't know how we're going to solve this one."

"What about Bud what's-his-face?"

"We're looking for him. It's been a long time, but he's a mean drunk, and he's got a record a mile long. Piddly stuff, mostly, but he's violent enough. One arrest was for killing a dog. With a knife. I can see him stabbing a man in the back like that."

Fred changed the subject. "Were you still there when Joan found out about the flowers?"

"Flowers?"

"In church today. Chrissy gave them to her. Broke down and made it sound as if she and Dave were secretly engaged."

"You think it's true?" No flies on Johnny Ketcham.

"That's just it. The guy was such a flirt there's no way of knowing how much of it was in her mind. But he was out of circulation long enough, he might have been ready for something permanent."

"Or a quick roll in the hay with a kid half his age. Her mother looked like she kept her on a tight leash—or wanted to."

Ketcham had seen that. Good. "I don't know what that was about," Fred said. "But you might be right. He used to date her mother."

"Not that it gets us anywhere. We're going to have to look at some more of the people he defrauded. They're none of them around here, and that's going to be a slow business, begging for cooperation from all over. I doubt Altschuler would authorize travel."

Fred reached over and snagged one of the last fries.

"How long do you think I'll have to stay away?"

"How much vacation time you have saved up?"

"A fair amount, but this isn't how I'd planned on spending it."

"So take your wife on a trip."

"It's a thought." About the only one Ketcham had come up with. Somehow, though, he didn't think he could persuade Joan to budge just now, and there was no way he was going to take off by himself and leave her to face this alone.

He eyed Wilma's pie, but it had no appeal today.

"I don't suppose we could do a little unauthorized travel together."

Ketcham looked tempted, but he shook his head. "If it weren't for your mom, we might get away with it, but it's still in your family. And between you and me, you might want to get Joan out of town for a while."

"You're worried?"

"Let's just say it wouldn't hurt."

Chapter 28

JOAN AND ANDREW kept going through family pictures. Answering his questions, she told him family stories about his own childhood, and even though she knew he was pumping her to take her mind off the murder, she enjoyed doing it.

Looking again at Dave's senior prom pictures, she had a sudden thought. They had left Oliver the summer after that spring dance. As far as she could tell, kid sister that she was, Dave and Patty had been a couple when the family moved back to Ann Arbor. But he'd saved no letters from her, no more pictures, not even her school picture tucked in with the others. Had they broken up before he left? Or had he just decided to forget her? Was she still bitter? But then why had she even gone to his funeral?

Maybe only to support her daughter in the loss she was feeling. Or maybe she was mad enough even now to want to see the last of him.

Not that there had been anything to see. They hadn't even put an empty urn in the church. They'd probably scatter his ashes in his own woods. Surely that would happen long before his will was probated. But who was to know, anyway?

I'm getting silly, Joan thought. She wondered whether Patty would be working at Ellen's today. Even if she turned out not to be, going over there would be something to do. You're really stretching it, she told herself, but she gave herself permission to go, rather than just picking up the phone.

"Think I'll take a walk," she said.

"You want me to come?" Andrew asked.

"No, I'd rather go alone." Not a lot he could say to that. Besides, it was the truth.

"Okay. I'll wash up."

"Thanks, Andrew." Hardly looking back at that small miracle, she pushed her feet into her boots and went out.

The snow wasn't as deep as it had been, but there was still plenty for sledding. With the park full of kids and dogs, she had to keep her eyes open to avoid the occasional sled flying down the hill from her left and across her path to the next downhill. Below her, she saw an elderly couple trudging up the hill with a sled big enough to share. What fun. She wondered whether she could talk Fred into giving it a try. They'd have to borrow a sled somewhere. Or break down and buy one, if they could even find one.

A little ahead of her, she recognized Laura Putnam, pulling a small sled up the hill. Joan waved to her, and the little girl stopped and waited for her when she reached the path. She was well bundled in padded jacket, snowsuit, and bright blue mittens, but her red cheeks and nose showed that she'd been out in the cold for a while.

"Are you going sledding, too?" she asked, apparently overlooking Joan's lack of a sled.

"It looks like fun. I was thinking maybe my husband and I could get a big sled and go together."

Laura looked her up and down. "You wouldn't fit on mine."

"I sure wouldn't."

Laura's smile lit up her face. "Guess that means I don't have to share."

"No, I'll have to find a sled of my own."

"Mom has a big one. She might let you borrow it."

"Maybe I'll ask her sometime. Is your mom home now, Laura?"

"No, Patty's sitting with me. But she said it was okay to come out here alone." Laura suddenly looked worried.

"Then I'm sure it is. Maybe I'll go say hi to Patty." Maybe that was why Patty ducked out of the church so fast. Just a babysitting job.

"Okay. Bye, Joan." Her worry relieved, Laura turned back up the hill. She'd picked a small hill close to home, with no trees or other hazards to worry about. Joan had no qualms about leaving her to fly down it on her own.

When she reached Ellen's backyard, the dog didn't bark. It did wag its tail at her. Something to be said for having been introduced. Joan reached over the fence and patted its head before she pushed the gate open, sliding her body in so that the dog couldn't take off to join Laura in racing down that hill.

"Anybody home?" she called at the back door.

Now wagging its whole rear end, the dog joined her there.

Patty opened the door, wiping her hands on a dish towel. "Oh, it's you. I mean, I just saw you at the church. Come on in, but Ellen's not back yet. She's picking up some last-minute things for Laura."

Christmas was almost on top of them and the last thing on Joan's mind, in spite of Andrew's tree waiting and the gifts she'd bought and wrapped long ago, knowing there'd be no time with the wedding right before it. She thanked Patty and went in, stomping the snow off her boots outside before slipping her feet out of them indoors. Patty's face wasn't as tense as it had been at the church, but Joan felt anything but welcomed. "I hope it's okay to stop by like this."

"Of course. Can I give you anything?"

"Maybe something hot, if it's really all right. It's cold out there."

"I made cocoa, for when Laura gives up. She's out there sledding, and she's gonna be an ice cube before long."

Joan nodded. "I saw her. Right now, she looks good for a few more trips down the hill. But if you have enough, sure, I'll drink some cocoa."

Patty poured a cup out of a pan on the stove, plopped it on the kitchen table, and waved at a chair. "You might as well sit down."

She sat down obediently and sipped the hot cocoa.

Turning her back, Patty slammed pots into the sink. "Gotta get these scrubbed for the Christmas party."

"Oh? Who's having a party? I'd thought Ellen wasn't expecting much of anybody."

"No one staying here, if that's what you mean. Just a bunch of people in town who don't want to have to fix their own Christmas. Seems to me that's part of it."

"Depends on how many relatives descend on you, I suppose."

"Not relatives. Just paying back their social obligations for the year with a big bash during the holidays. Or rather, we are." She sighed. "It's a job. I suppose I should be grateful for that."

"But?" Even through Patty's back she could read the *but*.

"Oh, nothing." She finally turned around, though. Her face was less angry now and more sad. "Not the way I'd expected— hoped—to spend my life."

Joan nodded. After Ken's death she'd felt that way for a long time.

"He let you down, didn't he? Dave, I mean."

"Oh, I got over that." But the bitter look was back.

"Patty, I am so sorry."

"I managed. I still do."

Joan knew about managing, and how hard it could be. What could she say to someone who was still struggling? She could hardly tell Patty she might get lucky. It hadn't all been Fred, though. Joan hadn't waited for luck to come along. But neither had Patty. She was clearly a hard worker, and she had at least one grown child.

"Chrissy seems to have turned out well."

The look was back again. "Till now. Till he came back."

Oops. And not for you. Another blow.

"But I can't tell her anything," Patty said. "Not that I haven't tried, but she won't listen to me."

"Probably not. Rebecca goes her own way, too."

"Only she's landed on her feet."

"She has, hasn't she? In spite of Bruce's mother."

"His mother? You mean that awful woman is his mother?"

"I'm afraid so."

"Heaven help your daughter."

"They seem to be ducking her pretty well. The other day the woman actually showed up in my office to tell me I had to give her their new address and make them do things her way."

Patty looked fascinated. "What did you do?"

"I told her I didn't know where they were living."

"You lied?"

"Didn't need to. I wouldn't let Rebecca give me their new address. I'd repeated the calls Dave made from our land line, and I was afraid of one of the guys who answered. For all I knew, I'd talked to Dave's killer. I didn't want him to be able to find Rebecca."

"You're scared?"

"You would be, too, if someone in your family was murdered. You'd want to do what you could to protect Chrissy."

Patty turned around and attacked the pots again. "Gotta get these done before Laura comes home."

Was Ellen a tough taskmaster for her few employees? Or was it just a way to avoid answering?

"I'm sorry," Joan said. "I've taken up enough of your time. Tell Ellen I stopped by, and thanks for the cocoa. Forgive my butting in on you. It's been such a strange time."

"Yeah." Patty took the empty cup from her. "For me, too."

Joan didn't try to figure it out, but pulled on her still-chilly boots and coat. "Thanks again. I'll see myself out."

"Sure. And send Laura home if you see her, okay? Then I won't have to go out and chase after her. She's another one with a mind of her own."

"I'll be glad to." Not that she'd planned to go back the same way she came, but she could do that much for Patty.

What must it be like, to have your old boyfriend, so much older than your daughter, come back, only to go after her? Or was it all Chrissy's imagination? Either way, it had to make life difficult.

Shrugging, she set out into the park again, but she didn't have to persuade Laura to go home. The child met her a few yards down the path.

"Hi, Joan," she said. "I'm about frozen. You remember that if you go sledding."

"I will. If you scoot on home, you'll warm up fast. Patty has hot cocoa waiting for you."

"With a marshmallow?"

"You'll have to ask her. She didn't give me one."

"I don't need to ask. I know where Mom keeps 'em." She waved and took off for the house.

Chapter 29

STILL AT loose ends, Joan kept trudging toward home. No place else to go right now. Just as well Ellen wasn't there, she thought. I didn't really have any business bothering her, or Patty either, for that matter. So why do I keep wanting to go there?

She knew, of course. But it seemed mawkish to want to return to the scene of her brother's murder. Why don't I want to go to the scene of Rebecca's wedding, instead? Then she remembered that she'd been there only that afternoon. Now the service for Dave overshadowed that lovely day.

I knew he'd wreck it, she thought. But that wasn't fair. Dave hadn't brought his killing on himself. Or had he? What had he done to make someone kill him? Maybe old Vern had a point.

Had the police investigated that question? Now she had a purpose. Picking up her pace, she charged through the snow, not to her own house, but to the police station. For a change, she wouldn't have to worry about interrupting Fred there.

She met Ketcham at the door instead, in his parka and boots.

"Joan." He sounded surprised to see her.

"Oh, you were going home. I'm sorry." Poor man, why had she assumed he'd be spending Saturday afternoon at work, after attending her brother's funeral, at that?

"Not at all, come in. I'm glad you're here." He turned and held the heavy door for her.

She thanked him and followed him up to an interview room, where he stripped off the parka and hung up her coat.

"What can I do for you? You're not looking for Fred." It sounded like a half question.

"No, I hoped to see you." She took the seat he offered, and he sat opposite her at the small table. She could imagine being grilled at that table, instead of being met with such sympathetic courtesy. "I keep trying to figure out who killed my brother, and why. I know you are, too, and I had to come ask if there's any way I might… anything I could tell you at this point."

He nodded as if he had all the time in the world. "That's good of you."

"I mean, I know better than to ask what you know, but I just couldn't stay away."

"I understand. It's frustrating, with Fred not able to take an active role in this one."

"We understand why."

"Sure you do, but it's got to be maddening."

"Yes." Not much more to say to that. "Do you think it's because of something Dave did? I mean, we know he was in prison. There must have been people mad at him."

"We're looking into those old cases now. It's hard to do, because they didn't happen in Indiana, for one, and they're old, for another. He spent a fair amount of time out of circulation."

"Oh." Of course. What had she expected, anyway?

"And there doesn't seem to be anything recent to account for the anger that would provoke that kind of attack."

She'd tried not to think of the specifics of it. He must have seen it on her face, because he reached out and patted her hand.

"I'm sorry, Joan. It was pretty horrific. At least we're sure Fred's mother didn't do it."

"She's a strong woman." Feeling disloyal, she made herself say it.

"Oh, I don't mean she couldn't have. But there wasn't anything to suggest that she did. From what I've heard, she's never been violent. Best we can tell, she thought she was saving his life, you see."

"That's what Fred told me. Poor Helga."

"He says she forgot it within the hour."

"I think so, too." There had been no sign of concern in Helga's behavior at the rehearsal dinner, much less at the wedding the next day. "She's lucky to remember her own family." Much less mine, she didn't say, but he nodded as if she had.

"What I keep wondering is why it happened here," she said. "Why not back in Pontiac, where he'd spent so much time and where he was living until he showed up here? You'd think there'd be a reason."

"Like old Bud, you mean?"

"Well, sure. Have you found him?" Too much to hope for.

"We're checking into it." A polite none-of-your-business, if she'd ever heard one. Or was it? Maybe they really were.

"We were looking at old family photos tonight." Her voice came out hesitant, though she'd tried to sound matter of fact.

He leaned forward. "Yes? You found something?"

"Not really. Just that Chrissy looks so much like her mother when she and Dave were dating. And now she thinks he was courting her. She told me today they were engaged. Sort of."

"Uh-huh."

"I have to wonder what her mother thought when she heard. Dave pretty much dropped Patty back when we left town."

"They were how old then?"

"Just kids. They both had another year of high school to go."

"So seventeen or thereabouts."

"Dave was. I suppose Patty was, too."

"Chrissy's a good deal older than that. Anyhow, thirty."

"Oh, she doesn't look exactly like Patty in high school. For one thing, she's not a blonde. But it's still striking. I suppose you've known them for a long time."

He nodded. "I grew up here. Older than Chrissy, younger than her mother. So I didn't know either one of them well."

Joan wondered what it would be like to spend your entire life in one small town. "Must be nice. Knowing everyone, I mean."

"It has its points." He sounded tired.

"I'm sorry. You were leaving when I got here. Your family is probably expecting you home."

He smiled. "A cop? Working on a murder? They know better. We'll be glad when Fred can give us some help."

"I'm sorry."

"Not your fault."

"No, just my brother and my husband." Only man in her family she wasn't apologizing for was her son.

He patted her hand. "You know better than that." Then he weakened. "I'm not telling you this, you understand."

"What?"

"I told you Bud Fleener hadn't been around here for a long time."

"Yes. But?"

"Turns out he was in prison, too, but he's out now."

"Where?" Could it be? All those years, she had no idea what kinds of trouble Dave had run up against. But if they were in the same prison, and Bud remembered him, she could imagine the kind of conflict that would make him go after Dave if he saw him out, right there in Oliver.

"I've already said too much. We're looking for him. According to his record, he's a real possibility. I'll let you know when I can tell you more."

"Thanks."

"Any chance you and Fred could get away for a little?"

She stared at him. "A cop? With a murder in the family?"

"In fact, that's why. We can always reach him—or you—if we need you. But right now it's driving him nuts. Take a little trip. He's got vacation time coming to him, and it would do him good to get out of here. With his mother holding the weapon and the victim being your brother, Altschuler won't let him anywhere near what matters to him."

Leaving town—it hadn't occurred to her. "You really think we should?"

"I think it would do him a world of good. Could you get off work? Think about it."

On the way home, she did.

Fred was waiting for her in the kitchen, where he had a pot of soup simmering. "You all right?"

She shrugged. "I guess. At least I got out of the house." She automatically started setting the table for soup.

"Where did you go?"

"Talked to Patty a little bit, and then to Ketcham."

"He was over there, or he had Patty at the station?"

"Neither one. I was too antsy to stay put. Went both places."

He looked at her. "You learn anything?"

"Well, yes, I did. Ketcham says Bud Fleener was in prison. Wouldn't say where, but he's out now, and just maybe he and Dave had some kind of run-in that would make him attack Dave when Dave showed up here. I think Ketcham knows Bud's here somewhere. I think he thinks Bud did it. And he's scared he'll come after me, too."

"He told you that?"

"Not exactly. And he made it plain he wasn't telling me what he did say. You know."

Fred nodded.

"He thinks we ought to get out of here," she said.

He nodded again. "He told you, too, huh?"

"It sounds crazy. You don't take a vacation because someone in the family gets killed."

"Because?"

"I don't know. It sounds all wrong."

"It's not like a missing child, you know. Those parents don't dare leave."

"No. But Fred, where would we go? It's almost Christmas. That's no time to travel."

"Maybe it's a perfect time. I can't go to work. How about you? Could you get away?"

"I suppose so. There's nothing much happening at the senior center, and the orchestra's not going to start rehearsing again until after Christmas. But what about Andrew?"

"Take him along, if he wants to go."

"Where?"

Now it was his turn to shrug. "No idea. I don't want to go see my folks."

That had occurred to her as a destination. Bishop Hill would be beautiful, with the candles in all the windows. "Why not?"

"With Mom involved, Altschuler would probably split a gut. But that's not why. I suppose I'm dodging responsibility. It's time to get Mom tested and make some better arrangements for her care. That means negotiating with my family. Maybe this would be the time to do it. No question about having the time. And with her holding that knife…"

She ached for him. "Do you know where to get her tested and all that?"

"No. I'd have to do some research before I go. I'm not ready. But that's an excuse. I really don't want to deal with the rest of them. And I'd have to neglect you in the process."

"That's all right. I could spend time with Helga while you mess with the others. I like her."

"Good. But I'm still not going to walk into that before I know what I'm doing. They're coping all right for now."

She wasn't so sure. The next time it might be Fred's father on the floor with the butcher knife in his chest. "What if…" But she stopped before it escaped her. "Never mind." She didn't really think Helga would turn violent.

"It's a dumb idea anyway. Leaving town isn't going to make us quit worrying. Look at us. Even thinking about going to Bishop Hill just turns on a whole new set of worries."

"I suppose…" She paused.

"What?"

"What do you think Bruce and Rebecca would say to a little help getting their moving done, so long as we didn't try to stay with them, I mean?"

"You want to go to the big city?"

"If we're getting away, we might as well do something really different. Bishop Hill is even littler than Oliver. You can't say that about New York."

He chuckled. "You just want to beat his mother to the punch."

"Well, there's that." It had a certain appeal. "You think I could keep my mouth shut the next time she asks where they are?"

"Not in a million years."

"We could drive their gifts to them and carry the trash home with us. That ought to make us popular."

"Drive?" he said. "People don't drive cars in the city. Where would you park?"

"Alternate sides of the street."

"In Manhattan?"

"I don't know," she said. "I think in Brooklyn, anyway. You don't know they live in Manhattan."

"You're right, I don't. We're out of our minds." But his face looked more animated than she'd seen it for days. Maybe Ketcham was right.

"So we'll fly," she said. "Pay for the extra luggage to take them their stuff."

"If they're even ready for it. They'd maybe rather have us arrive empty-handed and clean the new place, or paint or something." From what Rebecca said on the phone, he was right.

"I can paint!"

"All right, then. Call your daughter."

Chapter 30

JOAN WAS putting the finishing touches on supper and working up her nerve to call Rebecca when Andrew showed up. So she told him what they were thinking of doing.

"Leave town? What about Christmas?"

"They celebrate Christmas in New York, too. Remember the old movie you used to love? About Macy's Santa?"

"I know, Mom. But what about me?" He sounded like an abandoned child.

She looked at his woebegone face. "You could come, too."

"Where would they put all three of us?"

"Oh, Andrew, we couldn't land on Rebecca and Bruce. And they'd never live it down if Bruce's mother found out."

He rolled his eyes. "That's the truth."

"We'd stay in a hotel."

"At Christmas?"

"It wouldn't be so terrible."

"I don't mean that. I'll bet they've all been booked solid for months. Any you'd want to stay in, at least. Or pay for." He was nothing if not practical.

"You think?"

"Mom, that's when lots of people get time off work or school. Of course they travel, and people who travel book hotel space. In the city, anyway."

"You may be right."

"Besides, we've already put our tree up." He'd turned the lights on when he came in the front door. He had to feel special about this one—the first one he'd picked out himself.

"True. I wonder…"

"What?"

"I wonder whether they'd come here."

"They'd never get time off."

"We could ask."

"Mom, would you?"

"I'll have to talk to Fred again, but if it means that much to you to stay home—"

"It does."

Who knew? The men in her family were always surprising her.

She knew she didn't have to consult Fred, not really. Right now, he'd do whatever she had her heart set on. But did she want to ask Rebecca and Bruce to come for Christmas before they'd even begun married life without interference from family? No. Bad enough for Dave's murder to mar their wedding. All they didn't need was for her to turn into another Elizabeth Graham by playing for sympathy and laying on the guilt.

"We'll stay home, Andrew. We don't need Rebecca and Bruce. We weren't expecting to see them so soon anyway, and they for sure don't want us butting in. This is our family now. Who knows how much longer we'll have you here?"

"Aw, Mom." But he had to know it was true.

"Go tell Fred his soup's on."

After supper they sat by the tree and did their best to be a happy family. Only two more days till Christmas. Relieved at staying put, no matter what Ketcham thought, Joan curled up in Fred's arms on the big sofa.

"You didn't really want to go, did you?" she asked him.

"No. You?"

"No." But we'll have to start bolting the doors, she thought. Quit trusting so much.

"So what's next?"

"Whaddya mean, what's next?" Andrew said. "You forget about Santa Claus?" There was a lot of big kid in Andrew, sitting cross-legged under his tree. At least he wasn't the kind who expected an expensive ski trip for Christmas. "Remember when I used to worry Santa couldn't come to a house with no chimney?"

Joan remembered. "You never got much, even before Dad died. We never had a lot to blow on toys."

"I didn't know any better. I thought it was great."

Fred squeezed her. "You got lucky in your kids," he said.

"I did, didn't I? And now we have Bruce."

"Better not let his mom hear you say that," Andrew warned.

"Don't I know it. But I'm glad he's part of our family."

"Even if it means she is, too?"

"Even then." Maybe if they didn't threaten her, Elizabeth would come around enough to be tolerable. That moment she'd softened let Joan hope, even as she knew better than to trust it.

Andrew sat up straight. "What was that?"

"What was what?"

"That sound." Unfolding his legs, he stood up. "Someone's at the door." Before she could stop him, he went over and opened it.

There stood Patty, looking startled.

"I didn't ring the bell."

"That's okay," he said. "I thought I heard someone. Come on in."

"Am I interrupting?" She hesitated, standing on the porch.

Joan untangled herself from Fred. "Not at all. Come in, Patty. It's cold out there."

"I'm sorry." She hurried around the door and stood just inside while Andrew shut it behind her. "I didn't want to bother you. What a pretty tree."

Andrew beamed. "Thanks. I picked it out."

"Take off your coat and boots and sit down, Patty," Joan said. "Can we give you a cup of coffee? Maybe one of Fred's great sweet rolls?"

"I don't want to put you to any trouble." But Patty let Andrew take her coat and show her to a chair near the tree. She was still wearing the somewhat food-spattered jeans she'd worn for scrubbing pots, and her shirt, too, looked the worse for wear.

"It's no trouble." Joan headed for the kitchen, but Fred had beat her to it. He carried a plate with a cup of steaming coffee and a roll out to Patty.

"Here you go. My dad taught me to bake these. We pigged out on them this afternoon, but we left some for people who might drop in. A pleasure to have you."

But it didn't feel like a social visit, Joan thought. For that matter, why would Patty be visiting them? Earlier, she'd mostly looked angry. Surely she hadn't stopped by to apologize.

No longer looking angry, but a long way from having a social smile on her face, Patty accepted the plate and set it on the little table beside her. As she lifted the cup, her hand trembled. She sipped only a little before setting it back down.

"Joan, I had to come. I've been thinking about you ever since you were over at Ellen's this afternoon, and I had to come."

"Oh?" Joan had no idea what she was talking about.

"I could see how worried you were about Dave's killer going after your daughter."

"Well, yes."

"And you said if it was Chrissy I'd want to protect her."

"Uh-huh."

"You were right about that. I couldn't let you be so scared forever. I had to come tell you your daughter's safe. And so is mine."

Joan looked at Fred. How could Patty know? And then it hit her, what she'd half figured out while she was looking at the pictures and then listening to Ketcham. What she should have realized all along.

Her eyes met Patty's. "Because it was you."

"I couldn't let him do it, don't you see? He didn't care at all. She was in love with him, and she wasn't about to listen to her mother."

"Uh-huh."

"She wouldn't listen to me, and he didn't care. He was coming on to her, but he had no right to!"

The right age. Looking like Patty, but with Dave's dark hair.

Chrissy had to be Dave's daughter. Had he really not cared? But Joan remembered the night he'd gone too far with Rebecca for a loving uncle.

"Did he know he was her father? Did you tell him?"

"How could he not know? She even told him how old she was and when her birthday was."

"Does Chrissy know?"

"She has no idea."

Why not just tell her? Joan thought. It would be so natural to say, "Of course you love him, he's your dad." But she hadn't. "So you called in sick and then came in through the back door when you knew he'd be in there. How did you know he'd be there?"

"I didn't plan it like that. When I felt well enough to come in to work, I just came. I could see him in there with Helga. I waited till she wasn't looking and grabbed a knife.... I kept him from hurting my baby!"

She sat silent.

Andrew's eyes were round, but he didn't say anything.

"You know I'm a cop," Fred said.

"I know. But it doesn't matter about me anymore. Chrissy's safe from him. I had to keep her safe."

Even if it meant killing my brother, Joan thought. But the anger she'd expected to feel at Dave's murderer didn't come. This poor, confused woman. Had she, despite her words, taken her difficult life out on the man who could have made it easier for her? Who had left her pregnant before she finished high school—had she ever even managed to finish? And showed up again, only to reject her for her daughter—his daughter? Had Dave even suspected who Chrissy was to him? Did Patty really know he'd known? Joan wasn't convinced he had, hard as it was to believe she hadn't told him back then.

For that matter, she wasn't convinced Chrissy was right about his intentions. Her brother came on to women. Even Alex.

She'd been sure there was a reason for him to die in Oliver, and she'd been right. But had he brought his death on himself? Who knew what he would have done if he'd known about his daughter back when she was born? Or had he? Dave hadn't saved any letters from Patty. The answers had died with him.

Or maybe not. She'd stopped Nancy Van Allen from giving her the gossip after Dave's murder was in the paper. Had the whole town known about Patty, and Chrissy? Had they assumed she knew, too? Would it be that easy to find out for sure? But Ketcham had lived here all his life, and he didn't seem to know. It was hard to believe her parents, Chrissy's grandparents, had known and done nothing about it.

Fred was walking toward the door.

"What are you going to do?" Joan asked him.

"I've already done it. Ketcham's on his way."

⸺❧⸺

After they'd read Patty's rights to her and taken her off without siren or lights or even handcuffs, Joan sat quietly with Andrew. The tree had lost its warmth.

"Chrissy's my cousin," Andrew said finally. "I guess that makes Patty my aunt, kind of. What's going to happen to 'em, Mom?"

"To Patty? I don't know. She'll need a lawyer, that's for sure. And Andrew, we'll have to share what Dave left us—the timber— with Chrissy. I'm sure he didn't know he had a daughter when he made that will." And even if he had, it was only right. She had no more right to inherit from him than his child did.

"So what do you think would have happened if Patty hadn't killed him?"

"I don't know. I don't see how we'll ever know."